Heart's Whisper

"Let me take you home to your family, Moyra." William's voice was throaty and raw. " 'Tis where you belong."

"Nay." The side of her braid tapped his wrist when she shook her head. "I'll be going nowhere. Nae this night, the next and the ones after that."

"Blast it, Moyra, don't you understand? I—"

"I do understand. I'm nae fool." Her gaze narrowed, astutely scanning his rugged, moonlight-swept features. "I understand ye want me, William Armstrong. Almost as badly as I want you."

He swallowed hard. "You're a brazen wench, Moyra Elliot."

Tipping her chin, she surprised him by grinning saucily up at him. "Nay, nae brazen. Honest. You do want me. I can feel it."

"You'll regret this come dawn," he growled, as he hauled her close and captured anything else she may have said with a kiss.

DANGEROUS GAMES   (0-7860-0270-0, $4.99)
by Amanda Scott

When Nicholas Barrington, eldest son of the Earl of Ul-
combe, first met Melissa Seacort, the desperation he
sensed beneath her well-bred beauty haunted him. He
didn't realize how desperate Melissa really was . . . until
he found her again at a Newmarket gambling club—being auctioned off by her father to the highest bidder. So,
Nick bought himself a wife. With a villain hot on their
heels, and a fortune and their lives at stake, they would
gamble everything on the most dangerous game of all:
love.

A TOUCH OF PARADISE   (0-7860-0271-9, $4.99)
by Alexa Smart

As a confidence man and scam runner in 1880s America,
Malcolm Northrup has amassed a fortune. Now, posing
as the eminent Sir John Abbot—scholar, and possible
discoverer of the lost continent of Atlantis—he's taking
his act on the road with a lecture tour, seeking funds for
a scientific experiment he has no intention of making.
But scholar Halia Davenport is determined to accompany
Malcolm on his "expedition" . . . even if she must kidnap
him!

Heart's Whisper

Rebecca Sinclair

Zebra Books
Kensington Publishing Corp.
http://www.zebrabooks.com

One

The ceremony had been hastily assembled, and was wholeheartedly supported. No pomp, no circumstance. There was nothing similar to what would have been found in the hated English court to the south. No gentleman in velvets and hose, no ladies in satins. Not a farthingale in sight.

Instead, the somber crowd gathered inside the Church of the Holy Rood were garbed in the simplest wools and plaids. The significance of the ceremony they'd traveled far to attend was a great deal more important than the appearance of the loyal subjects in attendance.

In the past several years the situation between England and Scotland had spiraled from appalling to intolerable. It had taken the Battle of Solway Moss for the Scots to finally unite against England's tyranny.

Now, on this cold, cloudy September day, Scotland would boldly announce its stance of freedom by coronating the nine-month-old infant, Mary Stuart.

Hands folded tensely in his lap, William Armstrong

shifted uncomfortably atop the hard, narrow wooden pew. From the corner of his eye he noticed a man and child settle onto the pew in front of him. He spared them a brief glance, noticed there was something wrong with one of the man's arms, then immediately dismissed the pair from his mind. His attention was elsewhere; his attention was turned inward.

A frown etched deep creases between his thick, brown eyebrows. He tried to pinch the gesture away between the callused pads of his index finger and thumb, an adolescent mimicry of his father's favorite gesture, but the scowl was stubborn; it persisted, as dark and as brooding as the storm brewing outside the church.

Try as he might, William could not shift his thoughts from the court convened far to the south. Was the arrogant bastard, Henry VIII, even now plotting and scheming fresh ways in which to bring Scotland's sons and daughters to heel? Aye, William didn't doubt it was so.

Wincing, he remembered all too vividly the English King's most recent, unsavory methods. Among the men who'd been lucky enough to survive the ill-fated battle at Solway Moss were many of Scotland's finest nobles, who now languished in English prisons. Closer to home, the ashes of dozens of Scots Border towns smoldered from recent razings. Women and children had been cold-bloodedly slaughtered. No one had been spared from Henry's rampage. 'Twas only by the grace of God that William's own home, Cragmaer, in Dunmaerton, had been saved. Few towns had been so fortunate.

William's frown deepened. Hard though it was to understand, it appeared that Henry truly *was* so presumptuous as to believe brutality and violence was a sure way to secure a marriage between Scotland's infant Queen and his own son, Edward. 'Twas a grave error on his part . . . albeit not the first for a hated English monarch. One had only to glance at the history books to see England's past littered with similar blunders.

Not for the first time had Henry misjudged the lion to his north, and misjudged it severely. This time, however, England's ruthlessness and temerity went too far. Soon, *very* soon, its ruler would be made aware of his grievous mistake.

William smiled at the thought. To a man, the Scots had agreed young Mary's official coronation should be held on this stormy day. More importantly, the pledge of the Scots nobles' loyalty to their infant Queen would send the all-too-smug English King a sorely needed message: Scotland was a united nation unto the Scots themselves, a nation that *would not* tolerate his bullying, dominating ways.

"The Stuarts came in wi' a lass, they shall pass wi' a lass."

The voice snagged William's attention. Angling his head, he cocked one brow high and glanced to the left, at his father. "Aye, 'tis rumored James said as much on his deathbed, although I'm nae so sure I believe it. Nor does what I believe matter. Like it or nay, we werena left with a son tae crown. More's the pity. We've naught but the wee Mary now."

Robert Armstrong's burly shoulders rose and fell in a shrug. "Did ye see the clouds gathering on yer way in, lad?" he asked. The Armstrong was too busy watching the people gathering around the altar at the front of the church to see his son nod. "Mark my words, Willie, as if today's date isna bad enough, the coming storm is a ver' bad omen indeed."

" 'Tis only a storm. Naught more."

"Nay, m'lord, ye be wrong aboot that." The voice, lighter than air and softer than the first pink tinge of a summer morn, did not come from Robert Armstrong.

William traced the voice to its source—the pudgy, light-haired child sitting in the pew in front of him. As he watched, she scooted around until she was keeling backward in the pew. Had he been in a better frame of mind, William might have graced her with a smile; the hard bench was narrow, the child was not . . . 'Twas a wonder she fit that way at all! "And who might ye be, lass?"

"Who do ye want me tae be?" she countered with a sauciness that belied her meager years. Chubby forearms peeked from beneath the tattered sleeves of her too-large, dull gray tunic. Staking her beefy fists atop the back of the pew, she leaned forward and rested her dimpled chin upon the top fist. Her smile was broad and as guileless as her large, round eyes.

William's frown returned in force. Was it his imagination, or were the child's eyes the color of sun-kissed heather? Mayhap the dim lighting only made them appear so? "I dinna *want* ye tae be anyone, bairn. What I *do* want is for ye to turn back around and hush so I can watch the ceremony in peace."

The girl nodded gravely. "As do I. Howe'er, I thought it only fair to warn ye, yer da be right. Today isna merely the thirtieth anniversary of the Battle of Flodden, m'lord, 'tis also a day that marks the beginning of the end."

"Aye, sweeting, if ye say so," William replied in a vague, placating tone, his gaze drifting past her. "Now, be a good bairn and do as ye've been told. The ceremony is about to start."

"Ye dinna believe me?"

"There's naught tae believe," he scoffed. "Yer but a wee bairn. Maun tae young tae know aught of the world around ye, let alone what the future holds."

"Och! and I suppose *ye* know so much more at yer own grand auld age? Is that the way o' it?" Her soft shoulders stiffened with childish indignation, and her violet eyes flashed. "Ye arena so ver' much aulder than me, from the looks. What is it? Ten summers? Twelve at most, but I'm thinking ye canna be *that* auld."

"Mayhap more, mayhap less. Either way, 'tis summers of learning and experience ye dinna have. Enough, now. It matters naught whether I believe ye or nae, I—"

"Moyra!" The painfully thin, dark-haired man sitting beside the child sent her a chastising glare. "Did ye nae hear the mon? He told ye nae to bother him. Och! I should have known better than tae bring ye with me today. 'I'll be good,' ye promised. 'Ye'll nae e'en know I'm there,' ye swore. 'Tis just like yer mother, ye are . . . always wheedling and conniving and convincing me of yer sweetness and innocence, then turning around and causing naething but trouble. Hush ye now, or I swear by all that's holy, 'tis leaving ye deep in the forest on me way home, I'll be doing. Dinna be giving me that look, lass. This time, I *mean* it."

The child pursed her lips. If possible, her already

huge eyes grew larger still. Her lower lip trembled. William braced himself. He had a younger sibling, he recognized the signs. The girl was about to wail loudly enough to bring down the entire church.

Gritting his teeth, he prepared himself for the tirade sure to follow.

It was a tirade that did not come.

Instead, the lass surprised him yet again by winking and grinning mischievously. After another glance from those captivating violet eyes, she gave a heavy sigh, then reluctantly did as she was bid.

A moment ago William would have sworn nothing could drag his thoughts from the coronation about to commence. Yet with surprising ease, the plump child seated in front of him had done exactly that.

William's brown eyes narrowed. His gaze fixed thoughtfully on the back of the nymph's head. Her hair, he noticed absently, was the same shade as a meadow blanketed with freshly fallen snow: pure and soft and glossy, the strands were wedged between her back and the pew, making them of indiscernible length.

Leaning forward slightly, he glanced discreetly over the pudgy curve of her shoulder. Up close he could see that the strands of her hair were baby-fine, but she'd an abundance of them; he envisioned the ends curled in thick platinum spirals well past her shoulders. The bulk had been brushed back from her face and was currently being crushed between her slender back and the hard wooden pew.

Even from this angle, it was impossible to tell exactly how long her hair was. *And why should I even care?* he wondered as, the old pew creaking loudly beneath him, he forced himself to sit back.

The ceremony about to start, William forced his attention away from the mysterious child who spoke of the future as though it were the past, fixing it on the altar before them all.

He was surprised to see that Mary had already been brought in by Alexander Livingston, her Lord Keeper. Had the child seated in front of him been such a distraction that he'd missed what must have been a noticeable commotion when the bairn had been brought forth? Aye, he realized slowly, apparently so, for missed it he most certainly had.

Disturbing thoughts of stout, platinum-haired lasses soon faded from his mind, and William watched intently as Cardinal David Beaton put the coronation oath to Mary. Too young to answer for herself, it was her Lord Keeper who, in Mary's stead, solemnly pledged to "guide and protect Scotland and its people in the name of the One who had chosen her, God Almighty."

The Cardinal gently unfastened Mary's heavy robes, preparing to anoint her.

No sooner had the chilly air touched her chest than Mary's full lower lip began to tremble. Her dimpled hands bunched into tiny fists where they'd settled upon her heavily gowned lap. Tipping her tiny red-haired head back, the infant Queen let loose a wail that made more than one loyal subject gasp and wince. A few discreetly genuflected. Even more glanced hesitantly at the church's door.

'Twas apparent from the looks on their faces where the majority of their thoughts lay—on the storm brew-

ing outside. To a superstitious lot, the infant Queen's
reaction was a bad omen indeed.

Mary's cries grew louder. Sharp and piercing, the
helpless little one's shrieks reverberated off the
church's thick stone walls.

Cardinal Beaton paused. A teardrop of holy oil
plummeted from his fingertips onto Mary's gown,
where it was quickly absorbed. Unsure of what to do
about this startling occurrence, he hesitated in the act
of applying the liquid to Mary's diminutive back.

*Today isna merely the thirtieth anniversary of the
Battle of Flodden, m'lord, 'tis also a day that marks
the beginning of the end.*

Like a shout tossed over a vast, craggy mountain
range, the words echoed through William's mind. His
eyes widened, his gaze instinctively dipped. His breath
caught in his throat when he found himself ensnared
by huge, unblinking violet eyes.

Did I nae tell ye? said the fleeting gaze the child
cast over her shoulder before, perhaps afraid of catching another tongue-lashing from her father, she obediently turned back around.

Again, William was left to stare at the back of her
small platinum head. And stare at it he did, most hard.
He was only partially aware of when the Earls of Ar-
ran, Lennox and Argyll approached the altar, bearing
the royal crown, scepter and sword in turn.

'Twas the middle offering, a long silver staff
adorned with glistening crystal and shimmering pearl,
that caught the infant Queen's eye. Her tiny fingers
wrapped around the scepter, and her shrieks blessedly
trickled away until they were naught but a few inter-
mittent, hiccupy sobs.

Relieved sighs whispered through tension-tight lips. Mayhap the omen was not so dire after all?

"I canna see." The soft, high voice, now all too familiar, was, in this instance, also much closer than it should be. The words were accompanied by three sharp tugs on the elbow of William's tunic.

He glanced to his right and down. Then down some more. This time he was not at all surprised to find himself staring at the girl with the huge violet eyes and shock of thick platinum hair. He was, however, more than a wee bit taken aback to discover her sitting next to him.

When had she done that? He had no idea, but at some point in the last few minutes she'd scooted off her own pew and, apparently, under it, then scrambled onto his. No small feat for a child of her size!

Her legs were too short for her feet to touch the floor, and she didn't make the attempt. Instead, she perched on the edge of the narrow pew and, swinging her feet in the wide arcs that only a bairn could get away with on such a momentous occasion, repeated simply—not to mention loudly—"I said I canna see. Yer a fine muckle tall. I dinna suppose ye can heft me ontae one of those broad shoulders? I'm thinking I could see the other side of the world from there. Mayhap farther."

"Shhh," William scolded, his voice a soft hiss. He sent her what he hoped was a silencing glare. "I'll be doing nae such thing. Go back tae yer own seat now. Quick. Afore yer da misses ye."

She wrinkled her nose. A few stray platinum curls bounced around her face and shoulders and back when she shook her head decisively. "I'll be staying right here. With ye."

William gritted his teeth, closed his eyes and shook his head. A quick glance to his left told him his father was too absorbed in the ceremony to notice the goings-on beside him. William breathed a sigh of relief. At least he could be thankful for that much.

'Twas the first event of any significance—besides last autumn's Day O' Truce—that Robert Armstrong had allowed his son to attend in all the lad's thirteen summers. If William disgraced his father today, it could also be the last. Of that, he was very much aware as he opened his eyes and focused them once again on the proceedings at the altar.

He pretended to ignore the girl who sat quietly beside him, swinging her feet and occasionally banging the heels of her tattered leather shoes together. She did not ask to sit on his shoulder again. William found himself oddly grateful not to have a need to voice the brisk refusal hovering on the tip of his tongue.

As quickly as it had begun, the ceremony concluded. William wondered if the swift, almost anticlimactic finale had less to do with Scotland's rush to show independence than it did with the present company's fear that Mary would suddenly tire of the scepter and start wailing again.

While the Cardinal held the heavy, bejeweled crown lightly over her small red head, The Lord Keeper propped Mary upright. One by one the assembly left their seats and warily approached the altar, swearing allegiance to their diminutive Queen.

In hushed whispers, people began talking amongst themselves as they awaited their turn. William stood up to allow his father to pass, then reseated himself. Because of her size, the lass beside him was forced to scoot into the aisle . . . then just as promptly scooted right back onto the pew beside William again. She sat down with enough force to make the old wood groan.

"Ye dinna pledge fealty, m'lord?" she asked, thereby crushing any hope William may have had that she'd grown bored with badgering him. "Why do ye nae go up there with the rest of them?"

"There's nae need," he replied, more sharply than he meant to. Seeing a flash of hurt in her eyes, he took a deep breath and continued, his voice as strained as his quickly shredding patience, "Me da pledges allegiance for all clan Armstrong. 'Tis enough."

"But—"

"Moyra!" The child's father, apparently just now noticing his daughter's absence, turned in his seat. His blue eyes shot her a hot glare. "Och! Ye li'l devil. Mark me words, ye're the curse of clan Elliot. Dinna I tell ye tae stay put and leave the poor lad alone? Aye, I did. And were ye listening tae a word I said? Nay, ye werena. As usual. Now get back here a'fore I—"

"Och! He'll nae stop ranting now until I obey him. I maun go," the child said, ignoring her father's continued rumblings—this time the man threatened to lock her in the deepest, darkest cell of the nearest castle's dungeon and not let her out until she was ten summers old or of marriageable age, whichever came first. "Me brother says 'tis nae good for Da tae get upset," she confided as she reached out and took William's hand in both of hers. "If he starts coughing now, he may ne'er stop, don't ye ken?"

The contact of her hand upon his was startling.

Her pudgy fingers felt incredibly soft, brushing like rose petals against his older, tougher skin. Not much older, and not much tougher, he reminded himself, but older and tougher still. Had he been cold? He hadn't thought so . . . until now. The touch of her fingers was like being seared by blazing pinpoints of liquid-fire. In contrast, the flesh around her touch felt ice cold.

"Moyra, did ye nae hear me? I said—"

"Aye, Da, I think the entire church heard ye." Moyra shifted attention from her father to William. This time when she grinned, William found himself grinning back before he could think better of it. Just a small upward tilt of the corners of his mouth, but 'twas a grin all the same. "We shall meet again, m'lord. I swear it."

One sandy blond eyebrow quirked high in his forehead. "Is that so, bairn?"

"Aye. It shan't be for a ver' long time, though." She sighed, her thick chest lifting and falling with surprising melodrama. "Many winters from now, long after ye've forgotten all aboot me. Dinna doubt it. And when we do . . . Och! Weeell, I canna be telling ye tae much, now can I? 'Twould spoil the surprise."

She gave his hand a squeeze, then abruptly let go of him and pushed to her feet. Even in this position, with her standing and him sitting, the top of her head did not clear a chin that just weeks ago began sprouting its first few whiskers.

If the lass was intimidated by the differences in their height, it didn't show in either her stance or her gaze.

A movement near the altar caught William's eye. Distracted by the sight of his father kneeling in front of the infant Queen Mary, he did not at first notice what the young child standing next to him was about to do. Even if he had, William knew he'd have been too shocked to stop her.

Placing diminutive hands on his shoulders, the stocky, platinum-haired child called Moyra leaned forward and delivered a warm, wet kiss . . . first to one of his cheeks, then the other.

For years afterward William would wonder if the gesture had been purposely timed to coincide with Robert Armstrong doing the same to the infant Queen as he solemnly pledged clan Armstrong's loyalty.

Two

A drizzle of icy rain falling from the sky. Fog, layered upon the moss-strewn ground, wispily hovering around ankles that take slow, steady steps. Misty puffs settling hesitantly into place behind her.

Trees, tall and dark. Broad, thick trunks with tough, scratchy bark. Leafless branches reaching upward like bony, skeletal fingers trying to claw open the black velvet ceiling of the night.

Not a sound.

Even her footsteps are oddly silent.

The lack of noise seems resonant and heavy, like the water-drenched cloak hanging from slender shoulders, adding an extra burden of weight to her every dragging step.

A hill in the distance. Incredibly steep. Accessible only by a narrow, twisting path flanked by more winter-bare tree trunks and thickly overgrown shrubs. Needle-sharp icicles hang threateningly from the latter.

No snow. Odd, this time of year there should be snow.

High up, the sharp hoot of an owl. The sudden intrusion of noise is loud. Startlingly so.

Her footsteps quicken.

Gradually, more sounds intrude, magnify. The snapping of a dry twig. The crunch of dirt and gravel underfoot. The dull scratch of branches rubbing together.

Hurrying now. Gathering her cloak tightly about her, fisting it beneath her chin. Shivering with a violence that makes weary muscles ache. Almost running. Almost. Yet not quite daring to go that fast.

Fear.

Something lies over the hill. She knows what that something is, knows also that she can't stop, not even if she wanted to.

No option, no choice.

There'll be no turning back. Not now. Not ever.

Cresting the hill. Lungs burning with every inadequate, choppy breath dragged inward, breaths that freeze the air in front of her face to tendrils of vapor.

Cold to the bone. Shivering even more violently. Knuckles fisting the cloak, gripping it more tightly beneath her chin. Huddling inside the abundant, coarse woolen folds. Teeth clattering. Fingertips frosty and numb.

Blinking, eyes struggle to adjust to a scant sliver of moonlight. Scowling.

As if from nowhere, a castle slowly sketches itself against the black backdrop of night. Many slitted windows, but the glimmer of a torch light can be seen in only one.

Thick outer wall circling the keep like a stone fence guarding a graveyard . . . only broader, taller, stronger. The uneven stones as dark and as old as death.

An invisible hand at her back, pushing, urging her

forward. Shaking her head even as she takes a step forward.

"No. Please. I canna." Her lips form the words, but no sound pours forth.

The owl hoots again. This time the call sounds harsh, frantic.

Another step forward.

Another.

The hard, invisible force behind nudges her on, refusing to let her stumble, refusing to be denied.

Down a steady descent. The hill is steeper, twisting like the stripes on a narrow candy stick.

The fog thickens. Twists around her legs. Clings. Vaporous tendrils of it swallow her feet and ankles and shins, the hem of her plaid skirt. It feels cold and clammy against her skin.

In the forefront, the castle grows disproportionately larger as she nears. Walls and shard spikes of roof spurt up from the ground, melting, merging together, taking shape from the night . . . reminding her of a wildcat about to pounce.

The outer wall reaches for the mountain-peaked horizon in either direction.

Rises imposingly upward.

Looms threateningly over her.

In the distance, sounds grow like thunder. The pounding of hundreds of feet followed by great crashes of steel against steel. Grunts of pain. Bitter cries of anguish.

The noise goes on and on and on.

As abruptly as it started, it stops.

Silence so complete it is touchable. Until . . .

Somewhere, a lone howl of victory cuts the night like a sharp honed dirk.

A creak of old wood.

Blinking hard, she scrubs at her eyes with tightly clenched fists, frowns. Standing in front of the castle's main door now, yet with no memory of crossing the courtyard or of how she came to be here.

Taking a quick step backward, gasping when the door swings inward. As if from a long neglected vault, a blast of stale air rushes through the opening.

The rush of air feels as frigid as death.

Somewhere deep inside the belly of the castle, the lone cry—no longer of victory, but of misery—collapses in on itself and takes on human form.

A hand reaches out of the darkness . . .

Moyra Elliot awoke with a scream wedged in her fear-tightened throat. Her heart pounded, her breathing came in deep, choppy spasms. Despite the brisk winter chill in the air, beads of perspiration dampened her skin.

Years of practice made her swallow the scream back before it could break free. Until all that remained was the barest whisper of a tortured moan drifting away on the frigid night air.

Not that it would have mattered had she allowed herself to scream. As her brother, Jared, would have pointed out, "Ye can shout down these cursed, rotting rafters, lass, 'twill nae do ye a bit of good." Jared would have been right. Screaming would only make a difference if there was someone to hear her shout. There was no one.

Oh, aye, a passing fox *may* hear the racket and be drawn by curiosity. Mayhap even a curious hedgehog or twa? However, there was no one in the castle to hear if she cried out, nor had there been for almost a decade.

Moyra vaguely remembered a time, when she was a bairn, when Wyndehaghen had been teeming with people. That was when the keep had boasted the honor of being the seat of the Liddesdale Elliots, one of the most feared reiving families on the Scots side of the Border.

That time was long past.

When she was eight, after Wyndehaghen had been damaged in a raid by the Red Douglas, Moyra's father had begun erecting a new castle in a neighboring Liddesdale town. When she was ten, the Elliots had abandoned Moyra's beloved Wyndehaghen in favor of the new keep. While the new keep had commanding turrets and a fine new chapel, it lacked the elegance, charm and strength of its predecessor.

As the years passed, the Elliots came to realize they'd given up more than just their stronghold, they'd relinquished their dominant standing as a family to be feared on either side of the Border as well. Gradually their reputation for deeds of daring masterfully executed was surpassed by other Scots and English families. Families like the Maxwells and Armstrongs, the Douglases and Grays . . .

Now, if she listened closely, Moyra thought she could still hear the ghostly echo of footsteps in the cold, empty chambers below. The sounds were not real, of course. Not tonight. Not any night. She was as alone in Wyndehaghen tonight as she had ever been; the once glorious and now severely neglected keep was as cold and barren as it had been for the decade worth of nights that had come before.

Cold.

Aye, *very* cold, she thought as, shivering, she burrowed deeply beneath the two plaids she'd buried herself under hours before. The floor felt icy and hard beneath her; if the stone had warmed to her body at all, Moyra couldn't feel it.

A quick glance told her the meager fire she'd built upon retiring for the night had dwindled while she'd slept. All that remained of it now were smoldering embers in a thick bed of ashes.

A frown creased her brow. If she did not stoke those embers soon, and add more wood, she would need to restart the fire from scratch. That is, if she did not freeze to death whilst sleeping on this cold, harder-than-a-bed-of-ice floor!

Gathering the bulky plaids about her, Moyra rose to her knees. In that position, she scooted over to a hearth that, in reality, was naught more than an alcove in the thick—*bitterly cold!*—stone wall.

A skimpy pile of barely dry twigs and branches was stacked sloppily on the floor next to the hearth. Muttering something uncomplimentary in her native Gaelic beneath her breath, and still shivering enough to make her teeth chatter, she reached out and tossed a few handfuls of the precious fuel onto the dying fire, encouraging the wood to catch by poking at it with the tip of a long stick.

The fire needed little coaxing. The first, frail spark flourished into a teardrop of flame, and the teardrop quickly spread. In no time, warm fingers of heat reached into the room, wrapping themselves around her body like a lover's embrace.

Moyra's gaze narrowed, fixing on the dancing flames. But she didn't see them, and she barely heard the snap and crackle as the fire fed on fresh wood.

She swallowed hard, her thoughts abruptly turning elsewhere . . . back to the dream.

This time the shiver that raced down her spine had naught to do with the frigid chill in the air. Och, nay, nothing nearly so simple. It had everything to do with a ghostly blanket of fog, an unknown and imposingly large castle backdropped by a thick, moonless night . . .

And a hand reaching out of the impenetrable darkness.

A hand reaching for her.

Had she not known without a doubt whose hand it was, or why it was reaching for her, Moyra may have shrugged the dream off as being naught more than one of her many meaningless nightmares and gone back to sleep.

But she *did* know.

Just as she also knew the dream had been no mere nightmare.

It was a vision. A warning. In her life, she'd had numerous visions . . . certainly enough to recognize this one for what it was. Most of her previous visions had proved embarrassingly wrong, so much so that she'd ceased telling anyone of them years ago. Yet—

No vision in the past had been exactly like this one.

No vision in the past had been so strong and clear and . . . aye, *demanding*.

A part of her longed to ignore the dream, the vision.

But she could not. To do so would be disastrous, and not only for herself. She knew that as certainly as she knew, this time, her vision was accurate. The conviction of it pumped hot and fast through her bloodstream.

Eleven years of waiting—sometimes wondering, sometimes fantasizing—had reached an end.

It was time to find him.

How it happened was anyone's guess . . . but happen it most certainly had. Scarcely one hour ago William Armstrong had been ambushed.

Ambushed!

Just when he'd thought the situation couldn't get worse—when the sweet feel of escape was within his grasp!—he'd taken an arrow in the shoulder while trying to flee.

It did not soothe his conscience, or relieve his pain, to know the ambush had been set by Iain Douglas, a Border reiver renowned for such underhanded tactics. That William and his men had ridden, wide-eyed, smack into the trap was more than a little humiliating.

Bending low over his horse's back, William gritted his teeth against the pain piercing his shoulder and used his knees to nudge his mount to a quicker pace. The thudding of at least a dozen horses' hooves tromping over frigid, hard-packed ground echoed over the rolling hills behind him.

Were they closer now or farther back?

Bloody hell, he couldn't tell!

Beneath him, the horse heaved for breath; it came in harsh, surging gulps to match his own. Each exhalation fanned the frosty night air in wispy clouds of vapor.

Branches reached out from above, from both sides. Their brittle fingers clawed at the padded leather jack hanging from William's shoulders, trying to snag it and failing. The tip of one particularly tenacious branch scraped the line of his cheekbone. Wincing, he felt hot drops of blood trickle down his jaw, the side of his neck. They seeped beneath the collar of his jack and were absorbed, finally, by the thin, sweat-dampened tunic beneath.

Leaving the woods, he charged toward the closest of the seemingly endless, rolling hills etched against the midnight black horizon.

Both he and his mount were panting now. The muscles and tendons in William's back ached, protesting the cramped, hunched-over position, but he didn't alter it. The head of the arrow—the shaft had been broken off—was still embedded deeply in his shoulder and felt like a hot poker stabbing at him with every jostling stride.

Only when he'd successfully eluded the Douglas could he take the time to bind and dress his wound. There was no allowing for such luxuries now. Not with the villain in hot pursuit. It was imperative William gain as much distance as possible; if this painful position won him but a few precious seconds, the discomfort would be well worth it.

Every minute—nay, every *second!*—meant the difference between life and death.

Drops of sweat beaded on his brow, dripped into his eyes, blurring his vision. He swiped them away on the leather sleeve of his jack. His determined gaze never wavered from the next hill cresting the horizon.

His goal wasn't far now.

If he could somehow make it over the next hill, then carefully thread his way through the valley cradled between that hill and the one after . . .

Without the camouflage of trees, it would be only a matter of time before the Douglas picked up William's trail. Alas, there was no help for it. To hide in the meager layer of woods, hoping only the prickly covering of trees would conceal his presence until the search was called off, would be foolhardy at best.

William Armstrong had been foolhardy enough for one night, thank you very much!

Had Iain Douglas ever called off a hot trod once it was commenced? Nay, not that William could remember. There was no reason to think tonight would be different.

The hill crested, William chanced a quick glance over his shoulder. A sigh of relief poured in a misty cloud past his lips.

No one had followed him out of the woods.

Yet.

They would, of course. On that, he would bet his life. Indeed, he *was* betting his life upon it.

Clicking his tongue, he propelled the horse onward. Quickly they descended the lazy slope of the hill. In the direction of the valley that, for the moment, lay hidden in the black velvet folds of the night.

Somewhere in the distance he heard a shout of frustration. The noise sliced through the night, and skimmed down William's spine like chips of shattered glass.

A tight, unemotional grin tugged at one corner of his lips. The sound, not unfamiliar, could be easily traced to a frustrated Iain Douglas.

In his mind's eye, William pictured his enemy finally breaking through the barrier of trees. He could well imagine the man's irritation when he found the vague, night-shadowed hills stretching out before him . . . apparently empty of any sign of his maddeningly elusive quarry.

For the first time in the last hour, William allowed a small spark of hope to kindle in his veins and spread rapidly throughout the rest of him. Mayhap he stood a chance—slight, aye, but a chance all the same—of escaping with his head still firmly attached to his shoulders? 'Twas possible . . . yet something he didn't dare count on, he reminded himself as, again, he leaned as low as he could over the mare's back, wordlessly coaxing the shaggy Border pony to race faster still.

The tiny village—he couldn't even remember its name—that was nestled at the foot of the hill had been abandoned almost a decade ago, thanks to one of Johnnie Gordon's most nefarious raids. After the Gordon had cheerfully razed the town for the third time in as many years, the residents seemed to have come to the mutual conclusion that the spot was unlucky and moved on.

All that remained now were the ribs of a few charred, skeletal walls, each hinting at where thatch-roofed cottages had once stood. Most of the rickety frames had long since collapsed in upon themselves but, like the summer's last blade of grass before a heavy blanket of snow descended, one still stood proud and tall.

Slowing his mount, it was in that direction William headed. Rather, he led the scrappy pony a bit farther, toward the ruins of a castle cleverly hidden by the gentle curve of the hill directly behind the shack.

Like a playful bairn peeking out from behind a fence, the castle gradually became visible. William found its crumbling curtain walls and disintegrated outbuildings more than a wee bit discouraging, if only for the memory of how strong, how sturdy, how *alive* and bursting with activity Wyndehaghen had once been. That had been many years ago, aye, but he still remembered.

The *clop-clop* of his horse's hooves echoed upon scattered rocks and flagstones, giving the unbroken night around him an oddly hollow, eerily deserted quality.

While the keep itself remained intact, for the most part, one glance said the building had sustained massive damage. A large hole yawned in its southwest wall. At the top, the parapet had crumbled in numerous places; from this angle, the narrow walkway looked like nothing so much as a row of jagged, decaying teeth.

The keep squatted with its back closely and strategically guarded by the steep ascent of a treeless hill. A sneak attack from the rear was impossible. Two severely neglected moats ringed the curtain wall. The outer moat was dry—naught more than a smudged ridge of earth to indicate it had ever been there at all—while the inner moat cupped a mere few inches of thick, muddy water. To the southwest, far beyond the deserted castle or town, the outer moat converged with the River Esk.

Hooves splashed in the muddy water as William crossed the wide, shadow-strewn inner moat. The sludgy bottom slurped at the horse's hooves and fetlocks. Even in the depths of this shallow there could be hidden rifts. Should the mare accidentally stumble into one, she could twist a leg. A maimed mount would insure William's capture. Better by far to take a few extra seconds of caution now than chance his life to a single misstep.

It wasn't until William had crossed the second, inner moat that he reined the mare in and dismounted. Too many stray stones lay about. He'd do best to go the rest of the way on foot. After inspecting his aching wound—the bleeding hadn't stopped, but at least the majority of blood had been absorbed by the thickly padded inner lining of the jack—he pushed onward.

The security of the curtain wall, crumbled and ruined though it was, was reassuring. The tall, precariously leaning stones would provide an adequate screen when the Douglas and his men came charging over the same hill William had crested himself only a few short moments ago.

Skirting the inner wall, and tugging the mare into step behind him, he started toward the main body of the keep—only to abruptly stop short.

Frowning, he fixed his attention on one of the tall, narrow windows cut into the stone of the castle's third floor. Was it his imagination, mayhap a trick of the sliver-moon and the shadows, or did he see a vague light shimmering there . . . ?

Nay, it couldn't be. Wyndehaghen was deserted, had

been for nearly a decade. 'Twas rumored the castle was haunted.

Haunted? William shook his head. It must be loss of blood making him think such things, for he didn't believe in that sort of nonsense. Ghosts and goblins and creatures that stirred in the night. Nay, they did not exist.

Then again, if they did . . . ? 'Twould explain the light shimmering faintly in the third-floor window, would it not?

'Twas a light that, after he blinked hard, twice, and looked at again, was no longer there. If it had ever been . . .

A chill skated up William's spine, prickling the sandy blond hairs at his nape. Gritting his teeth, he wiped the sensation away with a roughened palm. The feeling faded, but slowly and with great reluctance.

"You're going daft, Armstrong," he muttered under his breath. There was a faint Scots burr to his voice, but it was very faint and muted by a harsh English accent. The mare's ears twitched at the deep, husky familiarly of its master's voice. "Next thing you know you'll be swearing you hear banshees wailing in your ears." He chuckled dryly, then shook his head and sighed. "Aye, and see kelpies dancing merrily about your feet, no doubt."

Putting the mysterious light in the window out of his mind, and concentrating instead on the grave matter at hand—outwitting the Douglas if he wanted to see the sun rise come morn—William continued on through the kirkyard, then ducked behind the craggy southwest corner of the keep. It was pitch black here; he had to use the bloodstained hand not tightly gripping the mare's reins to grope his way along the moist, icy walls. For her part, the mare seemed to have no trouble keeping pace behind him.

By the time he reached the rear of the castle, a few stray beams of moonlight had filtered over the hill and the thick stone wall. Not much, but enough for him to make out the dark, squat contours of what could only be a circular stone well.

William inhaled, a sharp gasp of relief.

Close. He was oh, so very close!

As his mother's seventh—and most current—husband had promised William, the well was there. Unless the man's memory had betrayed him as easily as Lizbet Armstrong had so casually betrayed the memory of all her husbands, the entrance to the secret tunnel *should* be located directly behind that well . . .

Three

Like the invisible hand haunting her dream, something—a force as invisible as it was strong—urged Moyra forward. Her bare feet absorbed the cold seeping up from the hard oak floor of the hallway. The icy chill invaded her bones, made her shiver.

She skirted around one dark corner, then the next. There was no need to worry about turning down the wrong hallway, or making a misstep; the layout of Wyndehaghen was as clear to her now as it had ever been. Mayhap clearer, since she'd roamed these abandoned corridors for the past several fortnights.

Gripping a handful of her plaid skirt in an untrembling fist, she hoisted the bulk of it up until the hem barely reached her knees. 'Twas indecent . . . but who cared? Who would see? That thought in mind, she quickly descended the tight, wheel staircase.

Down to the second floor.

The first floor.

The ground floor.

The staircase stopped at a meager foyer, then opened into the ground floor of the keep. It was on half of this bottom floor—the half she was now in— where supplies had once been stored. As soon as those in the castle knew it was under attack, the main door was sealed from within, leaving the occupants bolted inside. They could survive for weeks on the food and drink that had once been kept in this storage room.

Strategically, the layout was sound. If the main door of the keep was violated, the enemy still needed to cross the width of the ground-floor storage chamber. By the time the legion of reivers could trek that far, the alarm would surely have been sounded, the occupants above ready to meet the attack. Moyra could still hear the echo of steel against steel, remnants of the many battles that had been commenced atop that narrow, wheel staircase—the only entrance to the castle's upper stories.

Tonight, the ground floor was as open and as barren, as dark and uninviting, as the rest of the castle. When Wyndehaghen had been in its prime, Moyra would have needed to sidestep a crowd of crates and kegs of various sizes and shapes. Tonight, there wasn't a crate or keg in sight; she was free to cross to the main door without once having to alter her course, and that in itself caused a string of sadness to tug at her heart.

Her bare feet slapped against the hard, cold stone floor as she approached the main door, then hesitated. Through the tall, narrow windows cut into the outer wall, a few stray slivers of moonlight slanted down to the dust-strewn floor.

Nay, this was the wrong direction.

Moyra wasn't sure how she knew that, she simply *did*.

Lifting the heavy bolt, she dropped it into place. The clunk of solid wood hitting equally solid wood sounded oddly reassuring.

Aye, she was fully aware that anyone with a grain of determination could crawl through the castle's southeast wall—there was, after all, a gaping hole there the size of six brawnily built men!—but she could do naught about the keep's state of disrepair. Barring the door . . . now, *that* she *could* do something about.

The tiny wisps of platinum hair at her nape prickled and stood on end as the hot, invisible force relentlessly dragged her onward, the lure stronger and stronger . . . Och, well, she desperately needed to feel she was in control of *something*.

Turning on her bare heel, she hurried back in the direction from which she'd come. Instead of the wheel staircase, she turned at the last instant and warily approached what, to the untrained eye, looked like a solid stone wall. The entire length of it was ribbed with age-crooked wooden shelves. Only on exceedingly close inspection could one detect that, although the wood appeared to be constructed of single planks, the entire shelving was bisected down the center by a gossamer-thin fracture from floor to ceiling.

It was slightly to the right of this fracture that Moyra applied the heel of her palm, and pushed.

The creak of old wood assaulted the room like a powerful clap of thunder. At one point, the secret panel stuck, but she planted her bare feet determinedly on the hard stone floor and used her shoulder to shove it the rest of the way open.

A gust of moist, mold-scented air sighed out from the tunnel beyond. Wrinkling her nose, Moyra turned her face instinctively away from the stench, recoiling as her stomach muscles clenched and churned.

Dare she go on?

Dare she *not?*

Turning back was not an option. Indeed, it had ceased to be an option the instant she'd stepped foot out of the safety of her third-floor bedchamber.

The invisible force continued to pull at her; its grip was hard and cruel and relentless. The need to continue twisted around her like a thread of woven steel and became tied in an impossibly complicated knot . . . yanking her, unwilling but insistent, into the dark, damp, smelly recesses of the tunnel.

William gritted his teeth and tried not to notice the slicing pain in his shoulder, the pain that ricocheted all the way to the center of his spine with each cautious step. Tried not to, but did.

His stepfather's instructions, while so far welcomingly accurate, had only gone so far. William had found the trap door with surprising ease, but only because he'd known exactly where to look for it. Unfortunately, that was where the directions ended . . . and the pitch-black tunnel began.

William's palms were sticky with the slime coating the cold stone walls. The area around him was a sheet of unbroken blackness. With no light to lead his way, he'd only his palms skimming against the dank, moldy walls to guide him. With his sense of sight blotted out by the darkness, his other senses became honed to a sharper pitch.

The stench of the mildew-encrusted walls was almost overpowering, while the slime coating his fingers felt cold and wet and disgusting. Grimacing, he forced himself to continue on, deeper into the belly of the tunnel.

Not fond of tight, closed-in places, William could almost hear his heart pound. Between his wound, the fight that had caused it and the escape that had ensued immediately afterward, his nerves were chafed raw.

Where the devil was the opposite wall? Why couldn't he see it? Or even feel it when he stretched his uninjured arm out at full length? Mayhap the tunnel was wide at the base but narrow as it progressed? 'Twas possible, but . . . *how narrow?*

His breathing came hard and fast and choppy as he quickened his pace, well, quickened it as much as he dared considering the lack of lighting and the unfamiliar terrain. The *clop-clop* of his horse's hooves on wet stone, as the tough Border pony followed obediently behind him, sounded unnaturally loud.

What was at the end of this tunnel? William imagined it was the inside of the old, ruined keep . . . but what if he was wrong? What if he wound up emerging directly in front of a searching Iain Douglas?

Delivering himself up to the Douglas did not bear contemplating. Yes, the majority of Wyndehaghen lay in ruins, but so far this tunnel seemed intact.

Not a designer of castles, he could think of no logical reason for a tunnel to be built under the keep, only to have it eventually lead directly back out again. That would make no sense, even if the keep *had* been built by Elliots. Nay, more likely the tunnel through which he slowly, blindly guided himself emptied into some portion of the keep.

The question now, of course, was what portion? Did

it open into crumbled stone, or into the part of the castle that still stood . . . ?

There was only one way to find out.

Gritting his teeth over the almost overpowering feel of walls closing in on him, coupled with the grinding pain in his shoulder, William forced himself to move on, step by leaden, shuffling step.

Behind him lay Iain Douglas, and certain death. Ahead of him . . . Well, what choice did he have but to gamble his future on whatever lay ahead? Whatever it was, it had to be more merciful.

Moyra had taken no more than three steps into the tunnel when a gust of dank air wafted around her, tossing a few thick strands of platinum hair that escaped her plait around her face and shoulders. For a brief second, the plaid skirt molded to her legs, the thin, butternut yellow tunic to her shoulders and chest and belly.

Even the scant moonlight filtering in through the storeroom windows now was shut off, darkness, like a heavy blanket, enfolding her in its velvety blackness.

The moldy odor of the walls intensified, so thick and foul she thought she could taste the stench. The dampness clinging to the walls and floor made them feel cold and sticky to her bare feet and the hand she splayed over the stone wall as she leaned against it, trying to get her bearings.

In the distance, just up ahead, she heard a noise.

Something moved.

Moyra swallowed a gasp.

She'd been in the process of taking a step; the unnatural noise made her freeze in midmotion. Her eyes grew wide as she stared into the darkness, trying to see something, anything beyond the wall of blackness that seemed to start at the tip of her nose and go on forever.

"Is someone there?" she asked, and while she'd meant her voice to sound calm and controlled, it trembled almost as much as the knees knocking together beneath her thick plaid skirt.

Clearing her throat, she tried again. *"Mo chreach!"* Good heavens! "If there's someone there, ye'd best say so. I willna be responsible for me two—*ahem!*—four big, strapping brothers tearing ye apart thinking ye be an intruder . . ."

The noise came again.

Louder.

Closer.

Mayhap the sound was from nothing more harmful than a rat? This was a damp, dark place, after all. The kind of place a rodent would favor.

The noise came again.

Nay, if that sound was coming from a rat, 'twas a fearsomely *tall* rat. At least as tall as she, mayhap taller. 'Twas a rat that, as she heard it advance still more, seemed to be not at all afraid of the threat of four strapping brothers with swords at the ready.

A frown creased her brow. Didn't rats have claws? Aye, they did. Shouldn't she be hearing those claws scratching against the stone floor as it moved, *not* high up on the wall? Aye, she thought so. Och, well, that settled the matter. What she'd heard was not scratching so much as scraping.

Not a good sign. Not good at all.

Cursing herself for a fool—how could she let herself act upon one of her visions when she knew full well only a fraction of them ever came true?—Moyra spun back toward the tunnel's entrance. This time when she reached out and touched the wet, sticky stone, it was with the intent of guiding herself out of the darkness and right back out of the tunnel she'd entered.

The invisible, gut-wrenching tug that had awoken her and led her this far squeezed tightly in her chest, protesting such a cowardly retreat. Moyra refused to acknowledge the sensation, let alone pay it any attention.

Much as she'd have liked to believe it, she knew there was no rat, either deep in the belly of the tunnel or outside of it . . . not anywhere in the whole of Scotland was there a rat that could make *those* noises. The perpetrator was much larger, and much more intelligent.

She was not alone in the tunnel. Moyra could feel another presence close by as tangible as the cold, stale air on her cheeks.

Willing her feet to move, she advanced one step.

Two.

The slit of light that indicated the trap door was at hand gradually became visible. Heaving a sigh of relief, she lurched toward it.

Her relief was short-lived.

A hand—*the same one from her dream?*—manifested itself from out of the darkness, close to her right shoulder. Thick, powerful fingers curled with painful intent around the tender flesh of her upper arm.

Moyra opened her mouth to scream, but the shout never made it past her fear-parched throat. The hand around her arm pulled. Hard. Her back came up against something that felt more solid than the stone wall she'd just been touching. The breath left her lungs in a whoosh.

Another hand, equally as big and powerful as the first, coiled around the side of her neck. The palm—warm and solid—settled over her mouth, stifling any further noise she might have made. The hand was large enough for the webbing between her captor's index finger and thumb to partially cut off the air supply to her nose.

Moyra twisted and turned, her lungs burning for oxygen, even if the air did smell moldy and stale. The hand on her upper arm shifted, the man's—there was no doubt in her mind now that her captor was a man—steely arm encircled her waist, pinning her arm between the hot firmness of his chest and her softer, cooler side.

She opened her mouth, not caring that the hand covering it would muffle her shout.

"Samhchair!" a deep, husky voice growled in her ear.

The intruder's Gaelic was rusty, but decipherable. Obeying the brutal authority in his voice, she instantly fell silent.

The only noise to reach her was the ragged pounding of her heart in her ears . . . and the more ragged give and take of her captor's breaths soughing the cold, soggy night air.

Gradually, another sound began to intrude.

Like the low roll of distantly building thunder came

the tromp of horses's hooves pounding over the frozen earth outside. Moyra's breath caught. Without being able to see them, it was impossible to gauge how many riders were descending upon Wyndehaghen. One hundred men? Two hundred? Maybe more. The echo of gruff voices suggested the men outside were not trying to conceal their presence.

Who were they? And what could they possibly want with a long-abandoned, ruined castle?

Moyra stiffened as her thoughts swerved to the warm, hard body pressing against her. She was more aware than ever of the thick, powerful arms holding her, as if she were a bairn, to a thicker, more powerful male body, of the hand that stifled all but the most meager of whimpers . . .

Whoever was out there, surely they would not have braved such foul weather and treacherous terrain without good reason.

She'd been at Wyndehaghen for almost a fortnight, and in that time had not had a single visitor. 'Twas not unreasonable to suspect the man holding her had something—nay, had *everything!*—to do with this new, alarming presence gathering with raucous jeers and shouts just outside the castle's crumbling walls.

Except for her initial struggle, surprise had kept Moyra complacent. Her surprise soon melted into other, stronger emotions: fear laced heavily with confusion.

The forceful mental tug that had woken her and guided her downstairs and into this wretched tunnel had vanished the second her captor's fingers had curled around her arm. Had the strange, internal pull been leading her toward this man, whose arms were coiled with breath-squeezing tightness around her, or to the loud, tough reivers converging outside . . . ?

God in heaven, she didn't know!

Twisting her head to the side, she was relieved when the man shifted his hand enough to allow her to breathe a wee bit easier. Squeezing her eyes closed, she forced herself to inhale slowly, deeply, evenly.

With effort, Moyra cleared her mind, focusing her concentration solely upon summoning back that vague, breathless lure of sensation—a sensation so familiar, yet so very foreign and fragile.

After a moment, she sighed in frustration and opened her eyes. Like a rabbit stubbornly burrowing deeper within its hole, the sensation refused to resurface.

In another second she was exhaling and experiencing an entirely different emotion: panic.

The hand wrapped around her waist left her. The sliver of light indicating the entrance to the tunnel disappeared and she heard a soft click when the door was pulled closed. In another instant, the hand was back. A blade was pressed to her throat; the metal was colder than death, the hand that wielded it skillful and untrembling.

"Listen to me, wench, and listen well. I'll say this but once." His hot breath blasted over her ear and cheek and neck as he spoke. "If you value your life, do not move, do not cry out. The sound you hear is Iain Douglas and his men approaching. A very *angry* Iain Douglas, I might add. While I've no wish to spill your blood, 'tis a sentiment I doubt he shares."

Moyra inhaled sharply. The Douglas? *Here?* Sweet Lord, there 'twas a reiver to be feared, and with good reason. The tales of his nasty deeds on both English and Scots sides of the Border had echoed through her childhood, fueling more than one adolescent nightmare. If she'd thought the blade being pressed expertly to her throat was something to inspire terror, the prospect of being delivered into the unsavory hands of Iain Douglas was . . . well now, 'twas at least one hundred-fold worse!

Stifling the urge to struggle against the strong arms holding her was not easy, but it was something Moyra knew she'd no choice but to do.

The noises outside grew louder, closer. No longer was there the stomping of horse's hooves, instead she heard the muffled growls of male voices and the clatter of more than one bootheel upon the hard stone stairs of the wheel staircase as the Douglas and his men began searching the keep.

"Mpfh frrr!" The hand covering her mouth muffled Moyra's words. She felt the body pressing against her back ripple with tension.

"You are trying my patience, wench," the man growled softly in her ear, but Moyra shook her head insistently and repeated herself.

The hot, harsh rasp of an aggravated sigh washed over her. She could tell the man was debating what to do with his suddenly disobedient captive.

Moyra gritted her teeth in frustration. If he would but take his hand away from her mouth, she could tell him what had spurred her reaction!

As though he'd read her mind, one by one he pried his fingers reluctantly away from her mouth.

She sucked in great gulps of the mold-scented air, then softly hissed, "I've a fire lit in the third-floor bedchamber. 'Tis nae big, but 'tis big enough tae attract attention. When the Douglas finds it, he'll know the keep isna deserted and he'll expand his search. Och! The stories I've heard of the mon may nae be true, but if they are, he'll nae stop looking until he finds who lit that fire."

"Bloody hell." Though barely a whisper, the curse bounced off the damp stone walls. If Moyra had thought the body pressing against her felt tense before, 'twas nothing compared to the rigidity she felt in it now. "So help me, if you're lying to me wen—"

"Me name is Moyra, *nae* wench. And what reason would I have tae lie?"

"Good question." His pause was as heavy as the cold night air prickling at her skin. "Truly, I do not know." He sighed, and the wisps of hair clinging to her cheek were disturbed by the warm puff of air. "Are you certain the Douglas will discover your fire? Absolutely positive?"

"Aye. There's a wee chance he'll nae smell and hear it when he climbs the stairs, but he'd need tae be blind nae to see the glow when he passes the first chamber after the stairwell." Her voice hardened slightly. "Since I wasna expecting company, it ne'er occurred to me to douse the fire when I came downstairs tae, er"—she cleared her throat softly—"aye, tae sneak a bite tae eat."

" 'Tis a might late for that, is it not?"

"Me eating habits are none of yer concern, mon. We've more important matters to attend."

"Aye, of course."

The hand wielding the knife eased a bit; Moyra took advantage of the sudden lack of caution to swallow hard. Twice. Dryly. The chill of the blade lingered on her flesh long after the threat of it had been removed.

"Your fire complicates matters considerably. I don't suppose you've given any thought to getting rid of your other unexpected guests . . . ?" he asked huskily.

He shifted, and she detected a subtle catch in his voice. Had he just groaned? Frowning, she wondered at the cause, but only for a moment before swerving her thoughts back to the urgent issue at hand.

"Aye, I've been thinking on it," she admitted. "And, aye, I've an idea or twa."

"Such as . . . ?"

"Methinks it best tae keep me ideas to m'self for the time being. I dinna think ye'd like them."

"Considering the circumstances, wen—er, Moyra, I'm open to any suggestions you have. Try me."

"Well . . ." Moyra hesitated, then sighed. She shrugged as much as the strong arm around her middle would allow. "The fire will alert the Douglas that the keep isna empty, of course. However, methinks there's a chance—a wee one, aye, but a chance all the same—that he'll be satisfied if he but tracks down the source. Once done, he'll have nae reason tae continue searching, don't ye know?"

Again, she felt the muscles pressing against her back tighten with tension. "Surely you're not suggesting *you* go out there?"

"Would *ye* rather do it? I'll nae argue if ye do."

"Don't be a fool. I'm the one he's looking for."

"Exactly." She grinned smugly, even though he could not possibly see the gesture in the darkness of the tunnel. "I suppose ye've a better idea . . . ?"

'Twas yet another excellent question. Bloody hell,

but the woman was annoyingly full of them. As with the first, William had no ready answer. A sigh poured past his lips as he leaned heavily against the damp stone wall. The burning pain in his shoulder had intensified when he'd been forced to grab her. Her every move sliced through him like a knife, blurring his concentration and making his sense of reason unreliable.

Gritting his teeth, he contemplated his options. It did not take long; there were precious few. "A gentleman would not allow a lady to go out there," he said aloud, but to himself. "He would never even *think* of letting her risk her life in such a manner."

"True enough," came her ready reply. "Then again, a gentleman would ne'er hold a dagger tae a lady's throat, nor threaten her life . . . the way *ye* are doing right now. Och! mon, if that doesna tell me ye be nae gentleman, I canna think of what would! Logic, if ye have any, maun tell ye that my way is the only way. After all, ye be wounded and—"

"How did you know?"

"Me nose works perfectly well, thank ye ver' much. I can smell the blood. I can also feel it soaking intae the back of me tunic. 'Tis warm and sticky, and from the feel, ye've spilled more than a few drops. Dinna tell me ye are going to deny it!" She shifted her weight from one bare foot to another, her left shoulder purposely nudging his.

The man's swift inhalation and muted grunt of pain were answer enough.

"I dinna think so." She opened her mouth to say more, but quickly snapped it closed so fast her teeth clicked together painfully.

The muffled noises outside the tunnel had faded

while the Douglas and his men searched the upper floors, leaving them free to speak in hushed whispers. Now, however, the thud of heavy footsteps upon the stairs, combined with the roar of more than one husky male curse, suggested the time for talking was at an end.

Moyra shrugged from her captor's grasp, and noticed the way his arms grudgingly fell from around her.

She started toward the mouth of the tunnel, only to again be brought up short by those powerful fingers coiling tightly around her upper arm.

Softly, softly, a husky voice whispered uncertainly, very close to her ear, "Tell me true, Moyra, is your plan to save me . . . or turn me over for slaughter?"

Just as faintly, she whispered back over her shoulder, "If 'twas slaughtering ye I had in mind, could I nae have screamed and brought the Douglas down upon yer head several times already?"

"Aye, you *could* have."

"But I dinna."

"Mayhap 'tis because you have a more dire plan for me . . . ?"

"Yer trust is . . . inspiring," she hissed, her body stiffening with indignation.

"For good reason, don't you think? By letting you go out there and face Iain Douglas alone, I am putting my life in your hands."

"And by offering freely tae do it, *when I dinna have tae,* does it nae stand tae reason I'll be risking me own?" she countered coldly.

As the truth of her words sank in, his fingers loosed. Not a lot, but enough for her to slip free of his grasp.

A rustle of cloth and a quick inhalation said he'd instinctively lurched after her.

One quick step forward put her out of his reach.

Another and she'd slipped through the door to the tunnel and into the storage area beyond. As quietly as she could, she closed the secret panel, leaning back heavily against it.

It took a few seconds for her eyes to adjust to even this scant lighting. Blinking hard, she scanned the storage area. A sigh of relief slipped past her lips when she saw she was still alone.

For now.

That would not last . . . or so said the clomping of bootheels upon stone stairs.

Moyra's heart raced; the idea of facing Iain Douglas, a reiver she'd heard tales of but never actually met in the flesh, was enough to cause a surge of adrenaline to pump hot and fast through her bloodstream. The palms she splayed over the wooden shelves she leaned heavily against were damp with nervous perspiration. Her lungs burned for air, even though she filled them continuously with sharp, shallow breaths.

The footsteps drew closer.

They paused at the foot of the stairs, in the tiny, square, stone-box of a foyer that led either into the storage area or out of the castle.

There wasn't a doubt in Moyra's mind as to which direction those steps would take.

Mustering the tattered remains of her courage, she took a step forward. Two. Her bare feet felt as though they'd been encased in lead, yet she forced one in front of the other. What choice did she have? To be caught lingering near the tunnel's secret entrance was a mistake she was not willing, or foolish enough, to make.

Remembering the bloodstain that must surely be visible on her back, she quickly released her braid and fluffed the long, thick platinum strands around her shoulders. 'Twas the best she could do. With luck, her hair combined with the poor lighting would hide the incriminating bloodstain from view.

By the time Iain Douglas rounded the corner, Moyra was standing in the middle of the storage area.

Her spine was stiff and straight, her shoulders squared, her chin tipped at a proud, haughty angle that some said only an Elliot could attain. The generous folds of her plaid hid her quivering knees from view.

Four

"Willie Armstrong? Answer me, mon, I know yer in here. Ye'd best be showing that fair-bonnie face of yers, and showing it soon. I dinna want to hunt ye down, but I will . . . and I'll be *finding* ye if 'tis the last thing I do!"

The words exploded from Iain Douglas's barrel-shaped chest as he rounded the corner . . . and came to an abrupt halt. Even after he'd stopped speaking, his voice continued to ricochet off the cold stone walls; the echoes of it blasted over Moyra like deafening claps of thunder.

Lacing her fingers tightly in front of her, she took a deep breath and met the man's furious gaze with a level one of her own. Considering his brawny size and the hard, unforgiving glint in his eyes, she could easily believe all the tales she'd heard of this man true.

Her voice, when it came, was sharp and clear and steady. "What is all this racket aboot? Wyndehaghen belongs tae the Elliots. There be nae Armstrongs here."

A handful of men burst into the room behind the huge, redheaded man. They stopped short, forming a ragged-looking semicircle behind their laird. More than one surprised glance went Moyra's way.

She paid them no mind; 'twas the Douglas upon whom her gaze was trained, and she refused to let it stray. As she watched, his deep-set green eyes narrowed shrewdly. The suspicion glistening in them was as keen as that sharpening his tone. "Ye know me name, *lhuga towdie?*"

Her spine stiffened at the derogatory reference to her size. A scrawny hen, indeed! "Aye," she replied curtly. "Ye be Iain Douglas, the fiercest reiver on the Scots side of the Border. Or so yer reputation suggests."

" 'Tis a reputation well earned."

She shrugged. "Mayhap."

The Douglas's attention traveled over Moyra—slowly, assessively—from the top of her platinum head to the pink curls of her bare toes, then just as slowly back up again. "Ye dinna believe it?"

"I've nae reason tae *dis*believe it. Yet."

"Watch that tongue, lass, or ye'll find yerself lacking it come the morn." One bushy red eyebrow cocked high in his weathered forehead. Through the scraggly curl of his moustache she saw his lips purse. "Ye show nae fear in facing me squarely."

"Should I?"

"Few men on either side of these wild Borders would dare look at me with such arrogance."

This time it was Moyra's turn to shrug; the gesture was tight and strained. "I'm nae a mon."

"Aye, and well I can see it. Although there looks tae be barely enough of ye tae make up one lass."

The line of her jaw hardened, and her eyes narrowed

sharply. "I repeat, there's nae Armstrong here, especially nae William. Rumor has it the mon be long dead."

"Nay, lass, he isna dead. 'Tis a condition I'll rectify when I find him."

"Dead or alive, it matters naught tae me. Ye be wasting time looking for him at Wyndehaghen."

"Dinna listen tae her, m'lord," one of the men behind him said. "She lies. With our own eyes, twa of us saw Willie Armstrong riding this way."

Moyra shifted her attention to the man who'd spoken. Tall and lanky, with long, sweat-mussed brown hair, he shifted uneasily beneath her bold inspection. "I'm nae denying what ye say ye saw. He may well have ridden this way. Then again, he may nae have. Howe'er, just because he rode this way doesna mean he stopped here. And why would he? Wyndehaghen has lain in ruins for near a decade. Only a complete fool would hide amongst crumbled stone that is easily searched." Her attention shifted to the Douglas. "Ye need nae take me word for it. Look for yerself, ye'll nae find him."

"We *have* looked, wench. And on our first pass, we dinna see *ye.*"

"Then ye dinna look ver' well."

The instant the words slipped off her tongue, Moyra wished she could bite them back. Of course, it was too late to do so now.

As one, the men behind Iain Douglas, who'd begun talking in hushed whispers amongst themselves, fell silent when their laird took a quick, threatening step forward. Although it wasn't possible, Moyra could have sworn the hard stone floor shuddered beneath the pent-up fury of the big man's mighty step and weight. The Douglas's normally ruddy complexion had drained to ashy-white, then just as quickly darkened to a splotchy, anger-induced red.

With a hiss of frigid midnight air, the broadsword he clenched in his big fist arced up with deadly intent.

He stood close enough for Moyra to catch the pungent, leather-and-sweat smell of him. And more than close enough for the sword's powerful descent to do her nerves severe damage.

Her first instinct was to cry out, mayhap even cringe and take a swift, protective step backward.

In the end, she did neither.

Standing her ground, she planted balled fists atop the slender curve of her hips—more to keep her fingers from visibly trembling than to reenforce her stance, although the Douglas had no need to know it!—and tipped her chin up yet another proud notch.

Trapping her breath in her lungs until it burned, she met his furious glare with an unflinching look of her own.

The big man hesitated in midstep. Och! but he was sorely tempted to carry through on the blow, as was evident in the way his eyes flashed with outrage and the way a thick blue vein pushed at the leathery skin of his forehead. The vein pounded in time to his harsh, erratic heartbeat. His knuckles were white, aching from the strain of his grip on the sword's hilt. His brawny arm literally shook with the effort to hold himself, and his rage, in check.

"I've heard Iain Douglas isna opposed tae slaughtering innocent, unarmed women," Moyra remarked mildly—and wondered how her tone could remain so calm and smooth when her insides were churning so violently. "I'd nae have believed it, though, him being a fellow Scot and all. Until now."

"Ye test me sorely, lass," the Douglas growled, even as he slowly lowered his sword. More than one of the men gathered behind him tensed at the quiet fury reverberating in their laird's tone. "If ye've a mind tae keep that head of yers, ye'd best tell me where I'll be finding Willie Armstrong.

"I've already told ye—"

"And now *I* be telling *ye*— "

"—there's nae Armstrong here."

"—I dinna believe a word!"

Moyra glanced briefly up at the ceiling, sighed heavily, shook her head. The thick platinum curls trailing down her spine swayed back and forth with the gesture.

"Believe whate'er ye like," she said. "Surely there's naught I can say tae change yer mind." With a forced shrug, she gestured to the storage room stretching emptily around them. "Why ye think an Elliot would go tae the trouble of aiding a God-rot-em Armstrong is beyond me, Douglas. But ye need nae take me word for it. Go ahead, rip the keep apart stone by stone if ye maun . . . it shouldna take long; there be precious few stones left standing. The results will be the same. By the time ye finish searching, yer precious quarry will be halfway tae crotchety old Queen Bess's court."

Moyra took a small step forward, testing the strength in her knees. Finding the joints to be trembly but stable, she took another step. Another.

She was a mere hand's breadth away from the shadowy doorway when Iain Douglas's booming voice shot out from behind her. All the while, she expected him or his men to make some move to stop her progress, but they did not.

"So help me, wench, if I e'er find out yer lying tae me, I'll—"

"Rip me apart with yer bare hands?" she finished for him dryly. "Aye, I've nae doubt aboot it. And nae worries. I'm nae lying . . . as ye'll discover soon enough."

"Ye know the penalty for hiding an outlaw and interfering in a hot trod, do ye nae?"

"Of course. Everyone knows it. Howe'er, 'tis nae something I need concern m'self aboot. I'm guilty of neither." That said, she continued on, not allowing herself to relax until she'd succeeded in leaving the storage chamber unscathed.

The tiny foyer was degrees cooler. Not surprising since it lacked the heat of a dozen or so burly Douglas bodies to warm it.

Moyra welcomed the refreshing coolness. The air here was crisp and sharp and noticeably devoid of the sour odor of sweaty male bodies.

'Twas also devoid of the tangy scent of spilled blood.

Cautiously, Moyra began climbing the narrow, treacherously dark stairway. Her ascent was hesitant, for she still expected the Douglas or one of his men to stop her. When they did not, her thoughts strayed to the tunnel below. Nay, that was not true. More accurately, they fixed on the wounded man hiding within its dark, dank depths.

Was William Armstrong still there? Still hiding? Still waiting patiently for her to rid the keep of Iain

Douglas, as she'd promised she would? Or had he given up and retraced his steps through the tunnel, hoping to put distance between himself and the deadly man who hunted him?

She supposed the answers to those questions depended upon how badly he was wounded. In the darkness of the tunnel, she couldn't gauge the extent of his injury. All she'd known for sure was that he was definitely wounded; only someone with no sense of smell would have missed the unmistakable, sharp tang of blood in the air. Aye, he was bleeding and, judging by the remembered intensity of the scent on the moldy air, bleeding heavily.

Moyra's footsteps faltered when another thought occurred to her. She tripped, stumbled, came up against the cold stone wall gloving the stairway hard enough to push the breath from her lungs.

What if William Armstrong had already bled to death?

Moyra swallowed hard. Her knees trembled beneath the coarse folds of her plaid skirt.

Why, she wondered, should the idea disturb her? Reivers were slaughtered on both sides of this violent Border so often that the crime was heinously commonplace. Such was the price of basing one's livelihood upon thieving from one's neighbors.

Still . . .

She shivered, hugging her arms around her. While she wasn't sure why the prospect of William Armstrong perishing in her tunnel should bother her, she *was* sure that it did. It bothered her tremendously.

William Armstrong . . .

The name reverberated through her mind like one

of the Douglas's unholy roars bouncing off the icy stone walls in the storage chamber below.

She hadn't been lying when she'd told the Douglas she thought William Armstrong was dead. 'Twas a popular rumor; no one had seen nor heard from the eldest Armstrong son in well over half-a-dozen years, since shortly after his mother's third marriage, in fact.

Now that she knew William Armstrong was alive, however . . .

Och! What on earth was *he* doing here at Wyndehaghen? Was the man not a wee bit far from home? Aye, she thought, *more* than a wee bit, in fact. Surely he was too far west to be leading a foray into this untamed section of Liddesdale.

Besides, what reiver who cherished his unsavory reputation—not to mention his precious life—dared ride in the middle of winter? Being a lass, Moyra had never taken part in an attack, yet in years gone by she'd watched her father and brother participate in several; even *she* knew icy puddles and hard-packed ground were not conducive to raiding.

From the storage chamber below came the commotion of men talking and moving about. The sounds spurred Moyra to hastily finish ascending the wheel staircase to the third floor.

The fire had dwindled. Only a few meager tongues of snapping orange flame licked at the scant remains of charred wood. A quick glance said the pile stacked beside the hearth contained only enough fuel to get her through the bitter cold night . . . if she was stingy.

Gathering her plaid skirt in tight fists, Moyra hoisted it up to her knees and sat down cross-legged upon the floor. At least the stones here, close to the hearth, were still moderately warm. 'Twould make her wait a wee bit more comfortable.

And waiting, she knew, was all that could be done now.

She had done her best to rid Wyndehaghen of the Douglas. Whether or not she'd succeeded had yet to be proved. Until it was, there was naught more she could do.

With a sigh, she brushed a few stray wisps of hair back from her brow, arranged her posture so her spine didn't ache quite so badly, and set about waiting for the Douglas to leave as patiently as her naturally impatient nature allowed. Which was not very patiently at all.

William Armstrong leaned his good shoulder heavily against a wall that his pitch-black surroundings forbade him from seeing. Beyond the panel through which he'd not long ago glimpsed the woman disappear, he now heard muffled sounds.

Footsteps.

Talking.

He judged the latter to be too deep and fierce to belong to the woman he'd encountered in this dark, dank tunnel. That didn't mean Moyra wasn't out there, of course, it only meant he couldn't detect her voice.

The pain in his shoulder was sharper than ever, a vibrant, slicing ache that increased with his every ragged breath, shooting all the way down his side and up to the tension-bunched muscles in his neck. Movement of any sort was a torment equal to none.

A part of William wanted to turn down the unlit

tunnel and blindly fumble back the way he'd come. A larger, saner part of him recognized the urge as foolhardy in the extreme.

As though sensing his indecision, the mare nudged the small of his back with her nose. Well trained for battle, the horse did not so much as whicker to give away their presence.

William's thoughts volleyed between what awaited him at both ends of this damnably dark tunnel. Surely a man like Iain Douglas did not earn such an unsavory reputation for naught.

He couldn't imagine the Douglas venturing into the keep with all his men. Nay, 'twould be a reckless thing to do, and the Douglas was known for nothing so much as his great care. Especially the care he took in his ambushes . . . but William did not want to think about *that* right now.

More likely the Douglas would take only half his men with him into the keep, while leaving the other half to circle the outer walls, instructed to keep a sharp eye out for any attempt at escape.

Were the situation reversed, wouldn't William do the same himself?

Aye, he would. Which made the idea of slipping quietly away into the night an impossibility, even more so as the wound in his shoulder continued to shed blood despite his best attempts to stem the flow.

Blast it! If it wouldn't risk gaining the Douglas's attention, William would have slammed his fist against the damp stone wall in frustration. Instead, he settled for gritting his teeth and glaring into the unbroken blackness. Neither helped curb his festering irritation.

Being powerless to help himself was not a sensation

he'd felt before; it grated on his already chafed nerves.
Nor did he like any better the idea of putting his life
in someone else's hands . . . especially when the
someone in question was a *woman*.

Oh, aye, there was no question the latter fact rankled
him the most. His mother and her many marriages
had proven to him all too clearly how fickle and un-
trustworthy the feminine gender could be.

The muffled thuds of footsteps echoed on the other
side of the panel behind which he hid. They were
alarmingly close.

The sounds snagged William's full attention.

Holding his breath, he pressed his spine and the
back of his head against the stone wall behind him,
as if in so doing he could also somehow camouflage
himself should the Douglas accidentally stumble upon
whatever mechanism opened the secret panel from the
other side.

Pain ripped through his shoulder when his hand,
slick and warm with too much of his own blood,
inched lower. One by one, his fingers curled around
the hilt of the broadsword strapped to his hip.

"Are ye *still* here, Douglas?" Moyra stood poised
on the bottom step of the wheel staircase. Leaning
forward, she could only just see around the corner.
Out of the group of men gathered in the middle of
the storage chamber, her gaze sought and found Iain
Douglas. 'Twas not difficult; he stood a full head taller
than most of his men. "What are ye looking for now?
If 'tis food ye be foraging for, I'll warn ye now, I've
none tae spare."

"Ye know what I be looking for," the Douglas growled menacingly.

"Nae William Armstrong still." She shook her head. "I dinna understand. Surely by now ye realize he isna here."

"Aye," the Douglas said as, lifting his chin, he scratched the underside of his shaggy red beard thoughtfully. "I'm beginning tae think ye were telling the truth aboot that."

"And what reason would I have tae lie?"

" 'Tis a question I've been asking m'self o'er and o'er this last hour. I've yet tae come up with a reasonable answer. I'm of a mind ye have nae reason, nor were ye lying when ye said the lad ne'er stopped here."

Moyra smiled despite herself. "Does it always take ye so long tae come tae yer senses and see the way of things?"

"Nae usually." The big man's green eyes narrowed shrewdly. "Only when a woman is involved, I assure ye."

"Ye've nae hope of finding the Armstrong now. Ye know that, do ye nae?"

"Aye," he said, his tone lowering a dark, fierce pitch, "I know it . . . and more. It doesna mean, howe'er, that I'll ne'er find him. I *will*. Mayhap nae tonight, but another night for certain."

Moyra shrugged as though the matter was of no concern to her. If only the Douglas knew the truth of it! With effort, she made sure not to let her suddenly light, hopeful disposition seep into either her tone or expression. "I dinna doubt it. Nor would I want tae be the mon when ye do."

A few of the Douglas's men echoed the sentiment in hushed whispers and nods.

For himself, the Douglas ignored both his men and Moyra as his frustrated gaze swept one last time around the empty storage chamber. Shaking his head, he drew his bushy red eyebrows together to form furrows as deep as the river Esk on his weathered brow.

Without so much as glancing in Moyra's direction, he gestured abruptly to his men, spun on his heel and left the storage chamber. His heels echoed sharply on the stone as he crossed the small foyer in a single step, then disappeared out the main doorway, his men close on his heels.

Moyra waited a moment.

Two.

Two more.

As difficult as it was, she forced herself to wait for at least another handful of minutes.

Drifting in from outside were gruff shouts, followed by the thuds of retreating hoofbeats.

Moyra closed her eyes and sent up a silent prayer of thanks.

The Douglas had left Wyndehaghen.

Finally.

Och! now the *real* work would commence!

Five

"Och! mon, yer going tae have tae help a wee bit. I canna support another ounce of yer weight!" Moyra hoisted William's heavy arm around her shoulder, even as she stumbled against the cold, solid stairway wall.

His body collided with her side. Hard. 'Twas a wonder her ribs weren't crushed under the pressure!

Grunting, Moyra forced more strength into her knees than had ever been there before. Somehow, she managed to keep them both erect. Barely. The muscles in her shoulders tightened, the ones in her back pinched with the effort. Despite the frosty night air, perspiration coated her brow and the soft skin above her upper lip.

Had they not already reached the second-floor landing—*more than halfway to her chamber*—she might have succumbed to discouragement and given up.

William Armstrong felt like lead.

While he wasn't completely limp, he was dangerously close to it. What few words he'd spoken thus far were half Gaelic, half English, and completely undecipherable. The beginning of a fever had him in its blistering grip. Through both their clothing she felt the strong, damp heat of him seep into her own skin.

'Twas too chilly here on the stairway, too far from the fire's meager heat for him to be sweating so severely.

The third-floor bedchamber was but twelve dark, steep stairs above . . .

Moyra's body ached from bearing the bulk of William's powerful weight. How much farther could she go before collapsing from exhaustion?

He mumbled something under his breath, his words slurred and indistinguishable.

Moyra ignored him.

For the last quarter-hour, while she'd been struggling to get him upstairs, he'd said quite a bit. Since none of it made a bit of sense, she'd long since stopped listening or even trying to interpret his words. Lack of blood tended to addle the brain. She'd learned as much from a girlhood spent tending the wounds of her father and brother. 'Twas many years ago, aye, but some things could never be forgotten.

Gritting her teeth, she rearranged his big arm around her neck and, bracing herself for the pain in her back she knew was to come, shoved away from the wall.

William faltered into step with her; she used his own momentum to propel them both up the next step.

The next.

And the half-a-dozen steps after that.

She could barely distinguish the dim, flat shape of the landing from here. It appeared to loom far in the distance. The curving staircase seemed to tunnel around her, stretching on for an extraordinary long way . . . much farther away than it had ever looked before.

By the time they reached it, Moyra was panting and sore in muscles she hadn't known existed.

For his own part, William seemed to be barely conscious. His breaths heaved in and out of his lungs in agonized rasps. While he didn't groan often, when he did the sound was so softly tortured that Moyra swore she could feel the pain reflected in it all the way down to her cold, bare toes.

"The hard part be o'er, mon. We're almost there," she whispered encouragingly, her breaths hard and ragged as she guided him down the shadow-strewn corridor. "Now wouldna be a good time tae faint."

He grunted something that, she supposed, was an assurance he would stay conscious. Considering his pained, scratchy tone, she thought it less than reassuring.

The heat of the fire, skimpy though it was, hit Moyra the instant she hauled the man over the threshold. It must have hit him, too, for she felt William sigh in appreciation.

Lugging him the last few feet to the hearth tested her strained endurance, but she managed it. Somehow.

As one, they collapsed to their knees on the hard, fire-warmed stone floor.

His arm was still slung over her shoulder, his body pressed firmly against her side. For a split second, Moyra found herself wondering which was hotter, the dwindling fire . . . or this man's body.

In another second she shooed the thought away, as well as the liquid heat of sensation thoughts of his body caused to flood through her. Her own body was aching as she reached up and, as gently as she could, lifted his heavy arm from around her neck. Without the burden of his weight, the pain in her back immediately eased.

Like a bairn's rag doll containing not a stitch of its own life or strength, without her support William swayed then toppled to the side. He landed atop the hard stone floor like a thatched hut struck by a strong winter gust.

Moyra lunged for him, trying to break his fall as much as she could. However, he was a large, muscular man and she was but a tiny slip of a lass. He landed with a *thud* and a sharp hiss exhaled through tightly clenched teeth.

Had he still been conscious, Moyra might have offered an apology for such a rough landing. How was she to know he would tumble over the instant she let him go?

One quick glance told her that even if an apology had been offered, he'd not have heard a word of it. 'Twas just as well; she was more than a wee bit out of breath and doubted she'd have been able to voice it anyway.

Although her sore body cried out for sleep, there was no time for such luxury. Not when a fine muckle more needed to be done this night. William's wounds had to be evaluated and tended, the sooner the better—indeed, they should have been treated an hour or so ago—and she must see to his mount. Her own aches and pains and weariness, no matter how intense, were too insignificant by comparison to take priority.

Ignoring the discomfort in her arms and legs and back, Moyra shoved herself to her feet and glanced down at the man. Lying upon the floor as he was, William Armstrong did not look so large, nor so intimidating. Just the opposite, his softly relaxed features and pasty complexion gave him an air of vulnerability that she'd not have expected to see in any Armstrong.

While it was true she'd helped tend her father's and brother's wounds in the past, in truth, Moyra was not a nurturer by nature. Her mother had forced the chore upon her. Because compliance was expected, Moyra had never argued or objected.

Sighing reluctantly, she wiped her palms on the plaid covering her thighs, then cast a skeptical glance about the bare chamber. At least with her father and brother, she'd had resources available to draw upon. Tonight, with this man, she had naught but her own ingenuity . . . any healing herbs and dressings this castle had once stored were long since gone; those that remain would surely be too decayed from time to be of any use.

Her contemplative glance returned again to the man who lay at her feet. Reluctantly, she realized there was no help for it. If she was to tend William, and she seemed to have no choice in the matter, then she would need to utilize what paltry means were available—and pray to God they proved adequate.

First things first, however. She needed to peel off his jack, and the blood-soaked tunic beneath, in order to examine that wound. 'Twas the only way to determine just how badly William was hurt. Only then could she decide what, if anything, could be done to heal him.

Clenching her teeth so hard her temples throbbed, Moyra knelt upon the floor at his side. Wrinkling her nose and swallowing hard, she inwardly issued a silent command for her stomach to cease its nauseating churning, then reached reluctantly for the collar of his blood-soaked jack . . .

William would have liked nothing better than to languish forever in the sweet, painless, black velvet blanket he was wrapped tightly within.

Alas, he could not.

As he slowly regained consciousness, the pain in his shoulder reasserted itself. At first it was naught more than an uncomfortable twinge. Then, as the blackness receded and he tried to move, the sensation was transformed into a sharp, slicing pain.

His breath caught and his brow furrowed. Sharp stabs of agony tore through his mind and body like the tusks of a wild boar ripping through bare, unprotected flesh.

Sucking in a sharp breath, William forced himself to lie still until the pain subsided. It seemed to take forever. Mayhap longer. One by one he mentally coerced his muscles to relax. Eventually, he felt the world around him stopped spinning and dipping in great, sickening circles that threatened to drag him straight back down into the whirlpool of vast, painless darkness.

By all that was holy, he could *not* let that happen!

Having finally managed to grasp a bit of lucidity, he held on firmly, refusing to relinquish it. His instincts, always sharp, were screaming for him to stay conscious, pain or no pain. The Douglas may have left Wyndehaghen—aye, William remembered that much—but wherever the man had retreated to, William didn't doubt for a minute that he'd not given up the hunt.

Iain Douglas was not a man to give up easily, if at all; nay, the huge man was in possession of a dogged determination that put a pack of bloodthirsty, fox-hunting hounds to shame. Whatever mission the Douglas set for himself, he accomplished. Eventually.

Tonight, his mission had been to hunt down William Armstrong and demand retribution for the younger man's having so shamelessly raided his lands, pilfering his precious beasties.

The Douglas was well within his legal rights to launch what was known on either side of the Border as a "hot trod"—the immediate pursuit of thieving reivers in an attempt to reclaim stolen goods and exact vengeance for the time and trouble it took. Impromptu lynchings were not uncommon, nor were they illegal . . . provided the guilty party could be caught. 'Twas not an easy feat, that.

William's first raid had not gone well. Nay, not well at all.

Someone inside the Douglas's keep had sounded the alarm at almost the exact same instant William and his men absconded with over two hundred prime Douglas beasties. The Douglas, of course, had tried to stop them. When that failed, the man had launched a hot trod, meanwhile sending men ahead to set up one of his renowned ambushes.

The ambush had been embarrassingly successful. Not only had Iain Douglas succeeded in recapturing his prized cattle, he'd also captured twenty-eight of William's own men.

William had witnessed it all . . . a mere second or

two before all hell had broken loose. He would never know for certain whose bow had sent the arrow that had buried itself in his shoulder, who had shot it with such deadly precision. He had an uneasy feeling it had been the Douglas himself.

Before the pain had had a chance to hit him in full force, he and his men had abandoned the fight. Scattering, they'd ridden in all directions, scrambling for the cover of trees and hills.

Perhaps, had he been back on the Scots side of the Border longer, and had had more time to reacquaint himself with its craggy landscape, William would not have taken such a grievously wrong turn? 'Twas a turn that had him riding not west toward his own castle, but east . . . toward the crumbled remains of Wyndehaghen.

Ah, but it was far too late for self-recrimination now. What was done was done; hindsight, no matter how humiliatingly accurate, could change naught.

Setting his jaw hard, William pried his eyes open. The glow of the fire was vague, yet to someone who'd so recently regained consciousness, it seemed blinding. Squinting against the sudden light, he tried to ignore the way it stabbed into his eyes with a sharpness to rival the throbbing agony tearing through his shoulder.

Blinking hard, he gave himself a moment to grow accustomed to the meager brightness. Once that was accomplished, William scanned the small bedchamber. Like the rest of Wyndehaghen, it was discouragingly empty. No bed. No tables. No chairs. There was naught to even distinguish the room as a bedchamber, naught to set it apart from any of the many other vacant rooms in the ruined keep.

Frowning, he shifted his attention. His gaze fixed upon the woman standing beside a window whose glass had either been stolen or broken nearly a decade prior. The vacant casing was chipped and hanging askew.

A frigid winter wind rushed into the room like a cold sigh. The gust poured over the woman, tossing her long, unbound hair back over her slender shoulders. The strands flowed like a waterfall of moonlight down her back, their ends swaying almost to her knees.

If she was aware of either the wind or its bitter coldness, she gave no sign. William's frown deepened. He would have expected her to huddle tightly within the folds of the tattered plaid she'd tossed about her shoulders, seeking out its irresistible warmth the way a moth sought out a hot flame. Yet she did not. Instead she released a soft sigh and leaned a shoulder wearily against the broken window casing.

From this angle he could see only a small portion of her delicately molded profile. 'Twas enough to see that her gaze didn't waver from the distant, moon-swept horizon.

Did she realize he was awake? William thought not, and for that he was grateful. It gave him a chance to study her without her being aware of his scrutiny.

And study her, he did.

Most hard.

His gaze traveled from the top of her silky platinum head to the pink-tipped curls of her bare toes. She was a tiny woman, much smaller than he'd imagined she would be. The pale cloud of her hair seemed to add length to the narrow lines of her face. Her neck was long and smooth and tapered, her shoulders slender yet surprisingly solid.

William could not have said what he'd expected the woman to look like. Truly, he'd been in a good deal of pain during their time in the tunnel, not to mention dizzy from loss of blood; contemplating her looks had been the last thing on his mind. Still, when he'd put his arms around her, he'd gotten a basic impression of her size and shape.

Short, and scrawnier than a half-starved hen, had been his first impression. Now, looking at her in the mingling moon- and firelight, he was forced to reassess.

She wasn't bony and angular. Rather, her body was softly molded, appealingly slender. Her hips were lean, but pleasantly curved. He assumed the legs hidden beneath the baggy folds of her plaid, were also enticingly slim and shapely.

Curious, his attention strayed upward. Her complexion, he noticed, was smooth and creamy, with a healthy pink undertone. As he watched, a single tear trailed over the curve of her cheek, rounded the tightly bunched line of her jaw, dripped down the side of her neck until it was soaked up by the collar of her faded, butternut yellow tunic.

This time the stab of pain arrowing through William could not be traced back to anything as simple as the wound in his shoulder.

Frowning, he hardened himself against the instinctive softening thawing his insides. God blast it, she was a woman. He need know nothing else about her to realize that she could not be trusted. Oh, aye, she'd proved herself kinder than most of her gender—William could not imagine his mother risking her life for a wounded stranger—yet she was a woman all the same.

She was also, he reminded himself, an Elliot.

The Liddesdale extension of the two clans hadn't openly feuded for centuries, yet it was common knowledge on both sides of the Border that Elliots and Armstrongs were destined to fight again one day.

A woman *and* an Elliot.

A more wretched combination, William could not imagine.

Whatever the cause of her tears, 'twas not his concern. Lord knew, he'd enough troubles of his own at the moment. He was not about to offer to shoulder hers as well, even if she had saved his life. Gratitude went only so far!

"Is there a sound more haunting than the shrill of a lone bagpipe?" she asked suddenly.

William repressed a sharp inhalation of surprise. While her tone was strained, the calm Scots burr, coupled with the way she did not glance at him when she spoke, suggested she'd known he was awake for quite some time.

"N-Nay, none that I can think of," he answered after a thoughtful hesitation. "Then again, 'tis been several years since I've heard the wail of the pipe, lone or otherwise. And I don't hear it now."

"Och! That explains why yer accent sounds so heavily Sassenach . . ."

"It does not—"

"Aye, it does. Is there something wrong with yer

hearing? Canna ye hear yerself?" Even from this angle, William saw a dry, unemotional grin tug at one
corner of her lips. Her voice went gruff and low as
she imitated him in a most unflattering manner. " 'It
does not'." She shook her head, sighed. "Nae 'dinna,'
ye said 'does not,' and ye said it maun precisely. The
Sassenach inflection is there, e'en if ye be deaf tae
it."

"I've spent a good deal of my life in England," he
replied, feeling an annoying need to explain himself
and relieve his chafed, innate Scots pride. " 'Tis only
natural I'd pick up their coarse manners of speech."

Her shrug was tight. "Aye, well, methinks talking
like a Sassenach is a fine muckle better than being
dead."

"I beg your pardon—?"

"I said 'tis better than being dead. Dinna ye ken?
when ye mother married for the third time, and ye
disappeared o'er the Border, nae tae be seen nor heard
from again, 'twas rumored ye'd died. Mind ye, 'twas
nae a rumor anyone tried o'er hard to put tae rest, so
I assumed it true."

"You assumed wrong. As you can see, I'm very
much alive."

Slowly, purposefully, she glanced back at him from
over her shoulder. Her gaze—were her eyes green or
blue? In this light, and at this angle, it was impossible
to tell—fixed on him. Her attention tarried briefly on
his face before drifting down to the shoulder she'd
bandaged with strips of an old, tattered-but-freshly-
boiled sheet.

Even without words, her meaning was clear.

He was alive . . . barely . . . and only thanks to *her*. "How is yer shoulder?"

William tried to mimic her shrug, but winced instead when the aborted gesture made another sharp pain tear through him. "It feels like someone shoved an arrow clean through, then twisted it unmercifully," he admitted through clenched teeth.

"Nae clean through, but close." With her fist, she defiantly swiped away the moist trail the tear had left, then pushed away from the broken window casing and crossed to the hearth. Bending, she retrieved from the floor the remains of the arrow she'd so recently removed from his shoulder. The thin rod was in two pieces; the shorter piece, the part with the deadly metal tip, was thick with a crust of dry blood. "I thought ye may be wanting a souvenir of yer exploits. Few can claim surviving one of the Douglas's ambushes, dinna ye ken?"

"It may still be a wee bit premature to say I've survived my encounter with him, lass. I've a strong feeling 'tis just begun."

She nodded, and William found himself distracted by a thick strand of platinum hair, and the way it fell forward over her shoulder. The pain in his own shoulder kept him from surrendering to an odd, overpowering urge to reach out and touch that lock of hair. For a reason he could not explain, even if only to himself, he'd an uncanny desire to find out if that thick, glossy strand was as soft and silky as it appeared.

Up close, with the glow of firelight to caress her features, he could finally see her eyes. They were deep set, their color an unusual shade of violet that reminded him of a sun-drenched field of wild heather.

Like an itch he couldn't quite reach, a memory tickled at the back of William's mind . . . old and foggy and unplaceable.

Had he met this woman before? Nay. If he had, surely he'd remember. How could a man forget a woman whose hair and eyes were so vivid and striking? Aye, she was memorable in the extreme. Few women could boast of hair such as hers—thick and plentiful, each strand the color of a high, full moon. Fewer still possessed eyes of that odd, translucent shade of violet, so sharp and clear they seemed to look right through a man, and into his very soul.

"The Douglas will be back," William said, as much to distract his own wayward thoughts as anything. "You know that, do you not?"

"Aye," she murmured as, leaning forward, she tossed the broken arrow into the snapping flames, "but nae until tomorrow eve. We've time yet."

"I'm not so sure. Iain Douglas is known for many things, but patience is not one of them. I doubt he'll stay away that long."

"Trust me, mon, I know when he'll be back and when he willna."

Something in her tone snagged his attention. Frowning, William studied her profile, noting the firm line of resolve in her jaw, the sharp glint of certainty in her eyes as she stared deeply into the dwindling fire. "Do you know something I don't, Moyra?"

Again, that emotionless grin tugged at one corner of her mouth. The sight twisted at him in ways he didn't understand, and wasn't at all sure he wanted to.

"In a manner of speaking, aye, I know a lot most people dinna. I've The Sight."

His eyes narrowed dubiously. "I don't believe in such nonsense."

"Nae one asked ye tae. Howe'er, disbelieving doesna make it any less true." Rubbing her hands together, she stood and walked away from the fire, returning to the window. Her plaid skirt rustled softly around her ankles with each step. "Go back tae sleep, mon. Ye've lost a great deal of blood, and ye maun be exhausted. Ye'll ne'er start healing if ye waste yer strength talking the night away. Besides . . . Och! I be a fine muckle tired of hearing that hated Sassenach whine."

If Moyra had meant to insult him, she'd done a splendid job.

While he might have spent much of his life on the wrong side of the Border, he was a Scot to the bone, and his pride bristled under the criticism. He opened his mouth to tell her as much—nay, to tell her a "fine muckle" more!—only to find the words choked back by a sudden, unsuppressible yawn.

Blast the woman!

Again, she was right. He was exhausted, needed badly to rest and regain his strength. All things considered, he'd used up more energy than he realized staying awake for this long. His shoulder throbbed in time to his every heartbeat, and his eyelids felt scratchy and heavy, sluggish and less willing to lift with each blink.

From the corner of his sleep-heavy eyes, he sent Moyra Elliot a skeptical glance. She was staring out the window again, and for all intents and purposes seemed to have forgotten his presence.

While William doubted that was true, her lack of attention gave him the chance to close his eyes and relax. Only for a moment, of course. Aye, a moment or two of rest was all he needed to gather up what was left of his swiftly ebbing strength and . . .

Before he could even complete the musing, the swirling fingers of darkness had again risen up to enfold him in their sweet, painless, black velvet grip.

Two thoughts swirled simultaneously through William's head as sleep overtook him.

The first was brief and to the point. He prayed the lass was right, that the Douglas would stay away from Wyndehaghen this night.

The second, infinitely more confusing, was the way his tongue, as though on its own, soundlessly wrapped around her name in the same instant conscious thought scattered from his mind.

Moyra . . .

Moyra waited until she was sure William was asleep. It did not take long. In a matter of minutes his ragged breaths smoothed, growing slow and even, their rhythm shallow and lulling. A quick glance and she was sure. His pain-pinched features were still alarmingly pale, but the weathered lines in his cheeks and jaw and forehead had ironed themselves out, smoothing and softening in a way that only a deep, untroubled sleep permitted.

That his slumber was not restless, as before, she considered an encouraging sign. The makeshift herbal salve she'd spread liberally over his wound before dressing it must finally have done its job, dulling the sharp edge of his pain. With luck, he would sleep until dawn, although she very much doubted it.

The salve may have worked its magic for now, but like anything else, its healing powers were limited. Eventually, the blessed numbness would wear off. When it did, the stabbing pain would return in force.

As she watched, William lifted his uninjured arm. He rested a thick forearm atop his forehead, shielding the upper portion of his face from view. Her gaze drifted down his arm, over the light dusting of sandy-colored hair that coated it, settling finally on his hand.

Like drops of melting snow, a chill trickled down her spine.

Her mind's eye flashed her the image of a hand coming out of pitch-black darkness . . .

Reaching . . .

Reaching for her . . .

Moyra inhaled sharply and rubbed at the chill-bumps prickling the skin of her forearms.

The image was so vivid she might have just awakened. She could see each thick knuckle, each roughly callused fingertip. She could even see smudges of dirt clinging beneath each chipped fingernail.

There was no room for doubt.

William Armstrong's was not the hand in her vision.

As though the cold that assailed her also swept over him, William shivered. Groaning, he tried to huddle more deeply beneath the plaid she'd draped over him earlier.

At another time, Moyra would have laughed. A third

of the coarsely woven fabric had been torn away and used to secure his dressing. She'd tossed what remained over his brawny body.

The scrap of cloth was small. He was not. The plaid barely reached his knees.

Keeping warm beneath such an inadequate covering was comparable to throwing oneself in a mountain-fed loch to stay dry. It simply wasn't possible.

A scowl furrowed Moyra's brow as she watched his shivering increase. If his tremors became more violent, he could easily reopen the wound in his shoulder. If, in his weakened state, he caught a chill . . .

Mo chreach! She hadn't gone to so much trouble, facing down the notorious Iain Douglas and saving this man's life, only to have William catch a fever and die now. Moyra shuddered. Nor did she relish the idea of having to reclose and rebandage his wound.

She cast a quick, assessing glance around the room, although she already knew what she would find. Nothing. There was no other blanket to give him except the plaid tossed over her own shoulders. Although it was intact, it had been sewn for her and wasn't much larger than the one covering William now. Any heat the second plaid offered would be minimal.

So how on earth was she to keep him warm . . . ?

The answer, of course, was obvious. Aside from the fire, there was only one other source of heat in the room.

Herself.

Moyra hesitated, not wanting to put her body so close to the his again, yet at the same time not fully understanding her own reluctance. Eventually, she had to recognize the lack of choices involved.

Cursing in Gaelic, she reluctantly shoved away from the window and tentatively approached him.

Six

William had gone to sleep with two thoughts in mind . . .

He woke up with three sensations assaulting him.

The first was the undeniable return of the pain in his shoulder. It wasn't as sharp as before, rather it made itself known in a dull, insistent way that caused him to wince and grit his teeth against it.

The second, and infinitely more pleasant sensation, was the small, warm, heavenly soft body pressing against his good side. He felt the firmness of her curves, the warmth of her seeping into him. He knew immediately to whom that body belonged: Moyra Elliot. His petite, platinum-haired rescuer.

The third sensation was not nearly as pleasant as the second. It was the feel of a hand clamped firmly over his mouth, accompanied by words softly hissed in his ear, so close he could feel Moyra's breath sift through his hair and heat the flesh beneath it as she spoke. "Dinna make a sound, mon. Dinna e'en breathe. The Douglas is back."

If the words were meant to bring him fully awake, they succeeded. William's eyes snapped open, the pain in his shoulder abruptly secondary to the unseen danger at hand.

How the devil could the Red Douglas be back? Had this woman not claimed to have The Sight? And with it, had she not seen the cursed Douglas not returning to Wyndehaghen until the following night? Aye, she had, he thought, even as he remembered voicing his own claim that he did not believe in such nonsense.

Yet she'd seemed *so sure.*

For himself, William had been so dreadfully exhausted, and in such pain, that he'd let himself be lulled into believing her.

Moyra lay on the hard, icy stone at his side. The upper portion of her body was propped up on one elbow, making her loom over him. Her unbound hair floated down around her shoulders; more than one thick, glossy platinum strand curled feather-light upon his naked chest and belly.

If William had harbored even a fleeting hope that her outburst was the result of a nightmare, the sharp awareness in her deep violet eyes dispelled the notion. Whether there was truth to what she'd said or not, it was clear *she* believed Iain Douglas had returned.

He held his breath, his sharply honed survival instincts suddenly making him restless and edgy as he listened intently. Except for the ragged soughing of both their breaths, he heard naught.

One thick, sandy blond brow cocked skeptically high as he returned her gaze.

She shook her head, a quick, jerky, back and forth gesture, then pursed her lips in a soundless, "Shhhh."

A moment slipped tensely past. Another.

And then he heard it.

The sound was not loud. Just the opposite, he heard only a muffled *thump* of unknown origin, issuing from one of the rooms on the floor below. The noise would never have awakened him, yet now that he was awake and listening for any sound, he recognized it as being distinctly out of place.

The flesh on his forearms and shins prickled with awareness even as the hand of his good arm tensed between them and went instinctively for the hilt of his broadsword. The sword, of course, was not there. Moyra had removed it at some point when he was unconscious, before dressing his wound. All things considered, there had been no need to restrap it to his hip. Now, instead of the reassurance of solid steel against his palm, his fingers closed around the useless, coarse woolen folds of her plaid skirt.

Another soft, muffled *thump* came from the chamber directly below them. Was it his imagination, or did he truly feel the small, soft hand still covering his mouth tremble ever so slightly?

Whether she'd read his mind or understood his fumbling, her gaze shifted from his to the now virtually extinguished fire. Propped against the cold stone wall flanking the hearth was his sword.

She glanced at him again, meaningfully, then removed her hand from his mouth. Pushing away from him, she stood. His fevered body grew chilly without her warmth as he watched her pad soundlessly over to the hearth, retrieve the weapon, then return to him.

William Armstrong was not a small man; his sword reflected his imposing stature in its length and weight. The woman handled the weapon with an ease that surprised him, seeming not to notice the solid heaviness as she carried it back before kneeling beside him once more.

Her lips parted. The sound of something scraping ever so softly against stone in the chamber below made her snap her mouth shut.

This time it was *not* William's imagination. Moyra's hands shook visibly when she held the heavy sword out to him.

With his good hand, he took it. His fingertips brushed the backs of her knuckles, wrapped with white-strained tightness around the hilt. His heart skipped a beat, the muscles in his chest contracting sharply as he sucked in a quick breath.

The contact had not been nearly as innocent or uncomplicated as, given the circumstances, it should have been.

Still, there was no time to dwell on his unexpected reaction. In another instant Moyra put one hand beneath his good shoulder, while the other slipped beneath the small of his back. Straining under his heavily muscled weight, she struggled to help raise him up to a sitting position.

In the dimly lit room, his tunic seemed to appear from out of nowhere. She slipped it over his head, being careful not to disturb his wounded shoulder more than necessary as she gently guided his good arm into the sleeve. The cloth felt warm against his skin, and he had to wonder if she'd been sleeping upon his shirt; how else could the material retain so much heat in a room so bitterly cold?

The bedchamber's silence was so thick it was like a living, breathing thing; it pounded in time to the heartbeat throbbing in William's ears. 'Twas a heartbeat that echoed the hammering pain in his shoulder as, wrapping an arm about his waist, and taking on more of his weight than her slender form suggested she could, Moyra guided him to his feet.

Like hers, his feet were bare. Good. It saved him the trouble—not to mention the pain!—of having to stop and remove his boots—he was not so foolish as to dare risk any sound—for fear of alerting the intruders that their presence within the keep was known.

The stone floor felt colder than a frozen loch beneath the toughened soles of his feet as, step by agonizing step, they made their way to the door. They stopped once, briefly, for Moyra to retrieve his boots from beside the door, in so doing erasing the last trace of his presence from the dark, drearily barren chamber.

Once at the door she propped him against the wall and cautiously pressed her ear to the crack between the thick oak panel and its old, cracked casing. He used that time to strap the sword to his hip, and frowned when the fingers of his right hand fumbled. The wound in his shoulder flamed to vivid life with each movement.

William assumed Moyra heard no one in the narrow hallway outside, for she carefully eased the door open only far enough to allow them through.

Again, she wrapped an arm around his waist, plastering her side to his as her slender body took on a remarkably large portion of his weight. In this way, she led them into the dark, chilly corridor outside the bedchamber.

William had no idea of the layout of the keep. It took only a few steps for him to lose his direction.

Not surprising; he'd barely been conscious when the woman had somehow managed to drag him up the wheel staircase. How could he remember in which direction the staircase lay when he now had no light to guide him?

Moyra seemed to know exactly where she was going, and William quickly grew confident in falling into step with her. Her gait never faltered, never wavered, nor did she once career into the wall as they made their way silently down the tight, twisting hallway.

William was swept by a strong sense of powerlessness. Too many times this night he'd had to rely on this woman to save him, and he liked the idea now no more than he had the first time. It irked him to realize there was naught he could do but swallow back a surge of restless frustration and, yet again, follow her lead.

He knew the exact instant when they came to the staircase. Not because he could see it—in the unfamiliar, impenetrable darkness he could see precious little—but because her steps slowed and her elbow gently nudged his ribs. A rush of cold, musty air, reminding him far too vividly of the dark, crowded tunnel, whisked over his cheeks and brow. Moyra's shoulders dipped in a manner that indicated they were going downward.

To the floor below.

Where the sounds that had awakened her, but not him, had emanated.

Gritting his teeth, as much against the pain in his shoulder as anything else, William imagined every other wheel staircase he'd ever seen. In Border keeps, one wheel staircase was very much like the next. His mind's eye conjured up the width and breadth and spacing of each stair, even as he sent up a silent prayer that the architect of this particular stairway had shown no flair for creative design.

They descended the cramped, spiral staircase step by slow, agonizing step.

The sounds of bootheels scraping stone echoed with unnatural loudness, and as they drew closer to the second-floor landing, William thought he heard random, muffled whispers. Both sounds suggested the Douglas and his men were in the vicinity, but not too close by.

Yet.

Moyra's thoughts must have traveled a similar path, for William felt the arm encircling his waist flex with a sudden tension like that reflected in his own tightly bunched muscles. She quickened their pace, hesitating for a beat when they reached the second-story landing, as though to alert him they were again on level ground, then gently but insistently guided him to the right.

The veil of inky blackness was broken abruptly by an eery white glow.

A ghost!

Ridiculous, yet 'twas the first notion that sprung to mind. No doubt it had been inspired by Moyra's claim to have "the sight." Not skittish by nature, William was more than a wee bit surprised to feel his breath catch and his heart start to pound in wild, staccato bursts against his rib cage. The hand gripping his boots tightened until his knuckles were white and aching from the strain.

She was leading him down the last turn of the stairway to the main floor. Forcing himself to remain calm,

William squinted at the glowing white image, bringing it gradually into focus.

Swallowing back a laugh, he realized immediately what he was looking at. Nothing so ominous or unearthly as a specter. Oh, nay. 'Twas embarrassing to admit, even if only to himself, that what he saw was naught more than a few very ordinary, very *tangible,* streaks of moonlight filtering in through a large, crumbling hole in the keep's outer wall.

The farther down they descended, the chillier the air became. Had he been able to see, William knew his breaths would be naught but misty trails of vapor in front of his face. He couldn't see, though. His surroundings were black again, the hazy glow of moonlight obscured by the close crowding of the staircase's wall.

Pain stabbed at his wounded shoulder, shot frantic arrows down his arm and into his wrist and hand. So intent was he on biting back a tortured groan that he didn't at first notice when Moyra suddenly stopped. Didn't notice, that is, until he crashed into her.

She stumbled, slamming into the curved wall of the stairway. Her breath pushed from her lungs as William's big body collided with her considerably smaller one. Despite the situation, and the Douglas's nearness, William could not repress a groan this time, as a fresh blast of agony stabbed into him.

They both froze.

Although he couldn't see her in the darkness, William felt the violet heat of Moyra's gaze on him.

In the distance the sounds of bootheels on stone were no longer muffled. And no longer distant.

"This way, Iain!" someone shouted from the landing above. "He's on the stairs, trying tae escape."

"Mo chreach," Moyra murmured under her breath, while at the same time pushing against the hard male chest pinning her to the wall. Her fingertips encountered something warm and wet, and she knew William had reopened his wound.

Och! there were no help for it now. Iain Douglas was just above them. Judging by the undisguised racket he made, he was coming at them fast. If they didn't move—and move quickly—they might never move again.

Finding William's hand in the darkness was not difficult; her own hand seemed to know exactly where to go, as though it had done so countless times in the past. The fingers of her left hand entwined with the fingers of his right. One sharp tug was all it took to get the man stumbling blindly through the darkness behind her.

Since the alarm had already been sounded, there was no longer any need to creep quietly down the rest of the stairway. She detoured only long enough to shove the main door open, then plunged them both into the storage room. Scant slivers of moonlight flowed in through the narrow, solitary window, inadequately lighting their way as she hurried over to the wall with the wooden cupboard.

In less than two heavy heartbeats, Moyra had the tunnel door open and was shoving a badly winded William Armstrong through the opening. In another instant she was standing beside him, easing the thick panel back into place.

No sooner had she closed the door than she detected

the clamor—it was becoming all too familiar of late—of men hurrying down the stairway. She heard them tromping through the foyer, then straight out the front door. The noise had to vie for precedence over the racket her heart was making in her ears.

As she'd hoped, the Douglas assumed they'd left the keep through the only exit he was aware of. Even if he eventually recognized his folly, 'twould be too late; if he didn't know of the tunnel's existence, it stood to reason he knew even less of its location.

They were safe.

At least for the moment.

Moyra breathed a heartfelt sigh of relief and leaned back heavily against the cold, damp stone wall. Closing her eyes, she willed her heartbeat and breathing to regulate. Gradually, she became aware of the warm, thick, powerful fingers entwined with hers. Nay, more precisely, she became aware of the lack of strength in those fingers. She forced her tension-tightened grip to relax.

It was William who finally broke the thick, anxiety-riddled silence. "Did you not say you had 'The Sight'?" His deep, pain-husky voice cut through the inky darkness enfolding them.

"Aye, I did. And I do," she whispered, her spine bristling defensively. "Howe'er, I *dinna* say it was always clear. Or always accurate. Now hush. The Douglas is bound tae charge back intae the storage chamber soon. I dinna want yer whining tae give our position away."

Although she couldn't see it, Moyra somehow knew when William opened his mouth to say something, then just as quickly snapped it shut again. The sharp click of his teeth slamming together suggested that, in this at least, her perception was accurate.

Surely even William Armstrong could not argue with her wisdom, no matter how uncomplimentarily it had been stated. The Douglas *would* be back when he found no traces of the pair outside. Just as he had suspected they'd escaped through the front door, when he could find no trace of them, he would demand the keep be searched again, and searched much more thoroughly than before.

In that light, mayhap moving to the opposite end of the tunnel now was not a bad idea. The passage was crowded and narrow, but basically untwisting. If the Douglas were to discover the entrance, she knew they would hear echoes of his progress clear to the other end.

Moyra took a small, shuffling step to the right . . . and came up hard against William Armstrong's side. She felt his body stiffen, but ignored that as she nudged him gently with her shoulder and elbow.

Noise of the Douglas and his men returning to the keep through the front door came to them as muffled thumps; Moyra gritted her teeth against anything she might have said to alert William to her intent.

Instead, she nudged him again, more insistently, indicating they should proceed.

He must have finally understood her meaning, for he started to inch his way with excruciating slowness along the cold, damp wall.

Tightening her grip around his fingers, she matched him step for slow, cautious step. Her nose wrinkled at the feel of cold, wet, sticky puddles sucking at her bare feet. Already the dampness of the wall had penetrated the bloodstained back of her tunic; and the stone was scratching against her tender skin like the tips of bony fingers.

Grimacing, she dared not risk even the vaguest grunt or murmur of complaint. Not when she could hear the booming roar of the Douglas, deep and thick with frustration, as he barked orders at his men to search every crumbling corner and crevice of the keep.

"Dinna be showing yer grimy faces again wi'out those dirty mongrels in tow, or 'tis regretting it maun sorely ye'll be!"

Moyra didn't doubt for a second that the Douglas's hoarsely barked threat served as inspiration for William Armstrong to suddenly pick up his pace.

For a man so grievously wounded—hadn't she needed to support more than half his weight when they'd descended the wheel staircase? and her shoulders and back muscles ached from every second of it, thank ye ver' much!—he moved with astounding speed and accuracy.

They reached the far end of the tunnel in half the time she would have predicted.

Seven

One minute William was standing beside Moyra, poised at the cleverly concealed mouth of the tunnel—his fingers white-knuckled tight around his sword hilt as he readied himself to do whatever was necessary should either the Douglas or any of his men stray too close—the next he found himself lying flat on his back, and—

A frown etched deep creases in his brow. Was it his imagination or was the ground *moving*?

If so, his imagination was more vivid than he'd ever given it credit for . . . He could swear he heard the rhythmic *clop-clop-clop* of horse hooves, and the soft scratch of wood rubbing against wood.

The air no longer stank of mold and dampness and neglect. Instead, pulling a great gulp of it into his lungs, he noticed a pleasant, earthy aroma. While William still felt chilled to the bone, now there was a light, invisible warmth kissing his cheek and brow and chin.

His frown deepened.

What the devil?!

His eyes snapped open, then just as quickly snapped shut again when an unexpected blast of sunlight exploded in his vision, making him wince. Then again, mayhap the wince, and the grunt that accompanied it, were due instead to the sudden jolt of movement beneath him as whatever he was lying upon hit a good-sized rut?

The jarring activity came to an abrupt, not to mention blessed, stop.

Gritting his teeth against the light as much as the tearing pain in his shoulder, William cracked one eye open. Blinked hard. Several times. Slowly, he pulled into focus a gold- and gray-streaked sky.

More slowly still, his focus shifted to the head that, after a few seconds' hesitation, crept into his line of vision. The woman's platinum hair, delicately sculpted features and slender frame were as recognizable as the sharp violet gaze that inquisitively scanned his face.

'Twas Moyra Elliot. The woman who'd saved his life the night before.

At least he *assumed* 'twas the night before . . .

"Och! Yer finally awake, are ye?" she asked, her sarcastic tone a sharp contrast to the whiskey softness of her voice. " 'Tis about time. I was starting tae think ye planned tae sleep the day away." She'd been hunkered down beside him, her open palms pillowed atop the narrow cushions of her thighs. As he watched, she stood and, shielding her eyes with one hand, glanced up at the sky. " 'Tis past noon, dinna ye know? The sky be somewhat clear now, but I dinna think that will last. Mark me words, mon, there's a fine storm brewing."

William's voice, when it came, sounded scratchy and rough, even to his own ears. Oh, what he wouldn't give right now for a long, deep drink of cider. Or ale. Or whiskey. Anything wet would do. His throat felt cracked and dry, as parched as the roots of a tree after a long drought. "How do you know? Does 'The Sight' tell you?"

"Are ye making fun of me?"

"Nay," he replied, noting the way her spine had stiffened perceptibly. Even the thick twists of her braid seemed to go tight with indignation. With effort, William chased the sarcasm from his tone. This woman had saved his life, he reminded himself. Not once but twice. He was not so arrogant, nor in so much pain, that he couldn't recognize mockery and ridicule as a poor way to repay such a large debt. "I apologize. I meant no offense, lass. Truly. I was merely wondering how you can know if it's going to storm."

"Yer nae in England anymore, mon." When she glanced back down at him, William was surprised to see a glint of good humor shimmering in haunting violet eyes. The gesture was echoed in the faint blush warming her cheeks, the uplift of one corner of her mouth. "Here, it always rains. Have ye been gone so long ye've forgotten? A surprise *would* be this mild weather lasting just a wee bit longer. It willna. If I can promise ye naught else, I *can* promise ye that." She nodded to his shoulder, and her lips pursed. "How does it fare?"

"It hurts."

"As badly as last night?"

"More."

She murmured something under her breath. His Gaelic was rusty; it took a second to recognize the guttural-sounding words as the same mild curse he'd used often in his youth, a curse that had no English translation.

His back ached, no doubt from having lain on it for who knew how long . . . not to mention from being carried upon what he was coming to realize was a hastily constructed litter.

Wincing, William attempted to stretch the stiffness and tension out of his sore muscles and tendons. What he succeeded in doing instead was reigniting the blaze of pain in his shoulder.

He sucked in a sharp breath through his teeth, held it until his lungs burned. The world around him blurred, darkened and grew dangerously fuzzy and black around the edges.

"Humph! So much for being awake. I should have known a soft-bellied Sassenach wouldna be able tae keep his eyes open for long."

Her voice came at him from a distance, as soft and blurry as his vision had suddenly become. William latched on to the sound, focusing the crux of his concentration on Moyra's voice and face, while ignoring her insult. Both seemed to float somewhere in the dark haze swirling around him. Slowly, slowly, he willed the darkness to recede. It took far longer for the pain in his shoulder to retreat.

"Look at ye. Ye seem tae be making a fine recovery. Mayhap I misjudged ye. I dinna suppose ye can walk for a wee bit . . . ?

"I can barely stay conscious, lass." He almost laughed. Almost. "Nay, I don't think walking is a possibility."

"Och! well, 'twas a thought. Yer horse could use a wee rest."

"My . . . ?" Careful not to jar his aching shoulder, William shifted, then glanced up and to the side. His eyes widened and his jaw sagged open. "Damber?"

At the sound of its name, the mare's ears pricked. Turning her head, the horse glanced down and back at him as though to say, "So, you're finally awake, are you? 'Tis about bloody time!"

"If ye canna walk," the woman said, drawing his attention back to her, "we've little choice in the matter."

"How did you get near my horse, lass?" he asked, ignoring the riddle of her musing.

"We're only hours from—"

"Damber never lets anyone near her but me."

"—me brother's keep," she continued, speaking right over his words.

"The last time someone tried—"

"I dinna want tae see Jared again, mind ye . . . Howe'er, as I said, if ye canna walk, we've nae choice."

"—she bit him in the arse."

This last caught Moyra's attention. Her mouth snapped shut and she glanced down at him, her light platinum eyebrows rising high on her forehead. "Me brother ne'er bit anyone in the arse. I dinna ken what Border ballads ye've heard saying otherwise, but I tell ye, I know Jared well; he'd *ne'er* do such a crass thing. At least, nae when he's sober."

William stared at her, blinked hard, frowned. "I was talking about my horse."

"Ye were? Och! Then why did ye nae say so?"

"I thought I did."

"Er, mayhap. Who's tae say?" She shrugged self-consciously. "I maun admit, ye talk so fast, and me English be so poor . . . weel, I can barely follow that cursed Sassenach tongue." Again, she glanced at the sky. This time it was her turn to frown. "We'd best hurry if we're tae reach Glentroe Tower by sunset. When the snow starts, methinks it willna stop for several days. I dinna know about ye, but I've nae desire tae spend the night sleeping upon the cold, wet ground."

William shook his head, and winced when a shard of pain stabbed through his shoulder like a razor-sharp dagger cutting into an oven-warmed piece of soft bread. "It sounds less than appealing, I have to agree. But first, lass, answer a few questions for me."

"If ye're wondering about the Douglas," she replied, and sighed impatiently, "there be nae need. The mon will be of nae bother tae us for a wee bit."

"Excuse me? Perhaps my memory is failing, but I could have sworn you said much the same thing last night . . . shortly before he—"

"Aye, mon, I know what I said. And I dinna think ye'll be letting me forget how wrong I was, either. Howe'er, this time what I tell ye is a certainty."

"Does the, er 'Sight' tell you so?"

She shook her head. His attention snagged unwittingly on the thick coil of her braid and the way the fringed end of it scraped against the enticingly slim curve of her bottom with the movement. "Nothing so mysterious. I simply watched and waited at the mouth of the tunnel before daring tae creep about. I'll admit, the Douglas covered a fine muckle of ground in and around Wyndehaghen, and he swore enough tae make his poor dead mother blush, but in the end he found naught. Eventually he'd nae choice in the matter but tae give up and go home. When last seen, he and his men were riding back in the direction from whence they came."

It wasn't until William's muscles began to relax that he noticed the tension he'd been under. Even the pain in his shoulder seemed to ease a bit. The breath that poured from his lungs and whispered past his lips was thick with relief. " 'Tis good to hear."

" 'Twas good tae see."

William shifted his attention to the clouds edging the horizon. To his discerning eye they looked thicker, blacker, more threatening than they had even a few moments before. Whether the lass had 'The Sight' or not had yet to be proved, however she was right about one thing; 'twas going to storm afore the sun went down. He was growing more convinced of it by the second. "This brother of yours," he said, "how far are we from his keep?"

Moyra stiffened at the mention of her kin, but that was her only outward sign of discomfort. "Nae very. Just o'er the next hill."

"And he'll not mind the intrusion?"

A grin played about the corners of her lips. William was too intrigued by the unexpected sight of it to question its origin. "Och! make nae mistake, he'll mind a fine muckle. Howe'er, he'll nae turn me away."

"And me?" he asked, one golden eyebrow cocking high in his forehead.

Her shrug was too casual to be anything but forced. "Like I be saying, mon, he'll nae turn me away."

With that, Moyra slapped her palms together as

though to dislodge a clinging layer of dust, then spun on her bare heel and approached the horse.

Watching her through the shield of his lashes, William couldn't help but notice the way she ran a palm affectionately over the mare's silky black mane and glistening brown neck. He detected a gentle lilt to her voice when she crooned to the mare in Gaelic.

As though sensing her master's attention, Damber sent him a covert glance from over Moyra's shoulder, then whickered softly. Nostrils flaring, the horse affectionately nuzzled Moyra's palm with her nose.

William's eyebrows drew down in a scowl, and his lips pursed. Given to him by a stepbrother who'd trained the horse for battle, the fickle mare had been his companion for almost a half score of years. Yet never once had Damber looked at William with such blind adoration, nor had she nuzzled *his* hand with such blatant affection!

Moyra climbed up onto the mare's saddle.

Too soon the litter started moving once more.

Gritting his teeth, William braced himself for the teeth-jarring journey ahead.

The agony in his shoulder burst to life. Even through the gripping fingers of pain, a portion of his mind retained the sight of Moyra fondling his horse.

William closed his eyes, thinking to blot out the memory. Instead, on the inky blackness behind his closed eyelids, he was presented with the vision of her slender hand stroking slowly, slowly over the mare's glossy chestnut brown coat. As he began to slip into the soothing abyss of unconsciousness, the sweet lilt of her voice crooned in his ears . . .

Eight

"When ye left this keep, 'twas with a vow ye'd ne'er set foot in it again. Correct me if I'm wrong, but 'twas nae more than half a score of months ago. And already ye be back. Methinks ye've explaining tae do, Moyra Elliot, and a fine muckle lot of it."

The tightening of Moyra Elliot's jaw was her only outward sign of irritation. It was enough.

Only a scant year her elder, Jared knew his sister well. Oh, aye, the lass's gaze was averted to the untouched goblet of sweetened wine sitting on the table in front of her, but he didn't doubt for a second that, were she to glance up, those unusually colored eyes of hers would be flashing with hot violet fire.

That she'd come back to Glentroe Tower was surprising—truly, he'd thought to have seen the last of her, the damage wrought at their parting had been that great. But that she'd come back to his home so soon . . . Och! that was more surprising still.

And more than a wee bit disconcerting.

Weakness was something Moyra had no patience or tolerance for, in herself or others. As a bairn, he well remembered the way she'd always been the first to scamper up a tree or over the next hill, leaving him to follow more cautiously behind.

Had the girl ever asked for help? In his entire life, Jared couldn't remember it happening. Normally, she preferred to make her own way with things, in her own time. She'd always been quite bullheaded in that respect.

So what was different now? What had caused such an abrupt change of mind? What was so critical she had humbled herself by coming back to Glentroe Tower . . . ?

Dire need was the only thing that could force his sister to do something so uncharacteristic, Jared decided as his attention settled on the top of her platinum head. Especially when the help she sought was being asked from a brother she'd sworn to never speak with or see again.

Clearing his throat, he toyed with the cold pewter stem of his own goblet. "Should I ask how much the wounded mon upstairs has tae do with yer unexpected return, lass?"

"Ye can ask," she murmured. Her shrug was as tight as her tone, and equally uninviting.

"But ye'll nae tell me." He drummed his fingertips impatiently atop the scratched wooden tabletop. "Is that the way of it?"

"There's naught tae tell."

"I beg tae differ." The rhythm of his tapping fingers became more brisk. "The mon may have been unconscious when ye had him dragged in here—and he's stayed that way since, I canna argue that—but from the looks of him, I'd say there's a fine muckle lot tae tell, Moyra. Och! lass, *he didna wound himself.* Something, *someone,* wounded him. Just as something, or *someone,* caused ye tae panic and seek refuge here— as a last resort, I've nae a doubt."

Her spine stiffened. As Jared had predicted, when her gaze lifted from the goblet, her violet eyes were narrow and fiery with indignation. "I didna panic."

"Are ye telling me then that ye came here on purpose? That ye set out this morn specifically tae return tae Glentroe Tower and nowhere else?" He shook his head at the way she pursed her lips and, his own hazel gaze narrowed, stubbornly said nothing. "Aye, I thought as much. Ye came home because ye'd nae other choice." Pushing his goblet aside, Jared crossed his forearms on the table in front of him and leaned forward, toward his sister. His voice dropped a curious degree. *"Why?* Who or what were ye running from?"

Moyra tilted her chin up proudly and ignored the question. She averted her gaze to the window behind him, fixing her concentration on the rain that pounded against the pane like minuscule, wet fists. "Glentroe Tower is nae me home anymore," she said finally, softly, but with firm conviction. "Nae since the day ye killed our da."

Nothing else his sister said could make Jared Elliot's already ruddy cheeks suffuse with hot color. No other words could cause his hazel eyes to narrow so sharply, the line of his jaw to clench so teeth-grindingly hard.

He shoved to his feet.

The bench upon which he'd sat clattered noisily to the floor.

With a wary eye, Moyra watched her brother step over the fallen piece of furniture as though it were no more bulky than a bairn's misplaced toy. To him, she supposed it wasn't. Jared Elliot was firm and lean and unnaturally tall.

Raking all ten fingers through his light blond hair, he stalked over to the window, stared out it hard, pretending he could actually see even a hint of landscape through the drenched pane. His breath fogged the glass, he was standing so close; if he noticed the wispy puffs of vapor, he gave no sign. The lift and fall of his mighty shoulders was regular . . . too regular to be anything but tightly controlled.

A moment later when he spun back around to face her, the color in his cheeks had abated. Only the taut line of his jaw and the flash of months-old exasperation in his eyes hinted at the heat of emotion simmering beneath the surface. "For the last time, lass, I *dinna—* "

Moyra's open palm slammed onto the scarred wooden tabletop hard enough to make the pewter goblet in front of her jump, the sweetened wine inside it swish from side to side. "And I dinna want tae hear any more of yer excuses, Jared. Ye give tae many tae late, and there isna a single one that will bring our da back."

"Mother—" He started, only to have her interrupt him again, this time by slamming her tightly balled fist on the tabletop.

The goblet teetered on the edge of its round, flat, pewter foot, then toppled over. It's contents bled unnoticed over the chipped wood.

"Och! aye, our mother. Who, when last seen," she continued for him, her voice as hard and as cold as the metal that once held the wine, "had taken herself tae the west tower, locked herself in the room they shared, and wouldna eat nor drink nor talk to a soul."

"She comes down now." If possible, the line of his jaw hardened still more. 'The color flooded back to his cheeks, a flaming shade of crimson. "Only once in a wee while, aye, but 'tis a start."

The accusatory glare Moyra fixed on her brother spoke for itself. She opened her mouth to reinforce it, so there could be no more mistakes between them, but was distracted by a movement at the corner of her eye. Shifting her attention in that direction, she fixed her gaze on the old man standing in the doorway. His watery blue gaze volleyed undecidedly between brother and sister.

The intruder was short and painfully thin. Poking from beneath his kilt were two pale white legs the diameter of scrawny saplings. Even his wash-faded tunic could not hide the way his bony shoulders seemed to push at the fabric from beneath. In places, his dry, frizzy, shoulder-length hair was the same dirty-white hue as his shirt, in others, it was streaked with thick strands as black and as dull as soot. The same layered, salt-and-pepper pattern was repeated erratically in the overfull moustache and beard obliterating his mouth and chin and neck from view.

"Yer mon be awake," he said, jutting his bearded chin at Moyra. She searched her memory for his name, found it. Simon Ferguson. Once her father's clan captain, now the old man's son, Russell, loyally filled the same position for Jared. "He be asking for ye, lass. Maun loudly. Making quite the fuss aboot it, he is."

"He is named William," Moyra corrected sharply. "And, make nae mistake, he is*na* 'my' mon."

The way Simon's ancient shoulders rose and fell said he really didn't care to whom the man belonged. The fact remained he was awake and causing a fuss, and *she* was expected to do something about it before the entire keep was swept into the tumult.

A sigh whispered past Moyra's lips, soft and resigned. Her attention drifted briefly to the rain pelting the glass beyond her brother's lean shoulder.

Simon was right. Against her better judgment *she* had been the one to haul William Armstrong into Glentroe Tower. No one had asked her to do it, the decision had been made as freely as it could be, knowing Iain Douglas at any moment would be hot on their trail. Whether she liked it or not—and she most certainly did *not,* not one wee bit—it was *her* responsibility to take care of the man.

Like a cloak forged of lead, the responsibility weighed heavily upon her slender shoulders. And, like all the responsibilities that had come before it, and those that would come after this one had been met, she did not take it lightly.

Pushing to her feet, her gaze shifted to meet Jared's. And narrowed. Was it her imagination, or did his hazel eyes shimmer with hope that whatever words she chose to say would be kind, maybe even forgiving . . . ?

That she should thank him for providing shelter for herself and her unlikely companion went without question. Aye, he deserved that much. Yet when she opened her mouth to voice it, the words would not come. Her tongue felt oddly thick and heavy, refusing to budge from where it had flattened itself against the upper palate of her mouth. The words clogged in her throat like a fistful of under-cooked porridge.

That she *should* offer her gratitude seemed suddenly unimportant, for the fact remained, she *could not*.

When she looked at her brother now, she saw far more than his familiar blond hair, more than his lean, towering frame, more than the blue, black and red Elliot plaid belted at his narrow waist.

What she also saw was the look on their mother's face at being told of her husband's death.

The devastation in Helene Elliot's eyes had brought tears to Moyra's own. Swallowing back the gaping black hole of her own grief, she'd watched, helpless, as her mother's fragile features crumpled, as her knees buckled from beneath her. Her brother had been quick—he'd caught the older woman before she hit the stone floor—but the damage had already been done, life within Glentroe Tower would never be the same again. Not for anyone.

Aye, she knew without a doubt that if she closed her eyes right now her ears would fill with the sharp peals of her mother's grief-stricken wail. 'Twas that haunting ghost of a sound, invisible yet as undeniably present as herself, which trapped in Moyra's throat any conciliatory words she may have uttered.

Giving Jared one last glance, as harsh as it was unreadable, she spun on her heel and stalked from the hall.

In the enveloping silence that followed her departure, Jared could hear her small bare feet slapping at the stones in the hallway without. The sweetly innocent sounds were a stark contradiction to the reproach-

ful—and, aye, *mature*—violet gaze which had preceded them.

Jared stared at the empty doorway long after his
sister had gone upstairs, then, finally, shifted his attention to Simon, who now stood nervously beside the
table. The old man's eyes were crinkled in a natural
squint, yet even without visual proof, Jared could feel
the man's gaze on him. He opened his mouth, surprised to find the words that came out were not even
close to the ones filtering through his mind. "This
stranger me sister brought home . . . by chance, did
ye happen tae ask his full name?"

"Nay." The old man shook his head. "There was
nae need. He arrived with Moyra. She'd ne'er bring
an enemy intae Glentroe Tower."

"There was a time," Jared said, "when I would have
agreed." His lips pursed, and his expression clouded.
Both said what he would not voice: that the time for
agreeing to anything so logical and fundamental as
Moyra never bringing an enemy into their midst had
come and gone many long, hard months ago.

Moyra heard the voices long before she started
down the second-floor corridor. The first was too deep
and—Och! aye, too Sassenach—to belong to anyone
but William Armstrong. The other voice was young
and high; male, but cracking now and again with an
equal mixture of anger and adolescence. Without looking, she knew the latter belonged to Kenny, her nine-
year-old brother.

Her stride quickened. Judging from the irascible

tones in both voices, the two males were furious and making no attempt to conceal it.

"I'll see her *now,* you little devil!"

"Ye'll nae see her *at all* if ye keep shouting at me like that. I'm nae yer servant, and I'll be thanking ye tae stop treating me like I am."

"I don't care if you're the bloody Queen of Scotland, boy, I want to see her and I want to see her *now.*"

"Is that the way of it? Weel, now, *I* dinna care if *ye* be stodgy auld Queen Bess and the Pope combined, ye'll nae see *anyone* until ye—"

"Kenny!" Moyra came to an abrupt stop a mere step inside the small chamber's doorway. The sight that greeted her caused her violet eyes to open wide and her jaw to sag open.

Kenny, the youngest and usually most sedate of the three Elliot offspring, stood looming over the sickbed. His fingers were white-knuckled tight around the handle of a shallow pan. Thick tendrils of steam fingered the air above its iron rim; a rim, Moyra noticed suddenly, that was tilted menacingly toward the bed's sole occupant.

Speaking of the bed's sole occupant . . .

For his part, William Armstrong lay sprawled upon the straw-filled mattress like a king. Bare from the waist up, he was half sitting, his naked back cushioned from the cold stone wall by a pile of folded plaids, his legs stretched out before him and crossed lazily at the booted ankles. The way he slowly laced his fingers atop his hard, flat midriff was a study in both patience and defiance.

As she watched, his eyebrows quirked high in his

forehead . . . a blunt, albeit silent, challenge. Glaring up at Kenny, William seemed to wordlessly dare the lad to complete his threat and tip the steamy contents of the pan onto him.

Anger-induced red splotches stood out in sharp relief upon Kenny's soft, pale young cheeks. That, combined with the shrewd glint in his deep-set hazel eyes, suggested he was weighing the consequences of doing exactly that.

"Kenny!" she repeated, more loudly and firmly. "Put the pan down, lad. I didna risk me life saving this mon only tae have ye scald him with steaming bree. I've done enough nurturing for one night, thank ye ver' much!"

This time Moyra managed to snag her brother's attention. His gaze shifted to her, albeit reluctantly . . . and cautiously, as though he wasn't sure it was at all safe to let the brunt of his concentration drift far from the wounded man, whose gaze was as sharp as a finely honed dagger.

"You heard her, boy. Put down the pan or you'll be in a good deal of trouble."

Moyra shot a glare at William Armstrong, but he seemed not to notice. His gaze never left her brother—or, more accurately, the pan and its skin-blistering contents. His tone of voice, however, now that had been unmistakably deep and rich; the degree of immature gloating she detected in it scratched down her spine like ice-chips on a hot summer morn.

Trouble was something Kenny Elliot had tried to avoid his entire nine summers of life. For the most part, he had succeeded.

He wavered, torn between the gnawing hunger to

extract retribution and a deep, natural inclination to simply do what he was told, and do it promptly and well. In the end, he was not so far from swaddling that the former could overrule the latter . . . even if the latter didn't lose the battle without a strong internal fight.

Fingers trembling with an almost overpowering urge to do otherwise, Kenny leveled the pan, then lowered it. Turning, he bent at the waist and, with a clatter, set it down on the cold stone floor beside the bed.

When he straightened, the glance he shot his sister was in small part relief at seeing her again and in large part irritation that fate hadn't allowed him to see her a wee few minutes later . . . *after* he'd had the satisfaction of tossing the steaming bree upon the lap of the obstinate man lying upon the bed. *His* bed, no less!

The instant Kenny looked into his sister's familiar violet eyes, however, his anger drained away like wine through a hole cut into a wineskin. With Moyra, his anger never lasted long. Especially today. Och! nay, not when it felt so incredibly wonderful to see her again, alive and well, after months of thinking he never would.

Kenny's colt-thin legs started to carry him across the room. The clicking of his bootheels on stone wasn't nearly as loud as the excited knocking of his heartbeat in his ears. His knees felt weak and shaky, more watery than Cook's morning porridge. Tripping over his own two feet, he stumbled hard into the warm circle of his sister's embrace.

She staggered under the impact of the collision, but not too much and not enough for them both to topple to the floor. Almost, but not quite. Her arms came up, encircling his slender shoulders, holding him to her tightly. Mayhap too tightly judging by the way he groaned and squirmed.

Had it only been a matter of months since she'd last seen him? Aye. It seemed like much longer, though, for even in that short time he'd grown. Not a lot, but a bit. Enough for the top of his head to graze the underside of her chin. A few stray wisps of his silky blond hair—hair that smelled strongly of harsh lye soap—tickled her skin there. Moyra smiled and hugged him tighter still.

This time, Kenny's groan was audible, his squirm more insistent. He felt too good in her arms to be let go just yet, so instead Moyra loosened her grip. Kenny's sigh of relief felt warm and misty on her neck.

Her gaze drifted to the bed. Although Moyra's mind told her it was time to ease the smile curling her lips, it stayed stubbornly in place.

William Armstrong was looking at her strangely. His attention shifted from her mouth to her eyes. Back and forth. Again and again. Her flesh heated under the intensity of his gaze. It was like tangible fingers brushing softly, softly against her skin.

Moyra swallowed hard. She wasn't at all sure what to do with the unexpected surge of hot, tingly sensation that washed through her. Or the sudden breathlessness that accompanied it. In the end, she did the only thing she *could* do. In much the same way she handled her grief, she ignored it, buried it somewhere deep down inside her, quickly, before she could examine it too closely and be forced to decipher either it or its meaning.

As she watched, the seasoned creases between William's light blond eyebrows furrowed together in a scowl. The darkness of his expression suggested something about the sight of the woman and boy embracing at the foot of his bed had taken him off guard . . . and whatever it was, it didn't please him.

"Are ye causing trouble already, Sassenach?" she asked. Like a mirror being smashed against a rock, the sound of her voice bouncing off the chamber's cold stone walls shattered the tension that stretched taut between them.

"Nay," William replied, his whisker-stubbled chin jutting in the direction of her brother, "I'm simply replying in kind to the trouble being given to me."

The arms Kenny had coiled about Moyra's waist grew tight and stiff. He shifted to the side, not yet ready to leave the warm, familiar circle of his sister's embrace, yet also wanting to keep the wounded man on the bed within his sights. "I was only trying tae feed ye!"

"*Force*-feed me, don't you mean?"

"What does it matter?" Kenny shook his head against the soft hollow beneath his sister's shoulder. " 'Twas nae like I was trying tae kill ye." His young tone cracked on the last two words, then dropped a lethal pitch as his right hand strayed to the short sword strapped to his waist. His fingers curled tightly around the leather-wrapped hilt. "Were that me intent, ye'd be dead right now. Make nae mistake."

"I may be wounded," William snapped, "but I'm not an invalid. I resent being treated like one."

"Ye prefer being treated like a bairn, is that the way of things?" Moyra asked. William's gaze had drifted to Kenny; it now snapped back to her. His brown eyes were sharp and intense. "I'll be warning ye now, mon, if ye continue to act like one, 'tis how *I'll* be treating ye." She didn't miss the way William's eyes narrowed, their penetrating brown depths flashing her a dangerous challenge, she simply chose to ignore the sight. "Methinks ye owe Kenny an apology."

"For what? Not giving the little devil a chance to upend that steaming pan of soup on me?"

"Nay, I dinna ask ye tae apologize for *that.*" This time it was *her* gaze that narrowed, *her* eyes that flashed threateningly. "Howe'er ye *will* apologize for giving the poor lad unnecessary trouble. What did he do so wrong, except try tae carry out me own order tae feed ye? Or mayhap 'tis an odd Sassenach custom tae refuse help when it comes tae healing and regaining yer strength? As I recall, ye dinna refuse mine."

"You try my patience, wench."

"Nae as sorely as ye try mine. Now be a good bairn and apologize."

William's gaze narrowed, shifting to Kenny.

The silence that descended upon the room was deafening.

For one unnaturally long minute Moyra thought the arrogant man was not going to offer Kenny an apology. And what, she wondered, would she do then? There wasn't much she *could* do. Even with him wounded, she knew she was no match for the likes of William Armstrong. Surely she could not wrestle the words out of him if he'd no desire to voice them!

In the end, the matter was taken out of her hands.

With blatant reluctance, William briskly nodded in Kenny's direction, then abruptly shifted his attention to the fingers he'd entwined atop his stomach, studying the short, chipped nails with spurious interest.

By way of an apology, it was the best he was going to offer. That much was clear. 'Twould have to be enough.

Kenny stood on tiptoe and placed a quick, warm kiss on his sister's cheek before pushing from her embrace. "If ye dinna mind, lass," he said softly, so William could not overhear, "we'll talk later. I've chores tae do and . . . Och! the truth of the matter is, if I stay here a minute longer I canna guarantee I won't upend that pan of bree over yer mon's arrogant head after all."

"Mo chreach, Kenny, he's nae *my—*"

"It doesna matter whose mon he is, Moyra. He's still an arrogant *mueqata.* And a Sassenach. Nae a good combination, that."

Kenny gave his sister a weak smile, then quickly left the chamber before she could argue.

"What did he call me?" William asked from the bed, drawing her attention there. He was no longer looking at his fingers. His gaze had fixed on her, and fixed on her hard.

"A pig," she answered. Moving to the side of the bed, she sat down in the chair she assumed Kenny had recently vacated.

To her surprise, William grinned.

Why, she wondered, did the sight make her breath catch in her throat and her heart beat just a wee bit faster? Mayhap it had to do with the way his dark brown eyes flashed with amusement, or the creases that deepened at their corners and were mirrored in the weathered brackets flanking either side of his mouth? Whatever the reason, she found herself grinning in return.

" 'Tis nae funny." Was she chastising him . . . or herself? It was difficult to tell. "Kenny isna given tae fits of temper. Of us all, he's the calmest and most reasonable. Yet ye managed tae rankle his ire ver' fully and quickly."

"Aye, 'tis a gift. You have 'The Sight,' I have the ability to make people furious within a matter of minutes."

"Intentionally?"

"Not usually."

Moyra pursed her lips and thought about that for a second, then shook her head. Reaching down and to the side, she retrieved the pan of bree. "Methinks I'd rather have my gift than yers. Now open yer annoying Sassenach mouth and eat. Ye need tae heal and regain yer strength."

The spoon had fallen into the pan, the contents of which had cooled considerably. Moyra fished it out, then sucked the broth off her fingers. She wasn't sure what alerted her to William's gaze, but something must have, because in the midst of licking the broth from her index finger, she felt some unseen force tug her own gaze upward.

His attention was on her mouth.

This time Moyra's heart didn't beat faster, it skipped a beat entirely then gave two fast, strong ones that dumped a hot, tingly burst of adrenaline into her bloodstream. The feeling, unlike anything she'd ever experienced before, rippled through her chest and belly, spread into her legs and arms. Lastly, it infused her neck and cheeks and brow with a hot confusion of color.

For one heart-stopping instant, she wondered what it would feel like to have his tongue replace hers. The image was so jarringly vivid she could have sworn she felt his warm breath mist on her skin, his hot, wet tongue stroke her knuckles, lave at the sensitive pads of her fingertips as his lips formed a seal around . . .

The spoon fell from her suddenly slackened grip. It clattered against the edge of the pan before plunking back into the aromatic bree with a modest splash. A few drips of broth splattered onto her kilt, but she didn't notice, didn't care. The noise, thank heavens, had served to snap her back to her senses.

Blinking hard, she shook her head to clear it. Twice. It took a few seconds before she trusted herself to speak; even then she couldn't help noticing the slight tremor in her tone. "Methinks ye be right. Yer wounded, not crippled. Ye can feed yerself."

As she held the pan out to him, she mentally ordered her fingers not to shake. They almost obeyed her. Almost.

Using his unwounded arm, William reached for the pan. The tips of his fingers brushed against the backs of her knuckles. The contact was light, but jolting.

He froze.

So did she.

Was it William's imagination, or did Moyra's index finger still feel warm and damp from where she'd licked the broth from it? God help him, nay, it *couldn't* be his imagination—his imagination had never been *that* good.

"I—" Her voice came out as an embarrassingly high squeak. Moyra cleared her throat and, snatching her hand back, tried again. "I'm going tae go see aboot fetching more wood for yer fire." She nodded to the hearth on the opposite side of the room, but her attention never left the pan—rather, the strong male fingers that gripped it.

William nodded. He knew without looking that there was already a stack of wood beside the hearth. At least enough to keep the fire burning until morn. Kenny had carried the logs in earlier. Still, he was not going to point that fact out, nor try to dissuade Moyra from leaving.

After a brief pause, she nodded, as though to herself, then pushed to her feet. She gave him one last, curious glance before she left.

William swallowed hard. Oh, aye, he was sure they'd both recognized the excuse for exactly what it was, but he couldn't deny an overpowering urge to retreat from this woman's disturbing company. To give himself some much-needed time to regroup and reinforce.

Given enough time, surely he would be able to come up with a reason for why that touch—so fleeting, so innocent—had had such a devastating effect on him. Wouldn't he . . . ?

Nine

The mist . . . as alive and thick as ever. Circling the woman's legs, clinging like tenacious fingers. Cold and damp, settling against the naked, chill-pricked flesh of her calves and shins.

Muted crunch of moist leaves. The sound at first unrecognizable, then slowly traced to emanating from beneath her own small, bare feet.

Slow, stoic steps forward.

Mo chreach, *always* forward.

Her gait is careful, precisely paced, unrelenting.

Ahead, darkness so black it takes on a twisting, churning life all its own.

Her heartbeat accelerates, her slender shoulders tremble. Icy fingers fist the cloak tightly beneath her chin. Out of breath. Legs tired, aching, screaming for rest. Stomach muscles sore from so many quick, shallow breaths . . . breaths that turn the air to vapor.

Stop. Now. Turn back!

No, can't.

Something beckons from the darkness. Something she cannot see, doesn't want to know about. Something she only wishes to avoid.

A vague prick of light pierces the pitch-black fabric of the night ahead.

Her pace quickens.

From the darkness, an invisible claw reaches out. A gasp of pain is overridden by a loud—unnaturally loud—rending of cloth. Warm and thick, scenting the air with an obscure metallic undertone. Drops of blood drip down a slender, pale arm. They are absorbed eventually by the torn woolen cloak.

Fingers quiver, frantically searching the darkness. A whimper of relief. Naught more than a stray branch. Nothing extraordinary. Nothing to be alarmed about. The shallow wound stings and throbs yet the pain quickly loses its urgency.

What does not lose its urgency is the intrusive sound that makes itself heard in the distance. Low. Rough. Intensifying by the second.

Nay, mayhap 'tis not so distant after all.

The sound is closer.

Louder.

More plaintive.

A growl. Low and deep. The feral cry of a wounded animal. Horribly wounded. The oddly silent night magnifies the pain-filled shriek. Goosebumps sprout on chilled forearms. Not caused by the cold, but by that sound.

Feet abruptly ordered to stop moving. As though they had a life of their own, the command is ignored.

Dry twigs snap underfoot. The sound, unnaturally loud and crackling, accompanied by the moist-yet-somehow-soundless rustle of dying leaves as thick branches are shoved aside.

Forward.

Her gait is relentless. Persistently going forward. Into the belly of that piercing wail of pain.

Just around the next corner.

Not far now.

Icy sweat coating neck and brow, chest and arms, pelvis and legs. No cloth ever woven could be thick enough to thwart the chill seeping into fear-pricked flesh. Fear that seeps down into the bloodstream pumping hard and fast beneath.

The animalistic sound grows louder still. Coils around her, denser than the fog, more alive and demanding. Like tangible fingers, it wraps around her in a death-grip, trapping her on all sides like a living thing . . .

Moyra awoke with a gasp, and sat bolt upright in the bed.

The cold sweat clinging to her body transcended her dream, making the tunic and plaid skirt cling to her flesh. Shivering, she hugged her arms tightly about herself for warmth, of which there was precious little to be had.

The small hearth cut into the chamber's inner wall boasted a moderate fire, but the crackling orange flames did nothing to relieve the bone-deep cold that seemed to eat at her from the inside out.

Her heart slammed against her rib cage in hard, wild bursts. Her breath came in such rapid, shallow gasps that her head spun from an overabundance of oxygen. While she would have liked nothing better than to stay buried beneath the thick pelt of fur she'd tossed over herself earlier, a sudden sense of urgency forbade such luxury.

Something was wrong.

She could feel it, *taste* it.

Exactly what it was, she did not know. Yet. However, she had a feeling her dream and the suddenness with which she'd awoken would lead her to the answer soon enough.

Never before had she had visions on consecutive nights. To do so now was more than a wee bit disconcerting. Then again . . . Och! Even when she *did* have her infrequent visions, seldom were they trustworthy enough to act upon.

Except for last night.

Aye, last night's vision had been alarmingly sharp and clear—not to mention accurate and reliable. Should she trust her instincts? Dare she not? What if tonight's vision proved to be equally as portentous . . . ?

'Twas doubtful, considering her history. Still, Moyra hesitated to ignore the impending sense of doom that settled around her like a heavy, pitch-black cloak. Past history or not, would it not be more foolish to ignore her impulses simply because, more times than not, such feelings turned out to be shadows of nothing?

Nay, she decided finally, she could not ignore this, could not take the risk. Not when every muscle in her body screamed for her to get out of bed—*immediately!*—and seek out the cause of this frigid, bone-deep sense of dread.

With trembling fingers she tossed the fur aside. It landed in an unnoticed, rumpled heap at the foot of the bed. The mattress crunched beneath her as she pushed herself to a sitting position. Her knees felt oddly weak and watery, precariously unsupportive when she swung her legs over the side of the bed, then stood.

She winced as a shard of pain sliced through her right arm and shoulder. Her wincing gradually altered into a frown as she realized the pain emanated from the place where the branch had scratched her in her dream.

Had the injury followed her up out of sleep? Was that even possible?

Another thought—of another person, another injury, also in the same shoulder—struck her.

Swallowing hard, Moyra turned her mind in that direction. Like an underling who'd served his purpose and promptly faded into the background, the pain in her shoulder dulled, then disappeared entirely, leaving behind only a vague ache in tender flesh and bone to indicate it had been there at all.

She barely noticed the lingering pinch of sensation, for her concentration had swerved elsewhere. Her jaw sagged open in surprise. If she was right . . .

Not only had she never before experienced two visions on consecutive nights, she'd also *never* made two predictions in a row that were so easily interpreted, so crystal-clear, and so—*Mo chreach!*—so nerve-shatteringly *accurate!*

William had thought the pain intense before.

He was wrong.

Whatever he'd felt the night before was naught but a tickle compared to the agony now shooting through his shoulder. The pain traveled down his arm all the way to his fingertips, and in the other direction spread across his chest, tightening like an implacable steel band that pushed each ragged breath from his air-starved lungs and made it almost impossible to draw in another.

His head spun from lack of air, or from too much pain, he knew not which. Mayhap both. Every move he made was punctuated by fresh stabs of misery in his shoulder.

Despite the knowledge he was hurting himself still more, he could not lie still. Behind the blackness of his closed eyelids, William imagined the Douglas standing over him, stabbing his shoulder with a red-hot poker, over and over again, each thrust timed to coincide with his erratically labored breaths and heartbeats.

The bedding beneath him was bunched and wrinkled, soaked with sweat. More plastered his hair to his cheeks and brow and neck. Like splayed fingers, a half-dozen icy droplets of perspiration traced their way over his scalp; the twisting-turning feel of them was oddly confusing.

'Twas the middle of winter. He couldn't be warm enough to have created that much sweat. Could he? Nay, he was freezing cold, shivering so violently his teeth chattered! He could locate only one point of heat in his body, and that issued from his shoulder—the solitary, fist-sized portion of him was intolerably hot, and the flaming core of pain did not extend to any other part of his body.

William struggled to open his eyes, failed. His lids felt weighted, too heavy to lift. He didn't try a second time. From somewhere close by came a muted groan . . . It took several seconds before the rough, scratchy growl of pain could be traced back to his own unbearably parched throat.

"Hold still, mon. Ye've opened yer wound again and . . . Och! ye're burning up with fever."

The voice was soft, sweetly familiar, especially in the blackness behind his closed eyelids. Moyra. The woman from the tunnel. The woman who'd saved him from the Douglas. The woman who'd brought her to her brother's home, even though a strong, underlying tension made it clear she'd no wish to be there herself.

Elliot. To shift his mind from the pain, he tried to remember if hers was one of the many Border clans his family feuded with. There was a vague recollection of a blood feud several generations back, but he could not remember the cause, or even which branch of either family was involved. He knew for a fact the Liddesdale Armstrongs and Elliots had not openly warred for decades. 'Twas a relief, that. The last thing he needed was to find himself in the belly of one of his enemies!

Moyra . . .

Of their own volition his thoughts returned to the tunnel. To the woman.

Moyra . . .

'Twas an odd name, yet it fit her well. He liked the taste of it, liked also the way his lips and tongue could wrap around it . . . or would were he physically able to wrap either around anything; right now he was in no condition for it.

For reasons William didn't understand—*or didn't want to?*—a bit of the pain-coiled tension seeped out of his tightly bunched muscles. Gradually, he relaxed back against the mattress. His other senses took over where his sight left off, alerting him to the vague scent of lilacs overriding the more pervasive odor of his own sweat and the charred scent of ashes from the fire. 'Twas a ludicrous thing to notice at a time like this, the scent of a woman, yet notice it he did. And whether he wanted to admit it or not, the scent brought with it a warm, soothing wave of comfort.

It was all he could do to hold back a sigh when he felt the back of a hand graze lightly over his forehead . . . over the hard line of his cheek . . . down the side of his neck. Her skin was refreshingly soft and cool. Before he realized he was doing it, William had angled his head, turned into the touch.

His mouth grazed her wrist.

The hand froze.

For one fleeting instant he felt her pulse flutter against his fever-dry lips. The rhythm was youthful and vibrant and oh, so very *alive*. In a way he didn't comprehend, he found himself drawing on her strength, willing his own heartbeat to match the rich, steady cadence of hers.

Her fingers trembled. She hesitated, then pulled back. Quickly. Too quickly.

"With no one tending that fever, 'tis a wonder ye dinna die whilst I slept," he heard her murmur. Her voice was soft and . . . did he detect a vague quiver in her tone? Aye, he thought he did.

As though she noticed it, too, he heard her clear her throat. Twice. Hard. A rustle of cloth and shuffle of bare feet atop cold, hard stone suggested she'd moved away.

Again William tried to pry his eyes open.

Again he failed.

Blast it! He had an urge—as strong as it was strange and illogical—to glimpse the glossy platinum curtain of her hair, the elegant taper of her neck, the flash of her striking violet eyes . . .

Aye, the fever must be raging quite high indeed. Why else would he be entertaining such lustful thoughts, especially when his body was so racked with pain he could not think straight?!

A frustrated sigh slipped past his lips; the sound melted into another pain-riddled groan as a white-hot stab of agony knifed through his shoulder.

"Och! mon, quit yer moaning. Ye arena dying, although I be sure it feels that way. If ye think ye be in pain now, 'tis going tae hurt a fine muckle more when I cauterize that wee scratch."

Somehow, William managed to summon up his voice. While his tone was scratchy and rough, scraping painfully over his parched throat, he didn't complain; truly, 'twas a comfort to hear the sound of his own voice. "If you consider *this* a wee scratch, lass, I don't want to know what you'd consider a 'real' wound."

"A 'real' wound is one that bleeds profusely and threatens tae kill ye."

"I bled."

"Nae excessively."

"I'm bleeding again now. You said so yourself."

"A mere trickle. Enough tae threaten infection, aye, which is why it needs tae be sealed, but naught more. Me da, on the other hand . . . ah, now, *he* suffered a fine muckle of 'real' wounds."

"Worse than this? I find that hard to believe." The

words sounded childish, even to his own ears, yet William didn't try to bite them back. The woman had not too coyly suggested his masculinity was lacking. No Armstrong worth his broadsword allowed such an insinuation to go unchallenged!

"When he was a lad," she said after a pause, "me da's left arm was mangled by a wild boar. He dinna lose the hand, mind ye, but he was ne'er able tae use it again. 'Twas only thanks tae me grandmother's quick nursing that he lived tae tell the tale at all. And tell it he did—as often as he could, tae any who'd listen. 'Tis rumored he dinna shed a single tear, dinna e'en cry out loud, either when he was wounded or when he was tended." As she spoke, her voice faded, moving in the direction of the snapping, crackling fire. "Now, ye arena really trying tae tell me this wee wound of yers is worse than *that* . . . are ye?"

William snapped his mouth shut so hard his teeth clacked together. The line of his jaw hardened, a muscle there throbbed erratically. While he told himself the reaction was merely the result of the pain ripping through his body, he knew it was a lie.

A few tense moments ticked past.

With his eyes closed, William focused his auditory sense on tracking Moyra's movements around the chamber. The noises she made were accompanied by a few of his own muffled groans; he tried to swallow them back, but for the most part was embarrassingly unsuccessful.

She left the room briefly. When she returned, it was two sets of footsteps he heard trodding upon the stone floor. A questioning frown furrowed his brow, but his curiosity was soon appeased.

"Ye'll need tae hold him down," Moyra said. Her voice came from the left side of the bed, while the one that answered came from the right.

"Bloody hell, Moyra, canna ye get Jared tae do the chore?" Kenny's noticeably young, sulky voice cracked over his brother's name. "I've had a belly full of this mon."

"Jared is riding tonight, as ye well know. He's maun tae busy pilfering Graham beasties tae bother with such a menial task as this."

"But—"

"If ye dinna hush up and do as yer told, 'tis o'er me knee I'll be taking ye."

Remembering the size of even Moyra's youngest brother, William couldn't suppress a smile. The boy was almost as tall as his sister. The vision of her carrying through on her threat was humorous.

This time when William tried to open his eyes, he succeeded. The fire-lit room seemed overly bright and blurry at first, but not so much so that he couldn't see the young lad's face looming above him. Kenny's expression was tight with resentment; his hazel eyes narrowed, flashing with pent-up emotion. Glancing down, William noticed that the boy was clenching and unclenching his fists at the ends of rigidly straight, boyishly thin arms.

Shifting his attention, he squinted and saw Moyra crouched in front of the small stone hearth. She appeared to be poking something into the flames, but from this distance and angle he couldn't see what it was. A poker? A knife? Whatever the object, he'd an uncomfortable feeling 'twas what she planned to use to cauterize his wound.

The muscles in his stomach clenched like an iron fist snapping closed. The beat of his heart staggered. Gritting his teeth, he closed his eyes and prepared himself mentally for the pain to come. Blast it! If this woman's father could be mangled by a wild boar without shedding a single tear or crying out, then surely he could manage having red-hot metal pressed against his fevered skin long enough to weld a seal over his reopened wound!

While William wasn't entirely sure he believed the tale of Moyra's father, assuming it true helped fortify his courage . . . not to mention goaded his flailing male ego. If a mere boy could endure so much pain, surely he could endure less, and fleetingly at that. Couldn't he?

In another minute he was given the chance to find out.

His eyes still closed, William heard Moyra approach the bed rather than saw her. Her soft lilac scent was unmistakable. The silence that had enveloped the room metamorphosed into something heavier, something infinitely more tense.

Swallowing hard, he waited for what seemed an eternity before he felt Kenny settle one hand on his good shoulder, the other on the middle of his left thigh. William was in the middle of sucking in a long, deep, steadying breath when he felt the first burst of pain explode in his wounded shoulder. This time he didn't try to suppress a groan of agony.

The stench of scorched flesh was strong and ripe, clogging his nostrils. His spine bowed, his back arched off the mattress. Kenny might as well not be touching him for all the good the boy did; the lad was unable to hold William down no matter how hard he tried, and he did try with all his youthful might.

The minutes fused together.

The pain lasted for what seemed an eternity, clawing into his shoulder and washing throughout the rest of William's body in thrashing swells of teeth-jarring agony.

He didn't scream, but God, he wanted to! It took all his concentration to hold down the howl of pain, trap it between his lungs and throat; he wedged the scream there until it, too, blazed like a fire inside him.

It came as no surprise to feel the blackness roll in like easy, fast-moving storm clouds, blotting out the pain, blotting out everything. The darkness was a blessing, a relief from the agony tearing though his shoulder, and William surrendered to it gratefully.

The last thing he felt before slipping into unconsciousness was that small, wonderfully soft, refreshingly cool hand stroking his brow again. For reasons he didn't dare contemplate too closely, the darkness suddenly seemed less oppressive, and infinitely more comforting.

Ten

"Ye look tired as hell."

"Nae as tired as I feel. 'Tis nae possible, believe me."

Jared shook his head and sighed. His gaze scanned his sister. Truly, she appeared almost as wretched as on the morning she'd learned of their father's death.

Weary shadows smudged dark purplish-gray semi-circles beneath her eyes. In what little early morning light managed to sneak in through the tall, narrow windows carved in the far wall, her cheeks seemed unnaturally pale, almost gaunt. At some point during the night she'd pulled her hair back in a neat, thick braid at her nape. The silky platinum strands were now more out of the braid than in it; tousled curls clung limply to her brow and cheeks and neck.

"Get some rest whilst ye can, lass," Jared said, nodding to the stone archway leading out of the great hall. "Dinna worry about yer mon, I'll have one of the serving wenches watch o'er him for a wee bit. If ye insist, I'll e'en have her wake ye if he rouses."

"Nay, William is my responsibility." Moyra shook her head wearily, but insistently. "If anyone watches o'er him, 'twill be meself."

"Aye? Tell me, Moyra, have ye a reason for tending him so diligently . . . ?"

Moyra shrugged. A wince creased her brow when the tired, aching muscles in her shoulders and neck and back pulled taut, seeming to twist with the gesture. "As I said, he's my responsibility."

"And ye take yer responsibilities—real or imagined—maun seriously. Always have. Och! how well I ken it." Linking his fingers on the tabletop in front of him, Jared's attention sharpened on his sister. "What's the worst that can happen? He dies. 'Twill be nae great tragedy if the Border is less one Armstrong." His shrug was as casual as his tone, as though he were talking of nothing more serious than an approaching shower. " 'Twould nae necessarily be a bad thing."

"Do ye think I've gone tae so much trouble only tae have the mon die now?" she demanded sharply.

"Truth tae tell, lass, I dinna ken what tae think at this point." He drummed his fingertips atop the table, and at the same time used the heel of his other palm to support his chin. "Ye show up on me doorstoop yesterday afternoon after swearing ye'd ne'er set foot in this keep again. Ye ask for me help, after swearing ye'd ne'er ask anything from me again. Ye e'en *talk* tae me, after swearing ye'd never utter another word in my presence or direction." Sucking in a deep breath, he released it slowly, thoughtfully, through his teeth. "If e'er there was a person I thought as good as their word, that person was ye. Ye've always kenned yer own mind—and nae been shy aboot speaking it, much to our da's dismay. If ye e'er made a compromise of any sort, I dinna know aboot it. Yet in a single day ye've managed tae crush e'ery opinion I have of ye like a piece of dirt under yer heel." His eyes narrowed. "What is William Armstrong to ye that ye care so ver' much if he lives or dies?"

Moyra opened her mouth to answer, then just as quickly snapped it shut. No answer came immediately to mind.

Truly, *she didn't know* why it was so important to her that the man live. It simply *was*. Extremely important to her, in fact.

Important enough that she had selflessly risked her own life to save his. Important enough that she had sacrificed much-needed sleep, and was now suffering nagging pains of weariness and strain in order to tend him back to health. Important enough that—even now, when her mind was so fuzzy she could hardly link two coherent thoughts together—she still didn't entertain for a second the notion of seeking out the sleep her body craved. Nay, not until she could be sure William was out of danger.

Which brought her exhausted mind full circle . . .

She'd been away from his bedside too long. What if he'd awakened and found her gone? What if the herbs she'd forced down his throat had not worked, and his fever had escalated? Worse, what if he'd moved and torn open the fragile flesh she'd so carefully welded together?

Kenny was upstairs with him, of course, but Kenny was merely a lad. Also, she remembered all too vividly the scene she'd walked in on yesterday when the two were together.

'Twas clear she could not rely on her younger brother to tend William. She could not rely on anyone but herself to do the task correctly.

The wooden legs of the bench scraped against the stone floor when Moyra abruptly pushed herself to her feet. Glancing down, she locked her gaze with Jared's. "If William is well enough to travel, we'll leave afore sunset."

"Nay, Moyra," he said tiredly, "ye misunderstand me. Again. 'Tis nae what I meant. There be nae need tae—"

"Aye, there *is* a need. A maun pressing one, in fact. Ye were right in suggesting I've compromised me principles in bringing the mon here."

"I suggested nae such thing, I merely pointed out—"

"Aye, ye did suggest it, intentionally or nay," she said, and he frowned darkly to be so abruptly cut short once more. "Stop yer frowning, Jared. I said ye were right, did I nae? Ne'er disagree with a woman when she's letting ye win an argument. I *have* gone back on me word . . . several times. 'Tis wee compensation, and well I know it, but I did what I thought right at the time. Heaven knows I'd precious little choice. Och! brother, dinna fash yeself. William and I willna take advantage of yer kindness a moment longer than is necessary. As soon he can be moved, we'll be away from Glentroe Tower. Unlike the others I've broken, this be a promise I intend tae keep."

She was almost to the shadowy stone archway leading out of the hall when her brother's voice shot out from behind her. Strong and determined, Jared's words stopped her cold.

"What about our mother?" he asked briskly. "Will ye go back on yer promise tae her as well? Or is it a promise ye've conveniently forgotten now that you've taken up nursing wounded Border reivers?"

Like an arrow hitting its target, her brother's comment pierced Moyra's rigid self-control. Her breath caught. Her spine and jawline stiffened. Lifting her chin, she squared her shoulders, refusing to glance back at him when she answered. "Have a care, Jared. The promise ye speak of is between our mother and meself. Whether I keep it or nay is none of yer affair."

"Ye canna be more wrong about that. When yer actions, or lack of them, hurt someone I hold so dear, 'tis ver' much my affair. She was devastated when ye left, Moyra. Dinna ye know that? Especially so soon on the heels of da's death. If ye leave again, without e'en speaking tae her . . ."

"I planned tae see her before leaving, have nae fear of that."

"Do ye also plan tae upset her again, lass? She's maun more frail and weak than when last ye saw her. If ye start spouting yer wild accusations aboot me killing our da . . . weel, I dinna know for sure what will happen."

Moyra inhaled sharply, then released the breath slowly, slowly through tightly gritted teeth. "I'll do me best tae keep off that subject," she replied grudgingly. "Nor will I remind her that I think it ver' wrong she choose tae believe ye faultless in what happened. Now, if ye'll excuse me, I've a patient tae tend."

That said, Moyra squared her shoulders and quit the hall. She didn't spare her brother another glance. She didn't dare. If she had, surely Jared would see the contempt in her eyes, in her expression. Even if he somehow didn't, she'd a feeling he would sense it. What good could come of that? He already knew how she felt, she'd been most plain in that. Nay, there was no sense making an already intolerable situation worse.

Jared's eyes narrowed. The line of his jaw was harder than granite.

Drumming his fingers thoughtfully upon the table-top, he glared at the empty archway long after his sister had retreated up the stairs beyond it.

Eleven

It took several days before William was well enough
to ride.

'Twas on the morning of their departure that Moyra
found herself standing in the middle of her old bedchamber, a room that hadn't changed at all in the
months she'd been away. The bed remained unmade,
the covers rumpled, exactly the way she'd left them in
what felt now like a lifetime ago. Even the hairbrush
resting atop her dresser still had long platinum strands
of hair clinging to its stiff bristles.

Crossing to the dresser, Moyra picked up the brush.
The unadorned pewter handle felt thick and heavy in
her grip as she began dragging the brush through her
unbound hair. Her gaze lifted sightlessly to the dry
mortar where two thick stones converged, while at the
same time her mind reflected back on the last few
days.

The bulk of her time had been spent nursing William Armstrong. Then, when he'd become more alert
and restless, entertaining him with intricate tales of
her father's raids and daring. When he slept—since he
was still healing, his body needed frequent bouts of

rest—she often stole time away from him to visit her mother.

Jared was right. Never a large woman, Helene Elliot seemed more thin and frail than ever. Her light blue eyes had always been large and endearingly inno-cent—a precious rarity in one who lived surrounded by death and violence—yet now they had a detached, haunted quality that Moyra found disturbing.

More than once, in midconversation, Helene would stop talking and stare off at some distant point only she could see. Now and then her delicate blond head tipped to the side. Her brows would become pinched, as though she struggled to catch vague snatches of conversation that existed only in her own mind.

They spoke about Moyra's father often. In itself, Moyra did not find the topic disturbing. Oh, aye, 'twould be a lie to say her heart didn't tug painfully at the memories, or that it didn't ache when she real-ized she would never see his big, smiling face again, nor hear his roaring voice bouncing off stony castle walls that now seemed infinitely cold and empty.

What *did* disturb Moyra was the way her mother spoke of her late husband. While Moyra referred to her father in the past tense, as was customary when one discussed a dead man, her mother did not. Instead of alluding to what her husband *had* done, instead Helene boasted about what he *did* do, or what he *would* do in the future.

Had Moyra not known better, her mother's words would have led her to believe Ross Elliot was fit and fine and simply away from the keep on one of his infamous raids. That he was due to return at any mo-ment.

Indeed, more than once Moyra caught her mother's gaze darting anxiously to the open doorway. Only then would the woman's light blue eyes come alive, sparkling with anticipation. Only then would her too-pale cheeks take on that familiar, excited rosy hue. The way Helene scanned the doorway suggested that she expected Ross's burly form to materialize there, and she was most eager for the sight of it.

Like a thick, clinging ground fog, confusion and disappointment would eventually mist her mother's gaze. The woman's expression grew alarmingly pale once more when, of course, her husband did not appear. The sight was heart wrenching.

Her fingers trembling slightly, Moyra set the brush back down upon the dresser. What was it like to love a man so deeply and completely, she wondered, that your life ceased to exist when his did? And would she ever know such a love herself?

A frown pinched her brow when the image of William Armstrong scampered, unbidden, across her mind.

"Och, lass, 'tis lack of sleep making ye daft," she grumbled as, reaching up, she began working her long hair into a thick, tight plait. "Aye, what else could it be?"

What else indeed, she thought as she worked the glossy platinum strands in tight twists and turns. Her movements were harsh and jerky enough to make the roots of her hair pinch and burn. The twinges of pain were a welcome distraction. They kept her from wondering if her roughness was due to the fact that, like a tenacious shrub, the vision of William Armstrong had planted itself in her thoughts and thrived there . . .

Gritting her teeth, Moyra forced the notion aside. It did not go without a fight, but go it most certainly did. She saw to that.

Now that he was well enough to travel, William would be going home. Where he belonged. As soon as she'd deposited him upon his doorstep, her obligation to him was over. The chance of her setting eyes on him again was slim.

She hesitated in the act of tying off the braid with a thin blue ribbon. Her breath caught in her throat, and the slice of pain that stabbed through her midsection was as sharp as it was undeniable.

Why did the idea of never seeing William again bother her . . . ?

Moyra didn't know, but it did. It bothered her greatly.

A knock at the door snagged her attention.

Crossing the chamber, she opened the door to find Jared. Judging from the frown pinching her brother's brow, something was wrong. Nervously, Moyra waved him inside, then closed the door quietly behind him.

"Mother?" she asked when the wedge of breath that had lumped painfully in her throat finally eased enough for the words to slip past.

"She's fine. Sleeping soundly when last I checked on her."

"Then what?" The tightness of emotion squeezing her chest loosened, but did not entirely abate. "Something is wrong, Jared. I can tell. I can see it in yer eyes. Tell me."

" 'Tis yer patient. Or, mayhaps I should say yer *former* patient."

The tightness in her chest returned with enough

force to push the air from Moyra's lungs. "William . . . ?"

"Is gone, lass."

Gone?" She shook her head, sure she'd heard him wrong. "What do ye mean he's *gone?*"

"Exactly what I said. Whilst ye busied yerself bathing and changing, yer patient decided he was nae longer in need of yer tending and left."

Moyra frowned at her brother, but Jared's expression remained dispassionate. Her gaze narrowed on him sharply. "Are ye telling me he slipped past all yer guards? That nae a single one of them saw him leaving the keep?"

"I dinna say *that.*" Shrugging, he moved over to the bed and sat down upon it. The mattress crunched beneath him. "As a matter of fact, several saw him go."

Her eyes widened with shock. *"And they dinna see fit tae stop him?"*

"O'course not. And why should they? Their orders are tae keep rogues like him *out* of Glentroe Tower, nae *in* it." Tipping his head to the side, Jared studied his sister carefully. "The Elliots have nae quarrel with the Armstrongs at the moment, 'tis true, howe'er I'm nae the only Elliot in Glentroe Tower who couldna rest comfortably knowing an Armstrong slept under the same roof." Lifting his hand, he slapped his thigh and shook his head. "Och, lass, ye ken as well as I that the Armstrongs have a reputation on both sides of this godforsaken Border for a fine muckle of things, but trustworthiness isna one of then. A more bloodthirsty, unscrupulous family, ye willna find."

"William isna like that."

"Is that so?" This time it was Jared's eyes that

opened wide, their hazel depths shimmering with surprise. "I suppose ye be kenning this for a fact?"

"Aye."

"And ye would be kenning it . . . how?"

Moyra planted her hands on her hips. The line of her back went stiffer than the sturdy trunk of an oak tree. "It doesna matter *how* I know it, I know it."

"Ye arena thinking clearly, lass. The mon was ailing the entire time he was with ye. Nae in any condition tae show his true nature."

"Could that be because his true nature is—"

The hand Jared sliced through the air cut her words short. "His true nature is the same as that of any Armstrong, have nae doubt aboot it. Or did ye nae hear aboot his latest raid on the Douglas?"

Moyra's eyes narrowed. While she'd explained to her brother, vaguely, how she'd come upon the wounded William Armstrong, she'd not gone into detail. The Douglas's name was never mentioned, nor had she any desire to mention it now. While the feud between Douglas and Elliot was not as savage as some, it was a feud just the same.

"Either the mon is brave beyond reason," Jared continued, "or he is a complete and utter fool. If ye ask me, he's maun than a wee bit of both. 'Tis the only thing I can think of tae explain why he would go so far beyond a simple raid."

It was Moyra's turn to frown. "What do ye mean?"

"Dinna tell me ye've nae heard!"

"Heard . . . what?" she inquired cautiously. Like a teardrop of melting ice, a chill shivered its way down her spine. Beneath the kilt, her knees began to tremble; she moved to the bed and sank onto the mattress beside her brother. The feeling that settled like a chunk of lead in the pit of her stomach suggested she was not going to like the information Jared seemed so eager to share, just as the deep-rooted, irresistible pull of curiosity indicated she was going to listen, avidly, to each and every word.

Aye, she decided 'twas better to learn the truth from her brother, a reliable source, than to wait a few months and glean it from the inevitable Border ballad. 'Twas common knowledge that, enjoyable and entertaining though they were, facts in those ballads often could not be trusted; more times than not the truth was distorted and exaggerated beyond recognition!

In this particular instance, 'twas an unembellished truth she desired most to hear. The truth about William Armstrong . . . and about exactly what he had been doing the night she'd found him wounded at Wyndehaghen.

William pulled the string of the bow back until the muscles in his shoulder and back screamed at the pent-up tension. The pinched tips of his index finger and thumb stung, aching to release the string and let the arrow fly. Soon, but not quite yet.

Squinting now, with one eye almost closed and his brow furrowed, he glared down the length of the arrow, sighting the thick birch tree trunk that was his target. Yet it wasn't the gritty bark his gaze narrowed on. Nor did he see the puffs of his breath forming wispy vapor trails in the cold winter air. Oh, nay, nothing so uncomplicated. Rather, his mind's eye flashed

him an image of long, touchably-soft platinum hair
and wide, heather-colored eyes.

The impression of Moyra Elliot was not expelled
even after he loosened his fingers. The whistle of the
arrow as it shot toward its mark was overridden by
the memory of her voice . . . soft and sweet, echoing
in the darkness of the tunnel the night she'd saved his
life.

William gritted his teeth even as the arrowhead
stabbed into the three trunk. Even from this distance
he could see the thin stem vibrate from the force of
the impact. The quivers were scant when compared to
the tremors vibrating through his own body. Tremors
that commenced somewhere deep on the inside and,
like the ripples made by a stone tossed in a calm lake,
echoed swiftly outward.

A curse teased his lips.

He swallowed the words back when, startled, he
heard clapping coming from behind him. The sound,
too rhythmic to be enthusiastic, echoed off the dense
forest walls.

William's gaze snapped over his shoulder, narrowing on the man who stood on the edge of the clearing.

Tall, as thin as the trunk of the oak tree he so neg-
ligently leaned against was thick, the intruder had a
mop of long, ragged, light brown hair that looked as
though it hadn't been groomed in weeks; it hung
around his gaunt brow and cheeks like chunks of limp
straw. His clothes didn't fare much better. The tunic
clinging to his bony shoulders might have been beige,
although William doubted it. More likely, the shirt had,
at one time, been white, however, it had been worn
so often and for so long between infrequent washings

that the threadbare cloth was now tinged a permanent shade of dun.

As William watched, the man pushed away from the tree and, twigs and leaves crunching underfoot, walked toward him. Up close, it was evident the intruder was in the throes of adolescence. Old enough to shave, yet not old enough to do aught else with a blade. Like his appearance, his gait was lazy; he didn't swagger or strut, nor did he slouch or shuffle. Instead, he crossed the distance using an economy of motion, not expending an ounce more of energy than was necessary.

Stopping an arm's length away, the boy balled his hands into fists and planted them atop his lean hips. His attention volleyed from the spent arrow, to William, then back and forth again, finally coming to rest upon the latter.

"Impressive," he remarked finally. His words rang with a thick Scots burr. "Yer da would be proud." A crooked grin twisted over his thin-to-the-point-of-almost-nonexistent lips. The gesture reached his eyes, perhaps a wee bit too much—seeing the bright glint of amusement in those dark brown depths reminded William of an overeager pup.

The shrug that played over William's shoulders was tight and strained. "My father is dead," he replied flatly. "There's not much 'twould impress him these days."

"Our mother, then?"

"Aye, Duff, she would be. But then, the lady is easily excited." Reaching up over his right shoulder, William pulled another arrow from the quiver strapped to his back. "You need only change your clothes and bathe more than once every other fortnight to rouse her."

William didn't need to see his stepbrother's grin to know it broadened. While he'd not known the younger man long—his mother had married Duff's father scarcely two season previous—he knew him well enough.

Duff Pringle was as uncomplicated as the simple bow hanging limply from William's grasp. While another man would have been insulted, mayhap even enraged, Duff took the insult with no more concern than he showed the bitter winter wind tossing his unkempt hair about his face and shoulders. 'Twas rumored he'd slipped from the womb not caring a whit for what others said or thought about him. William was beginning to think the rumor held more weight than he'd at first given it credit for.

"I dinna come out here to bicker with ye, brother," Duff said.

When William sent him a sharp glance, his stepbrother merely lifted and lowered his eyebrows inquisitively. His grin remained firmly in place, and he did not retract the overly familiar designation. "Then what *did* you come for?"

"I've a message for ye."

"From . . . ?"

"Iain Douglas."

William had been in the process of lifting his bow and securing the arrow, readying it for another shot. At Duff's words, he froze. The brisk winter air crackled with the sudden, static alertness tingling through his veins. "Go on," he prodded, his voice reflecting the current of tension coursing through him.

"Weel . . ." Duff started, and the sounds of his feet shuffling in the winter-dead grass seemed oddly loud and grating. " 'Tis a wee bit confusing."

"Somehow, I think I'll be able to make sense of it." William lowered the bow and arrow to his side. In one swift, jerky motion, he turned to face his stepbrother.

Duff's grin faded until it reflected more confusion than amusement. Pursing his lips, he shrugged and said, "I was on me way tae visit Madelyn in Dundee when I stumbled upon one of the Douglas's men. Literally, I'm afraid. Apparently he'd stopped for the night and was getting ready tae ride again. Since we've no feud with the Douglas that I ken, I saw nae reason tae refuse the man's offer tae share his morning meal. 'Twould only set me back an hour or twa, and Madelyn is a fine bonny lass whom I've nae doubt would wait for me that long, so—"

"The message," William prodded, growing impatient.

"Aye, the message," Duff repeated. He hesitated, shook his dark head, shrugged his narrow shoulders. "When the man found out I have an Armstrong for a relative, he was curious tae ken from which branch of the family. Again, I saw no harm in telling him, although, thinking back on it, the way his eyes gleamed at the information, mayhap 'twas nae the smartest thing tae do. Immediately, he wanted tae know if I was related tae ye."

If possible, William's back and shoulders stiffened still more. "And you told him you were?"

"Aye. At that point, I could hardly deny it!" Duff's grin faltered, then faded away entirely. Nervously, he shifted his weight from foot to foot. "That's when he gave me the message. 'Twould appear he was riding here tae deliver it himself, but once he realized who I was—"

"Once you *told* him, you mean."

"Aye, er, whate'er." Duff fingered a stray strand of hair from his eyes and glanced guiltily away. "Anyway, in the end he must have decided tae save himself the time and trouble of an extra half-day's ride, for instead he gave the message tae me tae deliver."

Like a living thing, impatience clawed at William's gut. The fingers of his free hand clenched and unclenched at his side, and it was all he could do not to reach down the younger man's throat and forcibly yank the message in question free. Instead, his eyes sharpening on Duff, he waited for his stepbrother to speak again. It did not take long.

"Now, let me see if I have this right, for he said 'twas imperative I repeat it *exactly . . ."*

William sighed. The muscles in his jaw grew rigid as he bit back a curse.

"Aye, I have it. He said tae tell ye, 'There's a score tae settle. Be warned, the Douglas rides with the quarter moon, and this time his quarry is Elliot.' Och! but it makes nae a bit of sense, if you ask me, but—"

The bow and arrow dropped from abruptly slack fingers. It fell unnoticed to the frozen ground by William's feet. A low, feral growl emanated from his throat.

The unnatural sound made whatever Duff was about to say scatter like snowflakes tossed by a strong winter gust. The younger man took a quick, instinctive step backward when he caught a glimpse of the murderous glint in his stepbrother's eyes. For a split second he mistook the glare as being meant for him. His heart pounding out a hard, erratic beat in his lean chest, Duff found himself fearing for his life!

"I—I take it ye ken what the message means?" Duff stammered, but only once his initial panic had subsided.

"Aye," William growled, his tone as tight and strained as his expression, "I know exactly what it means. Mark my words, Duff, the man will *not* get away with this!" Eyes narrowing, his gaze sharpened on his stepbrother. "Go back to the keep and send someone with a message to both Scots and English March Wardens. Have them tell Robert Carey exactly what you told me. Maxwell will do naught, but tell Carey to ride for Wyndehaghen the instant he receives the message. Tell him 'tis a matter of utmost urgency, that an innocent life is in jeopardy."

"But—"

"Just do it!" William roared.

Startled, Duff nodded his head up and down even as he began to back away. The second he reached the edge of the clearing, he spun on his heels and darted into the thick, concealing line of trees.

William watched his stepbrother go, although his mind was elsewhere. His thoughts had shifted to Moyra Elliot, and they refused to budge from her.

In his chest, suspiciously near the region of his heart, was a tightening, like an iron fist jerking harshly closed and twisting mightily. 'Twas a sensation unlike anything he'd ever experienced before, and the sheer, breathless intensity of it left him feeling confused and shaken to the core.

Iain Douglas was going after Moyra.

That the Douglas had somehow discovered Moyra had deceived him went without question. How the man had unearthed the fact, William didn't know, nor did he waste precious time wondering on the matter. In the end, it was not important *how* the Douglas had found out, only that he had . . . and that the man's vengeful eye had turned on Moyra.

The woman had saved William's life. He'd healed quite nicely in the passing weeks, although his shoulder still ached, reminding him of all Moyra had so selflessly done for him. Oh, aye, his wound had healed all right, but only because Moyra Elliot had gone to such great lengths to tend him when he most needed tending.

How could William sit back and allow Iain Douglas to exact retribution on her, when her only sin was saving his life, and in turn risking her own?

He couldn't. There was nothing more to it.

William did not doubt that without Moyra's nursing, he would have died in Wyndehaghen's claustrophobically narrow tunnel. Nor did he doubt that he would not—*could not*—allow the Douglas to find and punish Moyra for the deed.

His conscience simply would not allow it.

At least he hoped 'twas his conscience that spurred him into the only decision he would allow himself to make. Surely there was nothing more complicated involved . . .

Or was there?

Gritting his teeth harder still, William forced the question from his mind even as he bent and retrieved his bow and arrow. Some things did not bear contemplating too closely, and this was one of them.

Telling himself he wished nothing more than to pay back his debt to Moyra in kind, William stalked toward the edge of the clearing, heading in the same direction in which he'd watched Duff so recently disappear.

Unfortunately, nothing he told himself relieved the breath-snatching tightness in his chest, or the restless anxiety that made every muscle in his body feel like it was coiled tighter than a spring ready to snap. Nor did it explain why the thought of seeing Moyra Elliot again quickened his footsteps to an impatient pace . . .

Twelve

From out of nowhere, a hand snaked around Moyra's shoulder and slammed over her mouth.

It all happened too fast, too unexpectedly, for her to react. One minute she was hunkered down in front of the hearth, stoking the dwindling flames with a gnarled stick, trying to coax the fire back to flickering life, the next thing she knew the hand was over her mouth and the stick had dropped from her suddenly slackened grasp. It toppled toward the floor; the hard, sharp edge struck the top of her foot with enough force to make her wince.

The hand over her mouth—*a big, powerful, male hand!*—trapped in her throat any sound she may have made, be it a gasp of pain or howl of surprise.

Moyra's body stiffened in protest. Struggling, she sent her right hand lunging for the dagger tucked in the cuff of her boot.

Another hand, as big and powerful as the first, shot out from the other side. Thick, strong fingers shackled her wrist, yanking her hand aside even as her fingertips grazed the body-warmed, carved wooden hilt of the knife.

"Lerf mmm ggg!" The words, muffled by the hand

over her mouth, were unrecognizable, yet Moyra felt better for having voiced them. Even though it was impossible to understand what she said, her tone was calm and cold and demanding. 'Twas a direct opposite to her inner responses, trembling with fear and apprehension.

Who would dare come to Wyndehaghen and treat her so harshly? Did this ruffian not know who she was?

A frown creased her brow. *Mo chreach,* now that she thought about it, who would dare come to Wyndehaghen *at all?* The keep was naught but ruins, the village beyond its decaying walls long since abandoned. Those who'd dwelled in or around here decades ago had found other clans to take them in and were well settled by now. Except for William Armstrong and the Douglas, in the whole time she'd been in residence in the ruined keep no one had even—

Moyra's eyes widened and her body went deathly still as that thought blasted over her like a frigid winter wind.

Her captor must have mistaken her stillness for compliance. Before she knew what he was about, he stood and in so doing dragged her to her feet with him.

The small of her back came up hard against his abdomen. Och! and what a hard, tight, well-muscled abdomen, it was!

Moyra felt like she'd been propped unwillingly against a carved granite wall. The fronts of the man's thighs blanketed the backs of hers; hot and hard, they were equally as sinewy as his stomach. The top of her head did not clear the broad shelf of his shoulders.

She knew that because, his hand still over her mouth, he jerked her head backward and it collided with the firm, sculpted plane of his chest.

His breaths, hot and misty, puffed down over the left side of her face. Had the hand over her mouth allowed any slack, she would have angled her head up and to the side to view her assailant. It did not. Instead, violet eyes narrowing with impotent fury, Moyra glared into the hot, glowing embers of the nearly extinguished fire. She concentrated on controlling her own harsh, uneven breathing because, at that moment, it seemed the only thing she *could* control.

'Twas a humbling sensation. One that chafed raw her integrally deep streak of Elliot pride. Humbled? Och, nay! An Elliot was many things but never, *never* humble!

It was only as Moyra lifted her booted foot, intent on crushing her captor's toes with the heel—she doubted it would do much good, but she was determined to try—that he finally spoke. "Shhh, lass," he hissed, his lips so close to her ear she could feel them move through the curtain of her hair, "do not make a sound or 'tis death to us both."

The voice, low and gritty and tense, wrapped around Moyra like a warm, familiar blanket.

She blinked hard. Twice. Her frown deepened. Although she wanted to shake her head in confusion, the man's grip on her was too tight to allow it. *"Wllm?"*

He didn't answer. Instead, hauling her along with him, William shifted to the side. Bracing his weight and hers on one rock-hard leg and hip, he used the booted foot of the other to kick at the thick, dark gray carpet of ashes scattered over the floor of the hearth.

In seconds, the few fastidiously cared for embers were doused.

Moyra sputtered a protest. Twisting, she tried to struggle free of his tight, restraining grip. Tried—and failed. As she'd known she would. Had William no idea how long it had taken her to coax those embers back to life?

Not only didn't he know, William didn't care. Matters of greater import were his utmost concern right then. Like keeping this woman alive.

His response to her silent rebellion was to tighten his hold on both her mouth and her wrist until, finally, her anger seemingly spent, she was once again still and quiet. Seething, aye, but silently. With an inward sigh, he realized 'twas the best he could hope for at the moment.

Again, he pressed his lips close to her ear. Trying to ignore the all-too-sweet lilac scent clinging to the silky strands tickling his cheek and chin, he whispered raggedly, "Be still, Moyra. I'm not here for my own health, I *am* here to ensure yours." Sensing her unasked question, he continued more softly, "I've a debt in sore need of repaying. People can say what they like about the Liddesdale Armstrongs—most of it, I'm sure, is true—but we've a reputation for repaying our debts, no matter what the cost. You saved my life once. Now, 'tis my turn to save yours."

Against the center of his palm, he felt her mouth open. Her warm breath, like liquid mist against his skin, was hot and branding until, obviously realizing she could say naught with his hand there, she snapped her mouth closed once more.

The shiver skating down William's spine had nothing to do with the chill that had settled in the small chamber. He was almost glad for the distraction of hoofbeats echoing outside the open window, coming from the direction of the overgrown courtyard below. It gave his mind something more constructive to concentrate on than the odd, burning sensation branded in the center of his hand, exactly where her breath had scorched his skin.

"We've no time to waste, Moyra," he hissed in her ear. "The Douglas is just outside. And this time, he is not coming for me." The revelation caused a shiver to make Moyra's slender shoulders tremble. "When I was here last, I was wounded and barely conscious. My memory cannot be relied upon. Tell me, which way to the tunnel?"

The back of her head still firmly pressed against the front of his chest, Moyra nevertheless managed to nod in the direction of the doorway. With only a quarter moon hanging in the black velvet sky outside, the light drifting in through the open window was faint. It reminded her uneasily of that first night, so many months ago, when she'd found him wounded and defenseless in her tunnel.

Tonight, there was barely enough of the wispy, silvery glow to make out the vague rectangular shape of the doorway, and none of it worked its way into the pitch-black, narrow corridor beyond.

Moyra needed no light to navigate the corridor, or the wheel staircase at the end of it. Each twist and turn was emblazoned in her memory.

William, however, had no such memories to rely upon. Whichever direction he chose to go in could only be a guess. He wasn't familiar enough with the

layout of the keep, and Moyra found his lack of
knowledge an unnecessary obstruction . . . especially
since he kept his hand over her mouth and continued
to haul her along with him as though she was a sack
of grain with no power of its own!

Nay, if they were going to make an escape, it *would
not* happen this way!

Having that in mind, when they reached the bedchamber's doorway, Moyra reached out. Locking her
elbow, she used her arms as a bar to prevent William
from leading them across the threshold. The sharp corner of the stone dug into her tender flesh; she winced,
but did not relax.

The curse that whispered in her ear was hot and
ripe . . . and Sassenach to the core. She ignored it
and its meaning—something to do with questioning
her ancestry—even as she stiffened her body still
more, refusing to let him haul her another inch.

"You try my patience, wench! Blast it! Put your
arm down. *Now.*"

Moyra shook her head adamantly.

From outside came the muted whicker of more than
one horse. The sound was followed by a husky male
murmur. The latter noise was quickly hushed.

Time was running out.

Again, William tried to haul her over the threshold.
Again, she held firm, refusing to allow it.

For a small woman, she was surprisingly powerful.
As powerful, William thought, as she was determined.
While he could hoist her higher and force her into the
corridor, he knew that the time it would take to accomplish the feat if she continued to be noncompliant
was a luxury he simply did not have. Then, too, there

was the amount of noise such an action would make. If the Douglas did not already know for a fact that they were here, a commotion like that one promised to be would certainly alert him to their presence.

Annoyed that a woman as small and as seemingly "delicate" as Moyra Elliot had so easily thwarted his intent and robbed him of any choice, William gritted his teeth and, one by one, reluctantly pried his fingers away from her mouth. The too-still, frosty winter air slapped at his palm . . . an instant before it was chased away by the hot blast of her sharp—relieved?—exhalation.

Something must have relaxed his grip on her wrist, because before he knew it, she'd shaken herself free. To his surprise, she did not pull away entirely, but entwined her fingers with his.

A sense of déjà vu made his senses spin. Her hand felt small and deceptively fragile, her grip tenuous but determined. Her skin was warm. Soft. Oddly nice the way it rubbed against his.

Scowling hard, William shook his head as though to shake the ridiculous observation off. Truly, this was no time to be thinking about how the woman's skin felt! Not with Iain Douglas and his men gathering just outside! So why, he wondered as his thoughts returned to the moment, did his skin continue to smolder with awareness of her touch . . . ?

If Moyra noticed his silent brooding, she made no comment. Instead, it was her turn to look toward him and whisper sharply. Annoyance thickened her accent when she snapped, "This way, and be quick aboot it. Och! mon, if ye ken what's good for ye, ye'll be staying maun close tae me. One misstep and ye'll stumble and fall down the stairway. If that happens, I'll nae be wasting me time stopping tae pick ye up."

She didn't wait for a reply. That was probably just as well; William would have been hard pressed to utter anything from between teeth so tightly clenched his jaw and temple throbbed from the pressure!

One sharp yank on his arm and he stumbled into step behind her. The darkness in the corridor was absolute, closing around them like a thick, cloying shroud. Much to his admiration, her steps never wavered. She seemed to know exactly where she was going, and William couldn't help but wonder if 'twas memory that led her, or something more enigmatic.

"I've The Sight," she had told him once, but he'd not believed her. He still didn't. He wasn't a man given to putting stock in anything that smacked of mysticism; quite simply, if he could not see or smell, hear or taste or touch something, it did not exist. This woman's "Sight" was nonsense as far as he was concerned. Hadn't she predicted the Douglas would not return, only to have him return after all? Aye, she had.

Still, as the darkness seemed to grow, and her steps never once faltered as he followed her blindly, inching with amazing speed through the impenetrable blackness . . . well, William couldn't help but wonder if mayhap the beliefs he'd always held fast were, in fact, a wee bit flawed . . .

While he may not have remembered his way to or from the tunnel, the tunnel itself was something William doubted he would ever forget.

The rank smell was unsettlingly familiar, as was the

feel of damp, sticky walls gliding beneath his open palms as he inched his way farther into the tunnel's narrow depths. Behind him, he heard Moyra quietly ease the door shut.

The sound was soft, yet it grated on William's nerves like shards of broken glass.

Once, many years ago, he'd been locked in a dungeon. Caught accidentally with a bunch of reivers who'd been raiding a neighboring family, he'd been taken hostage, his protests of innocence falling on deaf ears. They'd tossed him in the dungeon with the real culprits while his captors awaited ransom for his release.

Although his mother had furnished the funds quickly, it had not been quickly enough as far as William was concerned. In the end, he'd spent over three fortnights in the belly of the Forster's keep, locked in a small, cramped cell that spanned exactly four paces end to end in any direction, and stank worse than even this godforsaken tunnel. When he'd finally been freed, he'd sworn he would never, under *any* circumstances, allow himself to be locked up that way again.

Oh, aye, this was not quite the same thing, 'twas true enough; yet the restless feeling humming through him was uncomfortably similar.

Clenching his hands into fists at his sides, William gritted his teeth, closed his eyes and pictured himself back in the small bedchamber located three stories above. Compared to the crowded confines of this tunnel, the bedchamber seemed luxuriously spacious.

It took a good deal of concentration, but eventually his breaths slowed, regulated. Eventually the hard, erratic beat of his heart ironed itself out to a, while not quite calm, reassuringly steady rhythm.

"Methinks we've played this scene afore, mon," Moyra said, her voice just below a whisper. She stepped closer, taking her place by his side. Pressing her back against the stone, she inhaled sharply when the hard, cold wetness of the stone seeped through her tunic and plaid, seeping into the sensitive skin beneath.

A shiver trickled down her spine like chips of melting ice. It was followed by a gasp when she felt William's arm slip around her shoulders. This time when he hauled her roughly against his chest, she did not try to stop him, nor did she utter a single cry of protest . . . and not only because she abruptly lacked an ounce of breath with which to utter a thing. Och, nay, 'twas because the promised heat of his body was far too inviting to deny herself the feel of it.

"Ye dinna need tae—"

"Aye, lass, I do," he whispered back at her. The hand he trapped lightly over her mouth cut her words short. "Your teeth are chattering so loudly 'tis a wonder the racket did not tell the Douglas exactly where to look for us."

"Oh," she mouthed against his hand. Her heart stalled for a beat, then kicked nervously to life. She could taste his skin. The warm, salty flavor was a heady distraction, one she could happily have lived without. Did he sense how deeply the sensation disturbed her?

Squinting, Moyra tried to catch a glimpse of his face, to gauge his reaction. 'Twas no use. The darkness was complete and unrelenting.

A faint noise penetrated the door hiding the tunnel's entrance from the storeroom into which it emptied out.

A voice?

A footstep?

The rasp of steel against steel as a sword was drawn?

The sound was too faint and muted for Moyra to be sure, but she thought 'twas the latter.

Her breath caught and held. Without realizing she was doing it, she pressed herself more fully against William Armstrong's chest. This time it was not warmth she instinctively sought out, but strength, re-assurance. Security. To her surprise, she quickly found all three in the hard male body she leaned against, and in the powerful arm that tightened protectively around her shoulders.

Lifting her head, Moyra parted her lips, words of gratitude lingering on the tip of her tongue.

Angling his head, William opened his mouth, words of encouragement in his throat.

In the darkness it was impossible to tell the other's position exactly. Oh, aye, they knew where their bodies touched—all too well, they knew it!—yet that only suggested so much. Even the give and take of shallow breaths seemed oddly tenuous.

Neither planned for their lips to brush, it simply happened.

And when it did, neither turned away.

Instead, as one, they both froze in place.

Had they been out in the open, even in the dim shimmer of moonlight, the situation might have been comical. Imagine them standing there, paralyzed, their lips locked together in what, to an innocent observer, might have looked like a kiss . . . yet neither of them moving so much as a muscle!

The fact remained, however, that they were not in the open, and not a single ray of silvery light infiltrated the unyielding blackness. Nor did Moyra find anything funny about the feel of William's mouth on hers. Just the opposite, the warm flood of sensation pulsing like liquid fire through her veins was quite serious indeed, not to mention extremely wonderful.

They stood like statues, quiet and unmoving, neither daring to so much as breathe for fear of shattering the moment.

Would he pull away?

Would she?

He didn't.

Her eyes drifting close, as though she were ensnared by one of her visions, Moyra moved closer.

Hesitantly, she turned more fully toward him. Her hands lifted, opened, splayed atop the hard cushion of his chest. Beneath the warm, thin cloth of his tunic she felt his heart drumming against her overly sensitive fingertips. The beat was as harsh and erratic as her own.

Their breaths were choppy and ragged, entwining and mating on the cold, musty air.

Tentatively at first, then more boldly, she brushed her lips over his. Testing and savoring. Back and forth. Again and again.

She moved so very gently that their mouths barely touched . . . yet they did, and the effects of that touch flared like a handful of lightning through Moyra's bloodstream, heating her from the inside out in warm, radiating torrents of raw sensation.

Always before, her visions had come to her like strangers in the night, either while she was drifting off to sleep or, more often, during the dark, deep hours between dusk and dawn. This time, however, the vision came out of nowhere, blinding her with its strength and intensity.

There were no images, there was no sensation of impending doom . . . only pure, undiluted light bursting behind her closed eyelids like an exploding rainbow. Suddenly the blackness of reality was filled with vivid color and even more vivid sensations. With the feel of William Armstrong's warm, soft mouth pressed to hers . . . with his breath kissing her skin in small, warm puffs. Nothing else existed.

At first, William's response was no response at all. He didn't move, was barely able to breathe. He also didn't take a much-needed step backward, nor did he push Moyra away . . . and for good reason. He couldn't.

From the knees down it seemed he'd been encased in lead, or that he'd become a very real part of the hard, wet stone floor stretching beneath his feet, solid and heavy and unmovable. Even his arms felt unnaturally weighted. He couldn't have pushed Moyra away if he'd tried . . . and, heaven help him, trying wasn't an option.

The first touch of their lips had been accidental. In the unwavering darkness, was it surprising for either of them to misjudge distance, for perception to become tangled in the web of blackness? Nay, of course not.

That their lips continued to touch, however . . . that, even now, he could feel Moyra teasing him by brushing her soft, sweet mouth against his in a way that made his breath catch and his blood run hotter than a blazing bonfire . . . ah, now that was no accident. It was slow and deliberate and nerve-shatteringly intentional.

In a small corner of his mind, the only corner that remained unfoggy, William registered noises filtering in from the storage room beyond the tunnel door. The Douglas was out there, searching for this woman, and he would not give up until he found her and exacted his revenge. So why, William wondered, were the sounds of the search so easily overridden by the harsh, erratic pounding of his heart? Why did the fear of discovery fade before the feel of this woman's mouth brushing against his?

There was danger on the other side of that door, he knew it, could *sense it*. Yet he'd be lying if he didn't admit there was another, deeper and infinitely more complicated danger much, much closer . . . on this side of the door. A danger that sent his world upside down and jeopardized his very existence. The danger of surrendering himself to the kiss, and to the woman whose mouth tasted warm and sweet and inviting beyond reason.

Of the two, William could not have said with any certainly which danger posed the greatest risk. At that moment both felt life-threatening.

Without conscious thought, his hands lifted, settling on the slender curve of her hip. Beneath the body-warmed coarseness of the kilt, he could feel the heat of her soaking into his open palms. His fingers flexed, sinking into the fabric and into the hot, supple skin beneath.

Swallowing back a low, throaty groan, he parted his lips and his mouth opened hungrily over hers.

'Twas a mistake. William knew it the second he tasted the sweet, heady flavor of her on his tongue. But the realization came too late. Even though he acknowledged its existence, he didn't stop kissing her. Couldn't even if he'd wanted to . . . and suddenly, God help him, the last thing he wanted was to stop kissing her. Just the opposite, he found himself wanting to kiss more of her . . . *all of her* . . .

Moyra released a slow, breathy sigh. She'd been kissed before, many times. A pair of years ago she'd even been engaged for a fortnight to Neil MacFey; of course, kissing had been involved. Yet never, *never* had Neil or any other man kissed her like *this*.

William's mouth seemed to worship her. The tip of his tongue ran impatiently over the crease separating her upper lip from her lower, nudging them apart, then sliding over the pearly layer of her teeth.

His taste was warm and sweet, intoxicating; she felt drunk on the sensations that spiraled through her like an unstoppable whirlwind.

Her arms came up, her fingers spreading over the jack covering his shoulders and back. Flexing, she dug her fingers into the worn leather until she detected the hot, hard play of muscle beneath.

Her breath caught.

She felt him tense for a beat, then relax.

William shifted, and Moyra's body automatically shifted with him. They moved as one, as though joined together by some imperceptible yet powerful bond, as though both were merely one half to a whole.

The stone wall came up hard against Moyra's back. Och! how soft it felt compared to the firm male chest pressing against her front.

A noise tickled the back of her mind, soft yet intrusive, quiet yet out of place.

Hoofbeats?

Footsteps?

Aye, both.

Moyra knew the sounds boded ill, knew she should be concerned about them. Should be . . . but wasn't. 'Twas hard to be concerned about anything when William Armstrong's arms were wrapped so tightly about her, when he was holding her ever so close and his mouth was moving over hers in a way that left her shaken and breathless.

Moyra opened her mouth. Mayhap she would have said something—she knew not what—but William seized the advantage to deepen the kiss to a dizzying pitch.

His tongue probed and prodded, plundering the damp recess of her mouth, dancing and mating with her tongue until anything she might have said evaporated from her mind like steam off a boiling kettle.

A groan bubbled up in the back of William's throat. He swallowed it before it could break the surface. Moyra was so small and fragile in his arms. Hot and supple. Wonderful.

Her breasts pushed against his chest, small and touchably firm. Even through the obstruction of their clothing, the heat of her seared into his skin like a red-hot brand.

Keeping her quiet had not been his intent when he'd returned her kiss. In fact, the thought hadn't crossed his mind . . . until that very second. When it did, William seized upon the excuse like a drowning man clinging to a precious sliver of driftwood. Wasn't keeping her quiet, at any cost—to avoid discovery—by far a better reason for the passion with which he returned this kiss than the damnation of the truth? Oh, aye, it was!

Outside the door, he heard footsteps approach, pause, retreat. More plodded up and down the wheel staircase. In the chamber above, the embers in the hearth would be cold by now; only their faint, smoky scent would suggest that someone had recently occupied that chamber, and with the cold winter wind gusting in through the unpaned window, the smell of smoke would be so faint as to be virtually undetectable.

William's heartbeat stuttered with exhilaration. He told himself his reaction was due only to the knowledge that freedom was well within their grasp. He recognized the thought for the lie it was. Aye, he was overjoyed to have thwarted the Douglas, and to have safeguarded the life of the woman who had risked so much to save his, yet that joy was minimal compared to the feel of the warm, willing platinum-haired temptress in his arms.

The other maidens of William's acquaintance had always reacted to kisses with chaste coyness. Not this woman! There was nothing coy in the way her hands ascended his back, or the way her fingers opened, combing through his hair as she angled his head to the side, pulling him closer until she'd anchored his mouth down more firmly down atop hers. With wild abandon, her tongue met his every thrust and parry, then initiated its own.

In no time William's thoughts and senses were spinning out of control, and he was left to wonder if mayhap 'twas *she* who sought to silence *him*. If so, considering the blissfully seductive way in which she chose to go about it, he decided not to complain.

The noises outside again receded. Was it a natural occurrence, indicating the Douglas and his men had given up the search, or had the sounds been chased away by the thundering of his heart in his ears, the ragged soughing of both their breaths? William couldn't tell for certain.

His hands had been content to ride the slender curve of Moyra's hips, but only temporarily. Soon, his palms grew itchy, the muscles in his arms tight and restless.

Inching higher, he spanned the tight curve of her waist, turned inward, swept upward. The excess bulk of her thick woolen kilt had been tossed over her left shoulder and secured with a plain silver brooch— 'twas the way any of her clansmen would have worn the garment. The cloth felt scratchy beneath his fingertips as his palm crested the small swell of her breast.

Her nipple pebbled at his touch.

Instinctively she arched her back . . . arched into his hand.

William yanked back from the kiss as though he'd just been slapped. Gritting his teeth, he chewed back a tortured moan. How long had it been since he'd touched a woman thus? And felt such a needy response?

Never.

The single word cut through his mind as a sharply honed dagger cut through a fragile blade of grass. The instant he thought it, he knew it was true. Oh, aye, he'd had his share of stolen kisses and caresses, and in the past his bed had often been warmed by a willing maiden, yet . . .

Dear God, never had he experienced anything like *this*. Never had a woman's mouth tasted so inviting, never had her body been so passionately responsive. And never, *never* had he felt a need like the one raging through him now. The need to conquer and possess. A need so strong and desperate it jarred the breath from his lungs and the strength from his knees.

Never.

She was speaking.

William realized that in the same instant he realized he was much more fascinated by the feel of her lips moving against his as she formed words—by the way her breath puffed like a hot, silky mist against his skin—than he was with the actual words she spoke. Her voice was soft and smoky, breathless, her Scots burr thick and almost indecipherable. Almost.

". . . is gone. Ye can let go of me now."

"Gone?"

"Aye."

Suddenly, William was thankful for the unrelenting darkness. At least this way, she could not read his expression, could not see the surprise that must surely be registering there. "You're sure?"

"Aye."

Closing his eyes, William sucked in a long, slow

inhalation and released it with the same measured pace. "For how long?"

"Only a wee few moments."

Her voice came to him in the dark, soft and confused, reminding him again of that night many months ago.

He frowned ominously. She couldn't possibly be more confused than he was. When had the Douglas left? More importantly, why hadn't *he* noticed the man's departure? Had he been so swept up in kissing this woman that he'd lost all sense of time and reason?

'Twas a question William wasn't entirely sure he wanted answered.

"I said they be gone." She squirmed in his arms, and William clenched his teeth around a groan. Her pelvis ground against his. His body's response was powerful and sure; a hard, steady throbbing that was as strong as it was irrefutable. "Ye can let go of me now."

Never.

The unspoken response shot through William, as natural as breathing.

The small portion of his mind still able to retain a shred of rational thought assessed the darkness, the quiet. If there'd been a doubt in his mind, it was abruptly banished. Moyra was right, the Douglas and his men had gone. For now.

A larger part of his mind, however, was consumed with the mystery that was the woman in his arms. With the way her body molded so perfectly to his, the way she responded to him, the way his lips chilled without her mouth to warm them. And, aye, there was also the question of the degree to which *his* body responded to *hers*.

It was that larger, far-from-rational part of William that took precedence, goading him into bending at the waist and scooping Moyra into his arms. She was too shocked to protest, and in another instant, his mouth once again found hers. His kiss hot and hard and hungry, he swallowed any objection she may have voiced.

Moyra thought that was just as well, for suddenly she'd no voice with which to object to anything. And with every mind-numbing second that slipped past, she'd less and less inclination.

Mo chreach, why would she ever want to stop the blissful heaven that was William Armstrong's kiss, or reject the promise, of something mysteriously more blissful that lay ahead . . . ?

Thirteen

Moonlight skimmed over the ruined village that was cradled in the valley on the outskirts of Wynde-haghen Castle, washing over the lone cottage still standing, making the building shimmer and glow like a beacon.

The second he'd emerged from the tunnel, William had forced himself to stop kissing the woman he even now held cradled in his arms as he walked resolutely toward the cottage.

His confusion at the time had been ripe, magnified no doubt by the hard, anxious demands of his body, and the honey-sweet taste of her mouth lingering on his lips and tongue.

He'd wanted her.

Oh, so very badly.

He still did.

The way she'd kissed him back, wriggling her temptingly small body against him until he thought he would go mad, suggested the intensity of his desire was equaled only by her own.

Had the idea of Iain Douglas unexpectedly returning not been plaguing his thoughts, William knew he would have carried her up to her third-floor bedchamber and taken her right there, on the hard stone floor, in front of the cold hearth. But his instincts were sharp, and he'd learned long ago to heed them.

The hairs prickling at his nape suggested that lingering in the keep would be foolhardy in the extreme. Aye, it may look for all intents and purposes that the Douglas had given up his search, but that had happened before, and sometimes looks could be deceiving. It was not a chance William was willing to take.

Back in the tunnel, the memory of the lone cottage he'd spied on that long, pain-filled night when he'd been riding for his life toward Wyndehaghen had come to him unbidden. His mind had latched on to the memory greedily, the strong, hot urges of his body propelling him onward. Out of the ruined keep. Down the hill toward the deserted village.

It took scarcely a quarter hour to reach the cottage by foot. At that point, the freshly healed wound in William's shoulder was aching a protest, and he was more winded than he would have thought possible.

At any time he could have set Moyra down and let her walk the rest of the way herself. Could have, but didn't.

The idea of releasing her was something William found himself more than a wee bit reluctant to contemplate. He liked the way the silky heat of her penetrated through his clothes, into his skin, into his bloodstream. Liked also the way her scent wafted around him, clouding his senses until he felt himself enveloped in a warm, lilac-scented fog.

Her arms were looped about his neck, her platinum head was cradled against the hollow of his shoulder, and aye, the way her small, soft body curled trustingly into his much larger, much firmer one was an indescribable pleasure. Lack of breath and a sore muscle or two were a small price to pay. Definitely well worth the reward of holding this woman close.

The old, thatched roof of the cottage blotted out the moon as he approached the ruin.

Moyra stirred in his arms, shifted. William's breath wedged in his throat when he felt the moist heat of her lips graze the sensitive underside of his jaw. Her breath was hot and misty, puffing against his skin in shallow blasts.

A shiver skated down his spine. As he'd walked, William had kept a sharp eye on his surroundings, making sure there was no sign of the Douglas returning. Now, caution slipped away, to be swiftly replaced by the hard fist of desire.

The urge to angle his head and meet her lips with his own was so strong it was almost overwhelming. Almost. William resisted it, but only barely.

Applying the sole of his booted foot to the door, he sent it careening open. 'Twas a wonder the old hinges didn't give away under the force.

Inside, the shack was dark and dusty. By the time William carried Moyra across the threshold, he was beyond noticing the shadowy, cramped interior. And far beyond caring. He closed the door in the same way he'd opened it; hooking his ankle around the edge, he sent it slamming shut.

The action cast them into a velvet darkness broken only by a gleaming hint of moonlight slanting in through the small hole carved in the roof—a hole that, at one time, had served as an inadequate way to ventilate the shack of smoke from a cooking fire.

Unlike the keep they'd so recently left, this shack was not empty. An old, tarnished kettle was propped above a circle of stones in the center of the floor, while a crudely built, planked table had been shoved against the far wall. The latter was flanked on the closest side by a thin, rickety-looking bench. In a dark, cobwebbed corner stood a rocking chair that appeared so old and fragile William thought it might crumble to pieces at assuming the least bit of weight.

Moyra stirred in his arms, and any of his concentration that may have strayed elsewhere snapped back like a spring to the warm, soft feel of her.

Again, her lips brushed the side of his neck. This time, William didn't try to swallow the groan, but let it seep hoarsely from his throat. The sound seemed loud in the otherwise quiet interior of the shack.

Moyra shivered when William's groan trickled down her spine like drops of sun-warmed rain. Low and deep and throaty, the sound reverberated around her, *through* her. It reminded her of a wild, half-starved animal, growling as it caught sight of its next meal.

Her response, she was surprised to discover, was equally as basic and fierce. The pit of her stomach felt like she'd swallowed a ball of heat; hot fingers of desire radiated from that point outward, licking through her bloodstream, settling somewhere at the junction of her thighs. The feel of William's hot, salty-tasting flesh against her parted lips was a pleasure matched by nothing she'd ever experienced before.

When she'd been engaged to Neil MacFey, Moyra's father had warned her of the seduction of the flesh.

At the time, she'd thought his words so much nonsense. After all, hadn't she told him that kissing Neil had stirred as much passion in her as kissing Jared or Kenny? Aye, she had, and she hadn't lied. The urge to do anything more than kiss the scrawny, bucktoothed Neil had been nonexistent. Indeed, she'd lost more than one night's sleep since then wondering if the term "frigid" would apply to her. Now, however . . .

William shifted, and the supportive arm under her knees melted away. With the guidance of strong male hands under her arms, Moyra straightened her legs as her feet made their way toward the floor.

The front of her thighs and hips dragged with torturous slowness down the front of his.

It was Moyra's turn to moan. Low and deep, the sound tumbled past her lips, its tone as animalistic and hungry as the sound that had preceded it.

And then William's lips were on hers once more, his mouth consuming hers with an urgency that could not be denied. All sounds faded to the hammering of her heart in her ears, and the ragged soughing of both their breaths.

"You feel good, woman," he rasped raggedly against her lips. "Too good."

As though the words were a slap of icy water to his passion, William's fingers encircled her slender upper arms. Roughly, he yanked her away from him. The front of his chest, belly, hips and thighs suddenly chilly. He shoved the uncomfortable sensation aside and glared down at her.

The room was dark, but not so dark he couldn't see the flush of desire in Moyra's cheeks. The confusion shimmering in her eyes. Her lower lip—ah, God, so kiss-swollen and moist!—trembled beneath his stare.

Gritting his teeth, William attempted to guide his thoughts somewhere—*anywhere*—else. 'Twas like trying to move a mountain; they refused to budge. Desire, hot and raw, clawed at his gut. Not dragging this woman back into his arms, where he wanted most for her to be, took more self-control than he would have thought possible. Certainly more than he'd ever given himself credit for possessing.

Until tonight.

"Let me take you home to your family, Moyra." His voice was throaty and raw. " 'Tis where you belong."

"Nay." The side of her braid tapped his wrist when she shook her head. It was like being nudged by a warm rope woven of raw strands of silk. "I'll be going nowhere, mon. Nae this night, the next, and nae the ones after that."

"Blast it, Moyra, don't you understand? I—"

"I *do* understand. I'm nae fool," she interrupted him, clogging whatever else he may have said in his throat. "I understand maun more than ye give me credit for." Her gaze narrowed, astutely scanning his rugged, moonlight-swept features. William's lips burned when her attention settled on them. "I understand ye want me, William Armstrong. Almost as badly as I want you."

He swallowed hard. Twice. The erratic pounding of his heart did not so much as pause. His words, when they came were deep and rough, more like a tortured moan than a statement. "You're a brazen wench, Moyra Elliot."

Tipping her chin, she surprised him by grinning saucily up at him. "Nay, nae brazen. Honest. Ye *do* want me. I can feel it."

As though to prove her words, her hips thrust forward. Her pelvis brushed against his with a gentle, untamed seduction that made William inhale sharply.

Good Lord, did she have any idea what she was doing to him? *Did she care?*

The way her grin broadened alluringly said that, aye, she knew all too well the effect she was having. The passion-darkened glint in her beautiful, heather-colored eyes said it was exactly the effect she strove for.

Again, she moved, her pelvis brushing his, and . . . Ah, the gesture spoke for itself, and spoke volumes. Her body talked to his in a natural, timeless way that had the lower regions of William's body hard and hungry and responding in kind.

He could no more have stopped his hips from thrusting forward to grind against hers than he could have stopped breathing. Stopping either was not a consideration.

"Ye'll regret this come dawn," he growled, even as his fingers flexed around her upper arms and he hauled her close. Incredibly close.

His head angled, dipped; he captured anything she may have said with his mouth and a kiss that was hard and voracious and possessive.

She didn't push him away. Instead, her hands crept around the sides of his waist. Her fingers opened over the small of his back and her fingertips pressed, digging into him. Even through his jack and tunic William felt the warmth of her palms and the slender length of her fingers. Small and incredibly hot. It seemed she was burning her palm-print directly into his flesh, branding the blood that pumped hot and fast beneath the ultrasensitive surface.

His hands crept around her, he pressed her closely to his front. Ah, but the way her small, firm breasts pushed against his chest felt like a little piece of heaven!

His mouth never leaving hers, William lowered them both to the floor.

Moyra's back came up hard against the dirt floor.

William's front came up hard against the bed of her soft curves.

One of them sighed, the other shivered. Neither could be sure which did which. Neither cared.

Without thinking, William shifted, letting the hard-packed dirt floor absorb the majority of his body weight. But not all of it. He was not so charitable as to deny himself the ultimate pleasure of feeling Moyra Elliot's warm, willing body stretched out beneath him.

At some point, his hand had settled upon her stomach. The body-heated kilt was thick and scratchy against his fingertips. The muscles beneath were flat and firm, rising and falling with her every ragged breath.

Her hands lifted, skimming his back, his shoulders, his neck. Opening her fingers, she combed them through his hair, then cupped the back of his head.

There was no resistance as she pulled his mouth down harder upon hers. When her tongue darted out— warm and moist and teasing as it skimmed his lips— William groaned low and deep in his throat before opening to her. Meeting her hot, wet tongue's every thrust and parry, he deepened the kiss until they were both panting and dizzy.

For a little while, his hand was content to ride the firm, flat plane of her stomach. But not for long. Soon, a restless itching in his palm nudged his fingers into motion. He fisted the thick, generous folds of her plaid, released it, fisted it again. The cloth felt coarse and oddly unsubstantial. Not so oddly unsatisfying.

Tension was building inside of him, coiling tighter, demanding release. Opening his hand, his touch skimmed higher.

Moyra's breath lodged in her throat. Her heart skipped a beat, then clattered sharply to life when she felt his fingertips trace the gentle undercurve of her breast.

She didn't think 'twas possible, yet it felt to her like every muscle in her body was suddenly straining, tightening and tensing with an invisible, unbearable pressure.

'Twasn't enough. As good as this felt, she wanted more. Much more. How would it feel to have his hand there, under her tunic? She sighed softly, imagining his big, callused fingers grazing her sensitive, naked flesh . . .

Her sigh turned into a husky moan of pleasure when the elusiveness of the fantasy became a sensuous, breathtaking reality.

William's movements were jerky with strained impatience as he tugged at the hem of her tunic until it was bunched up around the slim curve of her waist. In the next breath, his fingers had slipped beneath the cloth; his fingertips lightly tickled the flesh of her belly before his hand skimmed upward with nerve-shattering swiftness.

She felt his fingers open, felt his palm settle over her left breast. The area felt oddly heavy, and the way her nipple hardened against the center of his hand surprised and . . . Och, aye, she'd be lying if she said it didn't please her.

The intimacy of his touch was better than anything she could possibly have imagined. William's hand was big, the skin slightly rough; it covered her breast fully even as his fingers flexed, testing the size and firmness.

Closing her eyes, Moyra arched her back and groaned, pressing more firmly into his hand. A feeling akin to being engulfed from the inside out by a burst of liquid fire swept through her. The sensation started where William touched her, then washed throughout the rest of her body in increasingly hot waves of raw sensation.

"By my word, mon, if ye ne'er stop doing that, I'll ne'er complain."

"By *my* word, Moyra, stopping is not something I'm of a mind to do. You feel . . . Ah, God, you feel too good."

So did his hot, damp breath misting over her passion-sensitized skin. Her nipple tightened in a way that was almost painful. The response was tame compared to the sensation that jolted through her when he lifted her tunic higher, dipped his head, and suctioned the aching peak into his mouth.

His teeth nibbled and teased, his tongue stroked and savored until she thought she would go insane. Moyra clutched at his shoulders, wonderfully warm and firm beneath her fingers, even as she ground her head back against the floor and lifted herself, craving still more intimacy.

"All in good time, lass," he rasped against her. "I've a feeling the Douglas will not be returning this night. And even if he does, he'll search the castle, but not this abandoned shack. We've all night."

Moyra shivered in anticipation at the sweet, velvety promise in his voice. A frown pinched her brow, but it quickly faded. When had his harsh Sassenach accent ceased to annoy her, she wondered with the vague corner of her mind still able to think on anything at all? She didn't know precisely, but at some point it obviously had, for now she found the abrasive sound of it oddly endearing.

In the space of one erratic heartbeat, the question scattered from Moyra's mind like so much dust. William's right hand had strayed back to her abdomen and was inching with breathtaking slowness lower, lower. His mouth was doing something to her which no other man had dared to do before, and eliciting a physical reaction that made logical thinking impossible. Och! aye, she cared not about anything save the acute, tingling sensations spreading throughout her body in rapidly building swells.

The need to feel him came upon her without warning. Skin to skin. That was what she wanted. Needed. *Craved.* Strong and determined, the yearning twisted inside her, impossible to overlook, more impossible to deny or resist. And she did not want to resist it.

Her hands strayed impatiently over his shoulders, down the hard-muscled length of his back. Grabbing fistfuls of the tunic, she tugged, awkwardly yanking it upward.

Did his breathing alter—become more harsh and choppy?—as he shifted to allow her to haul the garment over his arms and head? Moyra wasn't sure.

There was, however, one thing she was positive of— her flesh went deathly cold when the moist warmth of his mouth was taken away, then flooded with a tidal wave of heat when it almost immediately returned.

The rewards, she decided, were well worth the brief, physical discomfort. Instead of body-warmed fabric, her palms now settled upon hot, bare flesh. Moyra stroked his back.

Up and down.

Back and forth.

Again and again.

She reveled in the way his muscles bunched and rippled beneath her inquisitive fingertips. His naked chest brushed against the side of her rib cage, and she experienced a pleasant, tickling sensation when the thick pelt of golden hair coating his chest grazed her passion-sensitized skin.

His hand slipped over the curve of her hip, down the length of her outer thigh. He fingered the coarse hem of her kilt before slipping his hand beneath.

His fingertips felt hot and harsh against her skin as he slowly, slowly skimmed up over the valley of creamy flesh, separating her thighs.

Higher and higher and . . .

Mo chreach! Higher still.

He hesitated for a heartbeat when he encountered the tight nest of platinum curls. With a flick of his wrist, he angled his touch closer to the core of her.

Through the tips of his fingers William absorbed into his body the moist heat of her desire.

He swallowed hard. Twice. The muscles in his throat felt dry and unresponsive. If he was going to stop this madness, it would have to be now. Once he'd savored her dewy warmth, there'd be no turning back.

Closing his eyes and holding his passion in barely controlled arrest, William searched himself for a reason—any reason at all—to push away from this woman, to deny them both the satisfaction of the sensuous journey they'd so recently set out upon.

Oh, aye, 'twas true, Moyra Elliot's resilience and determination were bitter reminders of his own mother. Never had he been able to come to terms with Lizbet Armstrong's lack of respect for the memory, not only of his own father, but of her many husbands.

The similarities in the two were glaring. His mother was equally as tenacious as the woman who now lay soft and willing in his arms. Whatever heartache life threw her way, Lizbet Armstrong maneuvered her way through it with an ease that appalled her eldest son. While the Armstrongs were well known for their resourcefulness and adaptability, William thought his mother took both qualities to unadmirable extremes.

One question remained, however; it gnawed at his insides, demanding an immediate answer. Was Moyra Elliot like his mother in her disregard for men?

Gritting his teeth and forcing his eyes open, William gazed down at her. At some point the loose plait at her nape had come undone. Thick folds of glossy platinum hair were spread out on the ground and draped around her face and shoulders like a moonlit waterfall.

The muscles in William's stomach twisted and turned

over on themselves, forming an impossibly complicated knot. He fought an overpowering urge to scoop
up great handfuls of those silky, pure white strands.

How would her hair feel gliding through his fingers? Skimming his cheeks and throat and chest? The
hard plane of his bare belly?

To find out would mean moving the hand not sup-
porting his weight. The hand that was resting inti-
mately against her. The hand William was trying hard
not to move, but that wanted badly to move despite
his swiftly dwindling resolve—wanted to touch and
stroke her oh, so very deeply.

As he gazed down into her fathomless, heather-
colored eyes, the craving to do exactly that gripped
him.

His fingers flexed in instinctive response.

Not a lot . . . but enough.

Moyra's eyelids thickened, and the eyes beneath
them darkened with desire. Was it his imagination, or
did he actually hear her breath catch?

William frowned; he couldn't be certain. He did
know, however, that the erotic flush he glimpsed
spreading across her cheeks and down her neck was
not a figment of his imagination. Nor was the way
she slowly, with an awkward innocence that left him
feeling oddly weak and shaky, lifted her hips, pushing
into his touch.

The groan—low and raspy—spilled from William's
throat before he even realized it was there, let alone
had the presence of mind to stop or stifle it. This time
he didn't waste time attempting to separate right from
wrong, good from bad, rational thought from insane

desire. Instead, like a lamb led to slaughter, he surrendered himself up to complete and total sensation.

Nudging open her thighs, he wedged his hand between, his fingers stroking and arousing.

If the feel of William's mouth on her breast had been heaven, Moyra didn't know what to call the sensation that shot through her at the penetration of his finger. Her insides tightened as the place where he probed and caressed throbbed to vibrant life.

Moyra couldn't have kept her hips still if she'd tried.

The urge to move in time with each deep, sensuous stroke arrowed through her. It was too strong, too integral, to deny or resist.

Her hips came off the floor. Pushing her pelvis hard against his palm and wrist, she urged him to be faster, go deeper still.

As impossible as it seemed, she was breathing too fast, too deeply, yet at the same didn't seem able to pull nearly enough air into her burning, oxygen-starved lungs. Her head spun, and like leaves caught in a ferocious whirlpool, her senses began to spiral.

"William . . . ?" The voice that reached her ears sounded too shallow and tenuous to be recognizable as her own, yet she knew that it was. It had to be.

"Aye, lass, I know."

"Ye canna. I feel so . . ." Her words trailed away. She was at a loss as to how to describe these swells of exquisite sensation.

"Good?" William finished the sentence for her. His voice was husky, edged with pent-up desire. "It feels good, does it not?"

"Aye, but . . . Och! Methinks I need tae rethink the definition of 'good' sometime soon."

"Soon, mayhap. But not now."

"Aye." She sighed her agreement. "Nae now."

He murmured something, but the drumming of her heartbeat in her ears had reached a crescendo, the crashes of sound overriding everything but the sensuous tone of his voice.

A sensation had begun to stir low in her abdomen, tightening and building with each expert stroke of his hand. It flowed through her bloodstream in hot, tingly waves, settling finally in the secret place between her legs.

Where she'd been breathing heavily before, she now stopped breathing entirely as the whole of her concentration settled there in wonder.

"It's all right, lass," he crooned. "Go ahead. Let yourself go. Let yourself *feel*."

His husky breath washed over her naked breast as he spoke; as it settled on her skin, it felt as soft and as damp as a kiss, encouraging her to do as he bid. Free of any lingering inhibitions, Moyra clutched at his bare shoulders and surrendered herself fully to the sensations building and churning inside her.

The first wave of ecstasy slammed into Moyra, knocking the breath from her lungs and setting her heart to pounding at an unprecedented speed. She reeled under the sheer intensity of the sensation.

Lifting her chin, she closed her eyes and gritted her teeth hard. In the blackness behind her closed eyelids, she experienced yet another vision. Unlike the last, this one started as a minuscule, shimmering diamond pinprick against a backdrop of inky-black darkness. The image magnified, quickly gaining force before it exploded into a flash of blinding white light. The impression was so very real that Moyra thought she could taste and feel it as it crashed over her in hot, spasmodic waves of raw sensation.

Her fingers clenched inward, her nails digging into William's skin, slashing, drawing crimson beads of blood to the surface.

He didn't notice the pain. Indeed, he noticed nothing other than the sexual pleasure that had carved her beautiful features into an exquisitely tense mask. Her complexion was passion flushed. Her eyes, when she opened them, were dark and glazed with wonder.

Like a frayed rope, the tenuous leash to William's self-control snapped. Never in his life had he so strongly needed to bury himself deep inside a woman. Desire lacerated him from the inside out, sharp and demanding, impossible to disregard, more impossible to refuse.

Against his hand he could still feel her orgasmic tremors. The notion that he had satisfied her so completely was a staggering aphrodisiac.

In less than three throbbing heartbeats he'd divested himself of his boots, trews, sword and tunic. 'Twas while yanking off the latter he heard a loud rip of fabric, but he didn't care. With trembling fingers, William tossed his clothing aside.

Sighing long and deep, he lowered his body onto the sweet, soft bed that was her.

Dear Lord, she felt wonderful. Nay, better than wonderful! Small and soft and warm. Erotic and inviting.

He liked the way her shallow, choppy breaths washed over his shoulder, settling upon his skin like a hot, tangible mist . . . liked also the way she clutched at him, wrapping her arms around his waist and holding on tightly, as though she planned never to let him go.

Suddenly, resistance was a foreign concept, one William did not want to think about let alone familiarize himself with. He wanted this woman so badly he hurt . . .

"Ah, William," Moyra sighed.

He shifted, reached between their bodies, positioned himself.

"Ah, William!" Her voice was louder, sharp with surprise when, with one sure, powerful thrust, he buried himself deeply inside of her.

"Ah, Moyra," he murmured, his voice tight with the need to move, tighter still with the control it took for him to remain still. That she was a virgin, there was no doubt; he'd felt the resistance, as well as the minute tearing when her maidenhead gave away. However, he'd no wish to cause her more pain than was necessary.

Drawing on the last shreds of his restraint, William forced his hips to remain steady, unmoving—forced himself to temporarily squelch the desire to feel himself sliding against her slick, tight velvety heat.

Levering the upper portion of his weight on one arm, he glanced down at her, carefully gauging her reaction. Without thinking, he used his other hand to brush away a few stray wisps of hair from her temple and brow. Her skin seemed slightly fevered and damp to the touch, her hair every bit as soft and silky against his fingertips as he'd known it would be. "Are you all right, lass?"

She gazed up at him, her violet eyes shimmering with undisguised amazement. "Aye, fine. I dinna think

194   *Rebecca Sinclair*

I've e'er felt better. Er"—she blushed and glanced shyly away—"why did ye stop? Do ye nae want—"

"Aye, Moyra, I want," he said, his voice thick and husky, ringing with conviction. "I want very badly."

"Och! Weel then . . . ?"

William swallowed back his surprise. He'd little experience in bedding virgins; apparently, he'd not caused Moyra as much pain as he'd originally thought. The realization was twofold; not only did it set his mind to rest, at the same time it set fire to his barely suppressed desire.

His answer, when it came, was not verbal.

It was entirely physical.

His mouth crashed down atop hers for a long, deep, soul-draining kiss. At the same time, his hips began to move, their tempo strong and rhythmic.

Again, Moyra surprised him. Instead of being shocked, or timorously pulling away as he'd half expected her to do, she instead wrapped her legs tightly around his hips, arched her back, pressed against his buttocks with her slender calves and urged him deeper and faster still.

With unrivaled swiftness, William's own release gripped him. 'Twas almost embarrassing to feel his climax start so quickly—dear Lord, he'd only just entered her!—yet he had no more power to stop the liquid eruption of his completion from washing through him than he had to stop his heart from beating wildly in his chest.

Lowering his head, he applied his open mouth to the tapered length of her neck. Against his bare chest, he could feel the hard pearls of her nipples pressing into his skin. His lips moved against her, and he whispered something incomprehensible as the spasms of ecstasy crashed over him, drowning him in pure, wondrous sensation.

His climax seemed to last forever.

At the same time, it didn't last nearly long enough.

Making love to Moyra Elliot was the single, most powerful encounter William had ever experienced. It left him shaken to the core, weak and breathless. Vulnerable. Languid. It seemed as though his life force had been drained right out of him . . . and channeled directly into her.

His arms being suddenly unsubstantial, William lowered himself atop her. Again, he unconsciously shifted, careful to make sure the majority of his weight was atop the hard dirt floor. Her body felt oddly small beneath his. Delicate. Fragile.

A sensation twisted in his chest, the region frighteningly close to his heart. Although he didn't want to examine it too closely, he couldn't resist. The sensation coiling through him was a desire to shield and protect, and it was as unique as it was strong. He'd an unreasonably powerful urge to wrap this woman in his arms, to safeguard both her body and her mind in every way imaginable.

He wanted to protect her from Iain Douglas.

And—aye, William had to admit it—he also wanted to protect her from himself.

Inhaling deeply, he found himself blanketed in the lilac-sweet scent of her. Her fragrance filled him, wonderfully familiar, infinitely soothing. 'Twas lulling to his satiated senses.

Where he'd been wide awake only moments before, now sleep tugged at him with beckoning fingers. Wearily, his mind drifted back to that first night in Wyndehaghen's tunnel. Moyra's scent had been his first impression of her, for the unrelenting darkness had allowed no other intrusion but that of her voice. At the time, he'd thought—

Without warning, the door to the shack burst open.

William's heart stalled for one heavy beat, then slammed to erratic life. His tiredness evaporated like ground fog before bright, early morning sunlight.

In his arms, Moyra gasped and squirmed with equal surprise. The sound had no more left her than William had pushed himself to a sitting position. Shifting, he pushed her behind his back so the breadth of his naked body shielded her from view. He scrambled to find his sword.

Had the Douglas returned after all . . . ?

Sword in hand, William's gaze sharpened on the open doorway, and the burly figure that the moonlight pouring in from behind silhouetted there.

Fourteen

"Good God, William, *you bedded her?* Are you try-ing to start a feud where there's been none for gen-erations, or have you simply *gone insane?"*

William scowled. The voice teased his memory, but he'd be damned if he could place it. Behind him, Moyra shifted, pressing against his naked back and peeking cautiously at the intruder from over his shoul-der.

"Who the devil is he?" she hissed in William's ear, even as she snatched up her tunic and plaid and began to hastily tug each garment on in turn. "He be nae kinsman of *mine,* therefore he maun be a kinsman of *yers.* Och! Then there's that brittle Sassenach accent of his, which—"

"Shhh!" William silenced Moyra without sparing her so much as a backward glance. The movements behind him stiffened with silent indignation. He felt the rough scratch of wool against the small of his bare back, but he paid the sensation no mind. His concen-tration refused to budge from the elusive figure in the doorway.

Moyra was right, William realized, the intruder was

indeed his relative. Or so he strongly suspected. The question was . . . which one?

From his mother's many marriages, William had so many halfsiblings and stepsiblings and various other kin who were no real relations at all that . . . well, truth to tell, he'd ceased to keep track of them all at least a decade ago. Now, as he glared at the shadowy silhouette, his frown deepening, he wished he'd paid closer attention.

"Is the Douglas gone?" William asked the stranger finally.

The man grunted and shrugged. "For now. But, mark my words, he'll be back."

"Aye, I've no doubt of it. The question is *when?* And how many men will he have guarding his back this time?"

"Ah, Willie, your thinking, as always, is skewered." Taking a step forward, the man knocked the door closed with the toe of his boot. Steel rasped against steel as he withdrew his sword, bent slightly at the waist, and stabbed the crumpled heap of linen that was William's tunic with the razor-sharp tip. Holding the garment out to William thus, he continued nonchalantly, "What you *should* be asking yourself, and providing an answer to it posthaste, is whether or not you and the lass will still be here when he does return. Methinks *that* the question most in need of answering."

Like the harsh clanging of a church bell, a ring of familiarity pealed sharply through the back of William's mind. The man's tone, his casual-to-the-point-of-arrogance attitude . . . all of it combined to pinpoint the intruder's identity.

"Gray? Gray Collingwood!" A slow grin tugged at one corner of William's mouth as, careful not to prick himself upon the sword tip, he accepted his shirt, then tugged the cold, wrinkled garment over his head.

Behind him, he felt Moyra move. A tickle of silky hair against his back suggested she'd clothed herself and was again peering curiously over his shoulder.

Punching his arms through the sleeves of his tunic, William said, "What brings you to this wild side of the Border, Gray? When last I'd heard, you were squandering away your time at court . . . and creating quite a sensation as Elizabeth's newest favorite."

In the darkness surrounding them, William heard rather than saw his half brother shrug.

"Favorites come, favorites go," Gray replied. "Suffice it to say *this* favorite did not stay a favorite overlong."

"In other words," William clarified, "Elizabeth quickly discovered you for the scoundrel you are and tossed you out on your arse."

"Aye, something like that." Gray's chuckle was deep and thick. "Although she didn't throw me out, I left willingly. Such is the way of life at court." His tone grew darkly serious. "Dear brother, as much as I'd like nothing better than to share a pint or two while discussing at our leisure what's happened in the five years since last we saw each other, methinks this is neither the time nor the place for it." His gaze slipped meaningfully over William's shoulder, lingering on the vaguely discernible, blatantly feminine face peeking out from behind him. He hesitated, then focused his attention with renewed sharpness on his brother. "If we don't hurry and get the two of you safely away from Wyndehaghen, I've a thought Iain Douglas will do the deed. Somehow, I don't think 'safety' will be his primary concern."

William nodded and reached for his trews.

A grin curved Gray's lips as he politely turned toward the door. "I'll wait for you outside."

The door had barely shut before William had his trews yanked on, followed quickly by his hose and boots. When he stood to strap on his sword, Moyra stood with him.

Angling his head, he looked at her. In the dim light, her long platinum hair shimmered like a blanket of freshly fallen snow, the strands tousled appealingly about her face and shoulders. Her complexion was flushed, her lips kiss-swollen. Her fuller lower lip trembled before she caught it between her teeth.

"Moyra—" William began, only to have the vigorous shaking of her head stop him short.

"Nay, dinna. There's naught ye can say right now that I be wanting tae hear."

"You don't understand." He tried to reach out, to smooth away the determined tightness of her jawline with the callused tip of his thumb. "I'm of a mind I could start liking you, lass. Aye, given a chance, I could start liking you, too much."

Before he could complete the contact, she batted his hand away. "Och! is that the way of it? Humph! Mayhap 'tis better ye tell me this now, after ye've bedded me, eh? And whilst ye be of a mind, William, ye can also tell me something else. Do ye like every woman ye bed, or should I consider meself special?"

His eyes narrowed sharply. It was William's only reply, yet it was reply enough. His displeasure was clear in the way his lips thinned and the skin stretched tightly over his sculpted cheeks took on an angry, ruddy undertone.

Even in such dim lighting, Moyra could see the spark of warning shimmering in his eyes.

Saw it, and ignored it. Tilting her chin up, she met his penetrating brown glare with a proud, unintimidated violet glare of her own.

"I'd nae advise it," she continued finally. Crossing her arms over her waist, she casually let her gaze rake him from head to toe, then back again. Her heart skipped a beat when her mind flashed her an image of him naked, rising over her . . .

It was the only reaction Moyra allowed herself, and she took pains to make sure it did not show in either her expression or her gaze as the latter once again met his. "Och! Aye, mon, truth tae tell, I be liking ye just fine meself, but it makes nae a bit of difference. It canna. In the end it all means naught."

"Why?"

"Is it nae obvious?"

"Nay lass." Frowning, William scratched at the stubbled underside of his chin. The fringe of his shaggy blond hair scraped the shelf of his shoulders when he shook his head. "Explain yourself."

"All right." Moyra sucked in a deep, steadying breath, and on its release said, her voice ringing with conviction, *"Ye* can be of any mind ye like, it matters nae at all. Why, ye ask? I'll give ye a simple answer for a simple question. Because *I* be of a mind yer maun, *maun* tae much like me da for me tae e'er like ye o'er much."

"You let me—"

Her hand sliced through the air, silencing him. "I'm well aware of what I let ye do, mon. Please, I *dinna* need ye reminding me of it e'ery two seconds, thank ye ver' much. Our lovemak—" She fumbled over the word, cleared her throat, then awkwardly substituted a less intimate term as her disconcerted gaze abruptly broke from his. "What we did . . . Och! weel, it canna be changed nor can it be taken back. Have nae doubt, come the morn, I'll dwell on the right and wrong of *that* until I drive meself daft," under her breath she added, "although e'en a silly lass like meself kens that all the dwelling and self-recrimination in the world willna change a thing." Her gaze slid back to his, her eyes shimmering with a conviction that was also mirrored in her tone. "At the moment, howe'er, methinks we've more important matters at hand. Dinna ye agree? Matters such as leaving here before the Douglas returns, catches ye, and kills us both?"

William's frown deepened. Unfortunately, there was no arguing with reality. Only a fool would dismiss the urgency behind Moyra's warning. An Armstrong was many things, but a fool was not one of them.

"So be it." Gritting his teeth, William nodded tightly. Turning and striding purposefully toward the door, he said from over his shoulder, "I'll let the matter drop. For now, but not forever. Rest assured, this discussion is *not* closed. Most definitely not. 'Tis merely . . . postponed."

Moyra watched William's broad back as he disappeared through the open doorway, until he was swallowed up by the moonlit night beyond. Only when she was sure he was out of sight did she release the breath she'd been holding. It rushed past her lips like the last sigh of a summer breeze as the strength ebbed from her legs.

Her knees buckled, hitting the hardpacked dirt with enough force to snap her teeth painfully together and jar awake an ache that rippled all the way up her spine. Slowly, the rest of her weight sagged downward until she was sitting upon her shins, spine bowed defeatedly forward.

Her hands had landed open, palm down, on the floor on either side of her ankles. Moyra noticed this only when, inhaling sharply, her fingers clenched inward and she felt grains of dirt beneath her fingernails.

I'm of a mind I could start liking you, lass. Aye, given a chance, I could start liking you too much.

The words lingered in her mind, as taunting as a delectable piece of sweetmeat placed just out of a hungry bairn's reach.

A single tear clung to the curve of her lashes. She swiped it viciously away with the back of her fist. *Mo chreach!* She'd no time for being feminine! Nay, not when Iain Douglas was out there, somewhere, looking for her.

And looking for William Armstrong.

Her chin, which had sagged so it almost rested upon her collarbone, now lifted. Slowly at first, then more surely. Where her eyes had shimmered with unshed tears a second before, their violet depths now glistened with something else entirely. Something stronger and more integral.

Generations of stanch Elliot pride accounted for only a smattering of the emotions churning fiercely within her. The instinct for survival was there, and it was strong. Stronger still was the tickle of intuition that wrapped around her, entangling her curiosity in its elusive grip.

A vision?

Nay.

At least, 'twas not like any vision she'd ever had before.

Yet it was also not completely dissimilar, either. 'Twas more like an unspoken promise . . . for somewhere deep within Moyra was a burgeoning conviction that William Armstrong was right, the discussion—indeed, the entire situation between them—was not closed.

Just the opposite. It had barely begun.

Moyra was squirming again.

William gritted his teeth and shifted his gaze to his tree-strewn surroundings. He tried to ignore her. Tried to, but couldn't.

The three of them—Moyra, Gray, and himself—had camped for the night in a tiny valley tightly surrounded by thick, concealing woods. William felt reasonably secure, believing that any intruders would be announced by the sharp snap and crackle of winter-dry twigs and leaves underfoot. Still, he could not relax.

Sometime early tomorrow morning they would pass out of Liddesdale and into what was officially known as the Scots Middle March. 'Twas not a moment too soon, as far as William was concerned.

This hellishly craggy part of the Scots countryside was teeming with miscreants and outlaws. A man not recognized by his own kin was always welcome in Liddesdale, provided he lived long enough to enjoy the greeting. Most did not. Broken men roamed the hills in small bands, pillaging from enemies, neighbors and friends with equal gusto.

Liddesdale was not considered the most notorious stretch of land on the Scots side of the Border for naught; its unsavory reputation was the only thing Liddesdale and its unruly inhabitants came by honestly.

William sighed. Lifting one shoulder, then the other, he stretched a cramp from between his shoulder blades. While he'd succeeded in turning his thoughts away from Moyra Elliot for a wee bit, the reprieve proved all too short.

Before he knew it, his concentration, as well as his gaze, was magnetized back to her.

For two hours he'd been watching her covetously from the corners of his eyes. She sat in silence, her back propped wearily against a thick birch trunk, her eyes closed. The way she occasionally nibbled her lower lip and frowned suggested she'd not yet fallen asleep.

So did her almost constant squirming.

She seemed to be striving to find a cozy position, yet failing miserably. Or, if she did manage to find one, a scant few minutes later she would soon discover it not as soothing as she'd originally thought.

That she was in physical discomfort was obvious. A blind man could see it. The reason for her discomfort, while not as glaring, 'twas as clear to William as a sparkling sheet of glass.

At first he'd assumed she was cold. The night was frigid—he could see his exhalations mist the air in front of his face. However, on closer inspection, he noticed that she was not shivering as violently as one might expect. Nor did she huddle within herself or briskly chafe her arms and legs, as cold people instinctively do.

A thought occurred to William. Gritting his teeth together so hard now his temple throbbed and ached, he bit back a self-recriminating groan.

They'd ridden for hours, deep into the night, not slowing until they'd put a good deal of distance between themselves and Wyndehaghen and the Douglas. Until they could be reasonably sure the man was no longer a threat.

Lacking her own mount, Moyra had ridden on the saddle behind William. Even now, he could feel her fingers digging through his jack, gripping the sensitive skin beneath. Once or twice, they'd picked up the pace after hearing noises that could have been reivers on the way back from a successful raid. He'd felt her body stiffen against his back, noticed the way her breathing had gone rough and ragged.

At the time, he'd assumed her reaction was fear of being discovered. Now, as he watched her squirm, he was not so sure.

They'd made love. It seemed like years ago to him now, but in reality it had happened mere hours before. To a woman who'd never known a man's lovemaking, finding herself atop the hard back of a horse, riding for hours at a breakneck pace, would be uncomfortable in the extreme, he'd think. Why hadn't he realized that until now?

Moyra hadn't uttered a word of complaint. William felt a twinge of admiration. When he thought about it, he remembered glancing back at her and seeing a hopeful glint in her heather-colored eyes when he and

Gray had finally reined in their mounts. Against the nape of his neck, he'd felt the warm mist of a grateful sigh when it was agreed to stop and rest for the scant few hours remaining of the night.

Without hesitation, Moyra had unfisted his jack and slipped from the saddle without his help, her feet landing solidly on the frozen ground. She meandered stiffly over to the birch tree, then awkwardly sat down upon the hard, cold ground, her back propped tiredly against the thick trunk.

Head resting back against the tree, eyes scrunched tightly closed, she'd remained there while he and Gray took care of the horses. When they were finished, Gray had settled in for a quick rest. Judging from her unlined expression, William had assumed Moyra asleep and had sought out his own tree trunk to rest against.

Sleep would be a blessed reprieve, a much-needed time to reassess and regroup, to decide what he was going to do about the unexpected turn of events this night.

Or so he'd thought.

Pity it hadn't quite worked out that way.

Like a shadow looming just out of range of a bright light, sleep taunted and teased at the edges of his consciousness but never came into full view. His mind was foggy with exhaustion, yet his body felt alive and restless with the awareness of Moyra's close proximity.

At one point, William had closed his eyes, shoved all thoughts from his mind and at the same time invited the sweet blackness that was a deep, dreamless sleep.

It hadn't worked.

Even with his eyes closed, the core of his attention

refused to be uprooted from the spot where Moyra Elliot sat.

With her every uncomfortable squirm, he heard the soft rustle of her kilt; the noise seemed unnaturally loud, as though his senses were more in tune with it than they were to the soft, natural night noises echoing around him.

A few times William successfully managed to force his thoughts elsewhere . . . invariably, it took only seconds before they were right back to Moyra again.

Yer maun, maun tae much like me da for me tae e'er like ye o'er much.

The words tickled his memory in the same way her soft, honey-sweet voice had tickled his senses. What did she mean? He was nothing like her father. Ross Elliot was a hardened reiver, with hundreds of successful raids to his credit. William, on the other hand, had blundered at his very first attempt at a raid on the night he'd met Moyra. Not only had he managed to get himself wounded, he'd also stupidly fallen into one of Iain Douglas's notorious ambushes.

To his mind, the similarities between himself and Moyra's father were nonexistent.

Obviously, to her mind, the similarities were overwhelming.

William closed his eyes and frowned. He tried to understand the comparison she'd drawn. Could not. 'Twas a mystery to him. One that should not puzzle him over much. One that puzzled him in the extreme. The dilemma shoved the prospect of sleep from his weary mind and body until he felt consumed with the need to know the answer. The *real* answer.

There was, he realized, only one way to solve this more-irritating-by-the-second riddle.

Tired muscles ached a protest to sudden movement as William pushed himself to a stand. A dry twig snapped under his bootheel. Winter-dead leaves crunched. His gaze shot to Moyra; if she'd heard either, she gave no indication. Was that a good thing or bad? Truly, William didn't know.

Perhaps she really had fallen asleep? Nay, he thought not. She was squirming again; the movement was too restless and uneasy to be done whilst drowsing.

More twigs snapped, more leaves crunched as he walked toward her. On the other side of the clearing, Gray stirred, opening one eye sleepily, then closing it again after briefly focusing on the vague, moonlit shape of his brother.

Was it William's imagination, or did Moyra's body stiffen warily as he approached? With only a few glistening rays of moonlight working their way down through the lattice-work ceiling of branches above, he couldn't see well enough to be positive. Still, he was almost sure it did. Lord knows, the tired muscles in his own body were coiled tight with the tension of imminent confrontation.

He stopped beside her, hunkering down until his head was only slightly above hers. Without thinking, he reached out and dragged the calloused tip of his thumb over the hard line of her jaw, the curve of her chin, the soft-and-warm-as-velvet underside.

She didn't flinch, didn't pull back, didn't show any sign of surprise. If he'd harbored any doubts before, they were instantly abandoned. Moyra Elliot was wide awake.

" 'Tis time to finish our discussion, lass."

"And if I choose nae tae?" she countered tightly as, lifting her chin, she broke the distractive contact of his touch. She opened her eyes, glanced up at him, then just as quickly glanced away. "What then? Ye canna force me tae speak tae ye if I dinna wish it."

"Truth to tell, I don't know," he admitted softly. "Most women, it takes effort to get them *not* to speak."

"Och! mon, have ye nae figured out by now that I'm nae like 'most' women?"

"Aye, lass, I'm beginning to realize it."

William's hand dropped reluctantly to his lap. His gaze never wavered from the soft, delicate lines of her profile. In the scant gleam of moonlight that managed to reach her, her skin shimmered like fine porcelain bisque; white and creamy and tempting beyond reason.

The tip of his thumb still felt hot and tingly from touching her, and suddenly it was all he could do not to reach out and touch her again. The urge to feel her warm flesh gliding beneath his fingertips was almost uncontrollable. Almost.

"I'd be lying if I said I didn't find the contrast more than a little intriguing and," William added, softer, as though speaking only to himself, "challenging in the extreme."

"I dinna mean it tae be either."

"Aye, I'm well aware of that. Methinks you've no idea how much more fascinating that makes you."

"I dinna wish tae be fascinating," she snapped. "I

wish tae be left alone. I'm tired and . . . och! me body aches! Canna ye see I be trying tae sleep?"

"And failing miserably from the looks."

"Humph!"

Moyra crossed her arms tightly around her waist. Closing her eyes, she pretended she couldn't feel the way the heat of William's body chased away the chill that had settled inside her bones. Her jaw and chin smoldered from the memory of his touch; ignoring the sensation was akin to ignoring her breaths soughing unevenly in and out of her lungs, the coldness turning them to misty vapor or the kiss of winter-brisk air against her exposed flesh. In other words, 'twas impossible.

Och, weel, if she could do naught else, at least she could *pretend* to ignore him. *Pretend* to ignore how very aware she was of his closeness, of the way the scent of him filled her nostrils, surrounding her and wrapping her in a warm blanket of familiarity.

Aye, she could pretend she noticed none of it. She had to. The last thing either of them needed was for William Armstrong to realize the full extent of how his nearness—his oddly gentle touch, the spicy male scent of him!—disturbed her. To give indication of any of it would serve only to complicate a situation that was already hopelessly complicated.

"Moyra?" he asked.

She did not open her eyes, did not acknowledge him in any way. On the outside. How she felt on the inside was another matter. William's voice trickled down her spine like a drop of melted snow. The warmth of his breath puffed over the top of her head; it was more than a wee bit noticeable and . . . aye, highly pleasant.

If she'd hoped he would think her asleep, she found out soon enough she was mistaken. The ache in her lower regions made her shift uncomfortably. At the last minute, she bit back a moan of discomfort, but she didn't think to stop her brow from pinching, or her lips from thinning in reaction.

"Moyra," he said again. His voice, deep and husky, was subtly coaxing. "You said earlier that I remind you too much of your father for you to ever like me. I've thought on the matter"—indeed, he'd thought of precious little else, but did not mention *that*—"and I still don't understand. What does Ross Elliot have to do with any feelings you may or may not have for me? Answer me, lass. Please. The curiosity is gnawing at me to the point where I cannot sleep for the way it turns over and over in my mind."

One platinum brow cocked high. William couldn't sleep because of something she'd said? And why did she find that revelation ever so intriguing?

Cracking one eye open, Moyra angled her head and glanced up at him. Her gaze was narrow and assessive as it raked the chiseled angles of his face.

In the dim, scattered rays of moonlight, his cheekbones looked more harshly carved than ever, the hollows beneath deeper and more pronounced. The square line of his jaw resembled a slab of granite, much harsher than when viewed in the unforgiving light of day. Smudges of exhaustion smeared dark half-rings beneath his eyes. As for those piercing brown eyes themselves . . . they looked hooded and unreadable in this light, and at this angle. Moyra was positive she could feel tangible waves of tension rolling off him as he anxiously awaited her answer.

She closed her eye, leaned heavily back against the gritty tree trunk. Again, she shifted, squirming to find a comfortable position. Again, she failed.

When her voice came, it was soft and distant, as though she spoke as much to herself as she did to William. "When I think back, I've ver' few memories of me da whilst I was a bairn. As I've told ye—and as anyone ye ask can affirm—Ross Elliot was a Border reiver to the core. When the opportunity arose to ride against an enemy, he took it without second thought. When the opportunity wasna there, he made it. He was away from Wyndehaghen so much, my only true memories of him are of the times when he returned." Fully caught up in her memories now, she sighed, a small smile tugging at her lips. "Ne'er did I see me mother smile the way she did whenever me da rode intae the courtyard. Och! he was grimy and sweaty enough for twa men, yet she dinna hesitate tae throw herself intae his arms, hugging him tightly, as though she wished tae ne'er let him go again."

William swallowed hard. Shifting, he sat down beside her, his back also leaning against the birch trunk. Moyra's slender shoulder and upper arm pressed lightly against his thicker, harder arm. It was the only contact between them, but it was enough.

Closing his eyes, William tried to imagine his own mother relieved and overjoyed to see her husband—*any* of her husbands—return safe and sound from a raid.

Gritting his teeth, William shook his head. He simply could not imagine it. Lizbet Armstrong seemed to care about no one so much as she cared about herself. Her own happiness and welfare were of utmost concern to her. She moved from one husband to the next with such ease and regularity that it was doubtful she had the time or inclination to become fond enough of a current mate to worry about his safety, let alone miss him whilst he was gone or welcome his return with the zeal Moyra described in her own parents' reunion.

A pang of envy twisted in William's gut. The life Moyra described was incomprehensible to him; like day to night, his own childhood had been very dissimilar. How different, he wondered, would his life be if . . . ? Nay, how different would *he* be had he grown up with a single set of parents who loved each other to the exclusion of all others—the way Moyra's parents so obviously had—instead of a mother who buried her husbands with the same ease and regularity with which she picked out a new frock or decided the evening meal?

"When he returned wounded, maun times than nae," Moyra continued softly, turning William's attention back to her, "she nursed him herself, ne'er trusting anyone else tae get near . . . except me, but nae until I grew older. When he returned uninjured and victorious, she celebrated by his side. Och! and the Elliots knew how tae celebrate, dinna ye know? Sometimes for days at a time! That, I remember ver' well."

"Aye, but it still doesn't explain—"

"Hush, mon, I be getting tae it." Moyra hesitated, cleared her throat. "As I said, maun often than nae, me da came home injured. Usually the damage was minor—the graze of a sword blade, a knot on his thicker-than-granite skull. Howe'er, he wasn't always so lucky. A half score of times he was hurt badly enough that he would surely have died if nae for me mother's faithful nursing. 'Twas those times . . . Och! William, I remember those times all tae well. I remember Jared and meself as bairns—'twas afore Kenny was born—huddling together in one of our bed-chambers, nae daring tae talk, sometimes crying, all the while dreading the knock upon the door that would signal a summons for us tae go tae our da's deathbed. 'Twas torture, the waiting, the wondering if *this* would be the time me mother couldna save him."

"Consider yourself lucky, lass. At least *your* mother cared enough about her husband to try."

"Mayhap. Howe'er, I can tell ye, 'twas agony watching her nurse him, knowing there was naught I could do, naught anyone could do, tae help. His life was in her hands, and the strain of the burden was telling. I swore then I'd ne'er put meself in a life like that. I'd die an auld maid afore marrying meself off tae a reiver like me da."

As she'd talked, her voice soft but ragged with the rush of ill-suppressed memories, the frown had ironed itself from her brow. Something William had said now made it return in force, pinching the creamy skin between her eyebrows into deep, curious creases.

Opening her eyes, Moyra glanced at him curiously. At least, she glanced at the place where she'd last seen William to be, squatting down almost in front of her. He was no longer there.

Surprised, she snapped her gaze to the side. It was then she realized he'd sat down beside her, leaning back against the tree trunk in almost the same position as herself.

Of its own accord her attention strayed slowly over

him. Her gaze lingered on various areas of his body, absorbing the sight as though unconsciously striving to carve into memory each minuscule detail.

His legs were stretched out full-length and casually crossed at the booted ankles. The coarse, clinging layer of the trews offered a poor disguise for the muscular thighs beneath. While those muscles appeared dormant, Moyra did not think William nearly as relaxed as his pose implied.

Something . . . och! something indefinable about his too-casual position hinted at a crackling current of underlying tension. Perhaps 'twas the fingers linked atop the hard, flat plane of his belly? Instead of being loosely entwined, his grip looked tight, his knuckles white with strain. If she looked closely, the way he leaned against the thick, gritty tree bark was equally as stiff and tense.

Moyra had the impression that William was ready to spring into immediate action should the situation warrant it.

And if the situation *did* warrant it? What then? What if the Douglas stumbled upon them right this minute? Would William leap to her defense, sword drawn, ready to do whatever was necessary to protect her from harm?

Aye, she thought he would.

And why, Moyra wondered, did the idea make her feel so very warm and secure?

"You're smiling," William observed dryly. "Did you think what I said was funny?"

"Nae at all." The hint of a smile quickly disappeared from her lips. "I was . . . er, thinking of something else, is all. What did ye mean when ye said I be lucky? Did ye mean lucky to have twa parents who loved each other so ver' dearly? Or lucky tae have a mother who wasna shy about nursing her husband? I dinna understand. Are ye telling me yer mother ne'er did the same for yer da?"

"Which 'da' would you be referring to, Moyra? Or did you forget, I've had quite a few." It was William's turn to grin. The gesture was strained; it did not reach his eyes. Moyra noticed more than a wee bit of sarcasm etching his expression into hardness.

"Aye," she said, and groaned self-consciously. "I did forget." This time when she squirmed the gesture had nothing to do with the soreness in her lower region. Her left arm pressed more firmly against his right; the hard-muscled length of his upper arm felt reassuringly solid and warm. Nice, she thought. It felt nice. Succumbing to a powerful, unusual need for more contact, she shifted to face him and rested her hand upon his shoulder. The muscles beneath her fingertips tensed at her touch, but she did not remove her hand. "I'm sorry. I shouldna have asked."

His shrug was too forced to be casual. "No need for apologies. As you said, you forgot how dissimilar my upbringing was from yours. 'Tis no crime, Moyra, and I'm honestly not offended. Why should I be? You came to a natural conclusion . . . one that, unfortunately in my case, also happened to be very wrong."

"Thank ye kindly, but 'tis a maun flimsy excuse. I should have been more considerate." Her lips pursed. "Jared tells me often that I could save meself a good deal of trouble if I were tae think aboot what I'm going tae say *afore* I said it. Mayhap someday I'll heed that advice."

"Somehow, I doubt it." He grinned; 'twas a genuine smile this time, one that made his brown eyes sparkle. The creases shooting out from their corners deepened appealingly.

Moyra couldn't resist, she grinned back. Her fingers lightly squeezed his shoulder before she took her hand away. The warmth of him lingered on her palm for a long while afterward. "Aye," she said, "yer probably right." Her eyes widened, her grin broadened. "Och mon, did ye hear that? An Elliot and an Armstrong agreed on something. Methinks that's nae happened for at least a century."

"Mayhap two."

" 'Tis a cause for celebration, is it nae?"

His answer surprised her. He did not reply verbally, but rather physically and in a way that stole her breath away.

Twisting to the side, William angled his head, his mouth coming down on Moyra's before she could figure out what he was about to do.

Back and forth, his lips brushed against hers. Oh, so very gently. The fingers gripping her arms tightened reflexively as her own lips parted; she could taste his breath on them, and the flavor was something to savor.

The soreness that had plagued her greatly for the last several hours manifested into another, entirely different sensation. Had the feeling struck her this morning, she would have been confused by its sheer intensity. Tonight, however, she easily recognized the deep, throbbing longing for exactly what it was. Desire, wild and raw, pulsing through her bloodstream like liquid fire.

William's kiss was warm and wet and . . .

Och! Lord, it was *entirely too short!*

It seemed that no sooner had he begun kissing her than his mouth and body pulled away.

Moyra shivered, suddenly cold. Moaning throatily in disappointment, she leaned forward, her mouth instinctively tracking his, a hair'sbreadth away. He'd awakened the hunger in her again, and she was ravenous for a deeper, fuller taste of him.

William's hands settled upon her shoulders. His fingers, thick and powerful, dug into her skin as he held her firmly away from him. They were separated by barely an arm's length. In reality, 'twas a very short distance. So why, Moyra wondered, did the gap feel unnaturally long, and too insurmountable to breach?

"Ah, lass," he said, his voice ragged, "let's not start that again. After this afternoon, we both know all too well where it leads."

"Aye," she replied on a sigh, feeling not at all reluctant to let the kiss lead where it may. She would follow more than willingly. Even against the steady grip of his hand, she began to lean toward him once more.

"You misunderstand. Where 'twill inevitably lead is down a path you've sworn never to travel."

The frown was back, puckering her brow, a silent question that he instantly answered.

Resisting the urge to smooth her scowl away with the pad of his thumb, he elaborated, "Marriage to a reiver, that which you've sworn never to do, is where 'twill lead. Mark my words, Moyra, this afternoon took us both by surprise. 'Twas a mistake that should not have happened, a mistake that *will not* be repeated in the future. Were I to allow myself to take you into my bed again, I swear by all that's holy, 'twould be as my wife." His gaze narrowed, and a hard, indecipherable glint shimmered in his eyes. "You've made your vows, lass, and I've made mine."

The words struck her like a sharp icicle stabbing through her heart. His last cryptic statement puzzled her, but she did not tarry over it.

Instead, her mind refused to get past the fact that, even after making love to her with such wild, fierce possession not hours before, William Armstrong was *not* offering redemption by way of a marriage proposal.

That she hadn't really expected him to, that she would not have accepted the offer had he made it, none of it mattered in the least. That he oh, so casually declined making the offer, and that he had the audacity to tell her she was not worthy of being his wife . . . och! well, that mattered a great deal!

Moyra no longer needed William's hands to hold her back. Suddenly, the very *last* thing she wanted was to get closer to this man, let alone kiss him. The hot fingers of desire that had curled in her bloodstream only seconds ago evaporated like steam off a boiling kettle.

With a tight, jerky motion, she shrugged from his touch and squirmed away from him until they were no longer touching. The previous discomfort was back, prominent in her mind, but she ignored it as she leaned back against the tree trunk and closed her eyes. There was no way to know if disappointment shimmered in her gaze, and she wasn't willing to risk William Armstrong seeing it if it did.

Keeping her voice as tightly controlled as her expression, she muttered, "Ye've had yer talk, mon, now go away. Leave me in peace tae sleep."

That he'd said something gravely wrong, William was all too aware. What he'd said, or, more importantly, exactly how she'd interpreted it, was not nearly so obvious.

His gaze sharpened on Moyra's profile. The line of her jaw was hard and the muscle in her cheek worked as though she was gnashing her teeth. From the looks, getting her to talk any further would be as productive as trying to wring water from a stone.

He sighed, pushed himself wearily to a stand. If she noticed the movement, Moyra gave no indication. She didn't move a muscle as he stood towering over her, his attention fixed on the top of her platinum head.

Little did William know, Moyra was very much aware of him. Even with her eyes closed, her other senses marked his every movement.

She knew when he stood, knew when he raked his fingers through his shaggy blond hair, knew when he finally turned away.

Her mind's eyes followed him as he retraced his steps across the tiny, moonswept clearing. She almost, *almost* frowned when, with the snap of a winter-dry twig, she heard him stop. A rustle of linen and leather indicated he'd glanced back at her from over his shoulder.

It might have been her imagination, may even have been the slight winter breeze that was beginning to rustle the bare branches above, but she thought not. Nay, she was positive that, just before William resumed walking, he said so softly she could barely hear,

"Lay on your side, lass. 'Tis the only way you'll find comfort this night. By morn the soreness will have eased a wee bit."

A curiously foreign emotion—one she refused to acknowledge, let alone examine too closely—fluttered warmly, somewhere near the region of her heart. Moyra stomped the feeling down as if it were a burgeoning fire.

William's concern was touching, however, the unflattering blow he'd just dealt her was still too fresh and raw to allow herself to acknowledge it in anything more than a passing light.

Still . . .

A few minutes later, the scowl still locked firmly in place, Moyra shifted uncomfortably, shifted again. Finally, she pushed away from the tree trunk and lay down on her side upon the cold, hardpacked ground.

Mo chreach! William was right. This position was infinitely less painful. 'Twas both a good and a bad thing, for with the discomfort no longer a focus of her thoughts, she found herself instead turning over in her mind something he had said. Something she should have asked him to explain, and now wished she had.

You've made your vows, lass, and I've made mine.

Despite her resolve not to, she worried over the cryptic comment.

What did he mean by it? What vow had he made, and how on earth could it affect her? Moyra didn't know, nor was she certain why she should care.

But she did.

She cared more than she would ever admit.

While her life had taken more than a few uncertain

turns of late, there was one thing she was suddenly quite certain of: before long, she *would* have an answer to that question.

Aye, if need be, she'd make a vow to unearth it.

Fifteen

Like day to night, Smailholm Tower was as dissimilar to Wyndehaghen as it was possible for two castles to be. The primary difference being the fact that the former was not a crumbled ruin. Rather, not only did Smailholm appear to be newly constructed, it was also in the process of being completed.

Smailholm was situated atop a steep, rocky knoll, overlooking the small farming village from which it had taken its name. The keep was plain and unimposing. More a rectangular-shaped tower house than an actual stronghold. Its unadorned walls had been quarried and carved from local granite, the corners of each cemented together with sturdy blocks of red sandstone.

Moyra shifted in the saddle, noticing that, as William had predicted, she was not nearly so uncomfortable this morning. Shielding her eyes from the early morning sun, she assessed the building from her perch atop the rather restless mare that . . . Och! nay, she'd no desire to know where William had procured the horse. 'Twas enough that the mare had been tethered alongside William's and Gray's when Moyra had awakened this morning.

And what makes you think William is the one who fetched the horse? Could it not have been Gray . . . ?

Moyra shoved the thought from her mind and turned her attention back to the keep. From this distance and angle, she could see only one wall. 'Twas enough. The inhabitants of Smailholm must not appreciate sunlight, for she counted only two windows. One on the second floor, another on the third. Both were so meager they looked like nothing more than vaguely discernible pinpricks in the granite.

The protective barmkin they'd passed through was constructed of the same thick granite, surrounding the keep and—separated by a gloomy stretch of barren courtyard—the pair of outbuildings at the opposite end. 'Twas toward the latter Moyra shifted her gaze.

Thick tendrils of smoke curled up from the chimney atop the building to her left. The aroma of bland, unspiced meat scented the frosty morning air, drifting to her from that general direction. The kitchen, obviously.

Moyra wrinkled her nose. Frowning, she did a swift, mental calculation. By the time food traveled from the kitchen to the keep, wouldn't it be colder than the hard, uncomfortably lumpy ground she'd slept upon the night before? Aye, she thought with a grimace, it would. Apparently, unpalatable cold meals were as inviting to William Armstrong's family as dark, dreary stone walls.

She opened her mouth, then, before she could make a sound, shut it again so quickly her teeth clacked together. 'Twas *not* William's family who owned this keep, Moyra reminded herself, her blunder of last night still fresh in her mind. At least, the Liddesdale band of the Armstrong clan did not own it directly.

Smailholm was owned by Olen Pringle, William and Gray Armstrong's newest stepfather.

"If there's a more dismal keep on either side of this cursed Border, I've never seen it." Gray gestured toward the keep with a disgusted wave of his hand. "This place is . . . well, it's . . ." He seemed to be searching for a word but, apparently not finding it, settled instead for a disgruntled sigh and a shake of his dark head.

"Bleak?" Moyra supplied as, sitting forward in the saddle, she glanced past William and locked gazes with his brother. "Mayhap desolate?"

"Aye." Gray nodded. "Bleak and desolate are close, but neither quite describe what I had in mind."

"Uninviting, then?"

"Aye, 'twould be a good deal closer." Pursing his lips, Gray scowled and turned his attention to William. His hand smacked his thigh hard enough to make Moyra startle. "Whatever was going through our mother's head this time? When a woman remarries, she usually marries *up* in her class. But this! Ah, well, this"—he shuddered—"this *place* simply can't compare to the grandness of Riverdale."

"Or Buccleuch's." William nodded. "What was his castle's name? For that matter, what was *his* name?"

"Auld Wat," Gray answered distractedly. "I think. Don't take my word for it, though, since I could very well be wrong. She took two husbands while I was trying to get away from court . . . and Elizabeth's razor-sharp clutches. I never met either one."

"I did," William growled. "Pity both their estates passed to heirs. Mayhap if she'd a place to call home, she'd not have felt the need to marry. Again."

Gray shrugged, a tight lift and fall of his broad shoulders. "It wouldn't have mattered. She——"

"Excuse me," Moyra intruded, capturing both men's attention. Her gaze had wandered back to the castle at the opposite end of the courtyard, settling finally on the doorway . . . and the woman who stood there.

While Moyra had registered the detached terseness with which both men described their mother—"her" and "she," only once using the word "mother"—she chose to make no comment. Truly, 'twas none of her business. Instead, she nodded toward the castle and said, "Methinks that woman is trying tae get yer attention."

The woman raised a chubby arm and waved hesitantly in their direction. A brisk gust of wind plastered the drab gray frock to her abundantly round curves as she took a tentative step from the doorway. Another. A thick, vibrant curtain of copper-red hair swayed to the ample curve of her hips. Caught by the wind, strands of it played about her cheeks and brows, their soft curls serving to narrow her overwide features.

"William?" The woman called out, raising her voice in order to be heard over the whirl of the cold winter wind lashing through the courtyard. "And . . . is that you, Gray? My Lord, 'tis!"

The woman's pace quickened. Her steps became longer, more confident now that she knew the identity of the intruders.

As soon as she neared the trio, Moyra scanned the woman's age-rounded features. Her identity was obvious; William's and Gray's mother. The resemblance to her sons was faint—the shape of her dark brown eyes; the high, unfemininely rugged angle of her cheekbones—but undeniable. Her smile was wide and sincere, yet Moyra noticed a vague glint in her eyes that suggested a certain restraint, as though she wasn't quite sure what type of reaction to expect from her two sons, but had readied herself for any variety.

"For once, your timing is excellent, lads." Lizbet's accent was thick, indefinable and coarse. Part Scots, part Sassenach, part Welsh; as with a well-whipped batter each merged together to form a unique blend all its own. "At dawn the Gordon of Tynesdale was spotted roaming the hills not far from here. With Olen riding toward Leith, along with most of his men . . . Och! weel, suffice to say, I've spent the better part of the morning gathering up villagers and sealing us all within the safety of the keep."

"The Gordon has no quarrel with—" William had been about to say Armstrongs, but instead clamped his teeth around the surname, biting the word back. Smailholm wasn't an Armstrong keep, he reminded himself. It belonged to the Pringles. What little contact he'd had with his new family did not tell him whether or not his new family and the Gordon were currently feuding.

" 'Tis the Border, Willie. Don't expect rhyme nor reason to apply here. In the dead of winter, if a family finds themselves in dire need of food or blankets, they'll not think twice about raiding a complete stranger to get it. It has nothing to do with quarrels, 'tis simply the way they survive." Lizbet turned her attention to Gray. "Court life seems to agree with you. You're a wee bit pale, mayhap, but otherwise you look well."

"Who's Olen?" Gray asked.

"Why Leith?" William asked.

The questions, asked at the same instant, stumbled over themselves.

Lizbet patiently answered them in the order in which they came. Looking at Gray, she said with an uncertain smile playing over her lips, "My husband. Olen Pringle." To William, "Haven't you heard the news? Queen Mary is returning! She's said to be arriving at Leith, although no one is quite sure when."

"Och! and isna that exactly what Scotland needs right now?" Moyra muttered skeptically. Until that moment, the others' attention had been so focused on each other they seemed to have forgotten she was there. Now, one by one, their gazes shifted to her. She glanced at each of them in turn, then shrugged. "John Knox stirs up a fine muckle of trouble with his Protestant rantings and ravings. Mark me words, having our catholic Queen back on Scots soil will only make the situation a good deal worse."

"I'm afraid your friend is right," Lizbet said. Another gust of wind tunneled through the courtyard; her unbound hair billowed out behind her thick back like a soft red cloud. Although Moyra looked closely, if there was a streak of gray in those glossy strands, she couldn't find it. "However, there's naught to be done about it. With Philip dead, France no longer wants Mary. The threat she poses to the monarchy is more than enough reason to ship her back to Scotland."

Moyra nodded. "Aye, that I can understand, howe'er—"

William cleared his throat. Loudly. The sound was followed by a soft chuckle that may have come from Gray.

"If the Gordon is in the area," William said, changing the subject, "and you fear he may visit Smailholm, then wouldn't our time be better spent by finishing up fortifying the keep than talking politics?"

"Ah, Willie, you're always so bloody practical. Must be the Armstrong in you." Lizbet grinned and winked at Moyra, and it was in that instant Moyra decided she liked William's mother. She liked her very much indeed.

It did not take long for Lizbet's grin to abruptly fade. "Unfortunately, he's right. Put your horse in the stables, then come with me, lass. You and I can go inside and settle down the bairns and auld folk while these two"—she inclined her head in William's and Gray's direction—"recheck the village. I want to be sure no one was left behind before we seal the gate."

Moyra nodded and dismounted. She was halfway to the stables when a strange, tingling sense of awareness trickled down her spine like a captured drop of lighting; warm and tingly, the sensation raced from the nape of her neck to the small of her back. Stopping, she glanced over her shoulder.

Gray had dismounted. He was standing beside his horse, his dark head tipped as he spoke with his mother. William, on the other hand, was still astride and off to the side, as though trying to distance himself either from the two of them or their conversation. It was impossible to tell which. If he paid his mother and brother any attention at all, it wasn't evident.

Instead, his gaze was fixed on Moyra.

His brown eyes were narrow, dark and contemplative as he stared at her, and stared at her hard. There was no way to know the thoughts running through his head, yet the pinch of a scowl on his brow suggested that, whatever they were, he found them disturbing.

Their gazes met, locked, warred.

The visual contact lasted only a second, but a second was long enough.

Moyra felt the muscles in her stomach contract in response. Her breathing shallowed, her heartbeat accelerated. The fingers gripping the reins trembled. The reaction was as immediate as it was intense and uncontrollable.

She wondered if memories of the passion they'd shared so briefly the day before were running through his mind . . . the way they were running through hers.

Did he remember her touch as vividly as she remembered his? And, if so, did his body heat with the recollection, or grow cold with remorse . . . ?

There was no way to tell. His expression was as closed as his gaze, carefully guarding any feelings he may have. Shaking her head, Moyra hoped to also shake the questions—nay, the desperate need for *answers*—from her mind.

She faced forward once more, turned and entered the stable. The feel of William's eyes on her back lingered long after the cold shadows of the building had enfolded her.

It took ten minutes to tend to the mare. When she returned to the courtyard, William and Gray were nowhere in sight. Only Lizbet Armstro—nay, *Pringle*—was there waiting for her.

Moyra tried not to feel disappointed. Tried not to, but did.

"Ah, so that's the way of it," Lizbet remarked. " 'Tis

refreshing to know my instincts are still sharp after all these years."

Moyra halted in midstep. Either her disappointment was obvious, no matter how hard she tried not conceal it, or William's mother was extremely intuitive. The older woman's wise half-grin implied a wee bit of both.

"If the situation between you and Willie is what I suspect, then as soon as we've gotten the villagers settled, methinks you and I need to have a talk. A very *long* talk."

That said, Lizbet walked over to Moyra and slipped a hand in the crook of her arm. Any reply Moyra may have made, or explanation she may have demanded, was lost when the older woman gave her arm a tug and began leading her toward the entrance of the keep.

Sixteen

Lizbet Pringle set her unadorned pewter goblet of wine down atop the table in front of her. Resting her meaty elbows on the wooden surface, she leaned forward as far as her considerable chest would allow, and exchanged an unwavering glare with her eldest son. "Mark my words, you're wrong about Moyra Elliot, Willie. Very wrong."

"Aye, if you say so," William replied noncommittally. His gaze shifted to the floor of the great hall. The dozens of villagers who'd sought shelter within the safety of the keep had fallen to rest for the night wherever there was space. As on a field after a battle, bodies were strewn in every available nook and cranny. Unlike the remnants of a battle, however, these bodies consisted mostly of women and children, all warm and alive and unharmed.

The Gordon had never reached Smailholm. 'Twas doubtful now that he would. Still, Lizbet had insisted the villagers spend the night tucked safely within the keep. For their own protection, in case the Gordon returned. As she'd explained earlier, these were her people now, and she felt honor bound to see to their safety and welfare in her husband's absence.

Hearing the word "honor" from this woman's lips had not sat well with William, but he'd swallowed back any caustic comments he may have made.

His mind wandered to the top floor of the keep, where the family's private quarters were located. Somewhere up there, in separate bedchambers, Gray and Moyra slept. Both, understandably, had sought out their beds early.

As much as William's body bid him to do the same, he could not. Later, mayhap, if he was lucky, but not yet. Though every muscle and tendon in his body was sore and stretched to the limit of exhaustion, his mind was fully awake and racing, precluding any chance of sleep in the immediate future.

Instead, he'd sought a tankard of ale—actually, he was in the middle of his second—and the relative peace of the hall. Or, rather, the distraction thereof; the muffled snores and the occasional wail of a crying infant made the chamber anything but quiet.

'Twas here, only a few moments before, that Lizbet had found him, taking a seat on the bench stretching out at the opposite side of the table. He could tell from the tightness of her expression that she would not be leaving him to enjoy his solitude any time soon. Her jaw was set hard, and her brown eyes shimmered with determination. 'Twas an expression he recognized, with mixed emotions, from his childhood.

Lifting the tankard, William swallowed back a long drink of the honey-laced brew, then set the container down and again returned his mother's stare unflinchingly. Finally, he sighed, then said, "Tell me what's on your mind, mistress, and be done with it."

"Don't you listen, Willie? I just did." She lifted her

chin a decisive notch even as her thick fingers toyed with the stem of the goblet. "You're wrong about Moyra Elliot, and I wanted you to know it."

"Really? And would you mind also enlightening me as to what, precisely, it is I'm wrong about."

"Hmmm. Methinks the term 'everything' would be appropriate in this situation."

William scowled. " 'Tis a vague answer."

"To a question that needn't have been asked, it's more than answer enough. I'm of a mind you know exactly what you're wrong about. Whether or not you'll admit it, even to yourself . . . well, that's something else entirely."

Lizbet reached across the table, covered his hand, which tightly gripped the tankard handle, with hers, and gave his fingers a quick, reassuring squeeze. William's expression hardened, and he quickly slipped his hand free of her grasp.

Sighing regretfully, she pulled her own hand back. "You're a stubborn one, lad. Stubborn and unlenient to a fault. Och! how you remind me of—"

"My father?" The lift and fall of William's shoulders was too tight and strained to be casual. "I'm surprised you remember him. And, aye, I've no doubt 'tis the Armstrong in me. If naught else, we're a long-memoried, unforgiving lot. But then, you knew that when you married my father, didn't you?"

"We've had this discussion before, Willie. I'll not be having it with you again tonight. Tonight, I want to talk about Moyra Elliot."

"I'd rather not. Tonight, *I'm* trying *not* to think about her." He lifted the tankard, pulled in another long draft, and wished he'd instead settled for something stronger and more potent. Like a tankard filled to the brim with stanch Scots whiskey.

"You can try all you want, lad, 'twill not do you a bit of good. Some things are beyond resisting. This is one. You could no more stop thinking about Moyra than you could stop breathing."

William slammed his tankard down atop the table. Hard. The unexpected racket caused more than one of the bodies around them to stir. The old woman in the corner muttered groggily, but did not fully awaken. Out of respect for those sleeping around him, he kept his tone low. However, eyes narrowing, he made absolutely no attempt to keep the contempt he felt from entering his voice. "Have a care, mistress. You don't know me nearly as well as you think."

"Aye, you're right, Willie. I know you *better*. Or did you forget I was married to your father?"

"Not for very long."

"Mayhap, but 'twas long enough to give birth to you," she pointed out tightly.

"A mere six months after the wedding," William growled. "Rumor has it I was uncommonly large and hearty for being such a premature babe."

"Enough!" It was Lizbet's turn to smack the table. She didn't use the goblet, but struck the planking with her big, open hand. The blow packed enough force to turn her palm red and make the skin there smart. The repercussion of the blow shimmied all the way up her arm to her shoulder. "Why is it that all I ever do is explain and defend myself to you? Well, no more, I say! Quite frankly, I've had a belly full of it. I've already told you, I'll not be having *that* conversation with you. Not now, not ever again. Were the situation reversed, I'd simply be thankful I wasn't born a bastard. You've no idea how close you came to that fate, do you? Were the circumstances otherwise, or were your father any other man, you might very well have had to live under the shame of that label." Her eyes narrowed angrily. She picked up her tankard to take a sip, but her throat was too tight for it and she set it down again.

"I think I've heard enough," William snarled. Pushing the tankard aside, he splayed his hands on the table and started to push himself to his feet. Her next words stopped him in midstand.

"Nay, you've barely heard anything. Yet. And you'll be hearing the rest, whether you want to or not, while I'm still of a mind to say it. *Now sit down!*" Her voice was strong and commanding.

Surprised, William sat. He eyed her warily, but did not attempt to leave again.

Lizbet shook her head, the tail of her thick red braid swaying against her overbroad hips. "Oh, how you grumble and complain endlessly. Never do you waste the opportunity to point your accusing finger at me and claim 'tis *my* fault your life is so bloody difficult. I've news for you, Willie. You're wrong about *that,* too.

"The truth is, your life is not difficult at all. What few difficulties you have, you've made for yourself. Och! but I doubt you'd recognize *real* difficulty if it came up to you, introduced itself, bowed politely, then held a dagger to your throat and demanded attention. Let me tell you what *real* difficulty is, lad. *Real* difficulty is burying seven husbands, and each time feeling as though a large chunk of your heart had been torn out of your body and buried right alongside them. *Real* difficulty is stupidly allowing yourself to fall in love all over again—only to have *that* husband die as well. And the one after that.

"It took me an unbearably long time, and more heartache than you could ever understand, but I've learned my lesson. I've finally admitted I cannot—*cannot!*—go through such pain again. I can't lose another husband. I *won't*. Nor do I need fear it quite so much. Why do you think I married Olen Pringle? He's a good man, a devout man, a giving man, aye, but more importantly, he's is a farmer, not a reiver. He does not pick quarrels, does not wage blood feuds, he does not willingly partake of any of the nasty Border practices that have widowed me six times. He leads a simple life of cropping and protecting his people. If 'tis God's will, Olen will be hale and hearty for at least the next two score. Even you have to admit that, considering his infinitely more civilized way of life, he stands a much better chance of it than did all my late husbands combined."

Never could William remember his mother giving such a long, impassioned speech. That she had done so tonight shocked him almost as much as her revelations. Almost. His expression carefully guarded, he met and held her gaze, noticing the way her brown eyes sparkled with sincerity, her rounded cheeks flushed with unsuppressed resentment.

A tense moment of silence ticked slowly past.

Another.

William retrieved his tankard and lifted it to his lips . . . only to find the ceramic rim warm against them, the interior of the mug dry as a bone. Sighing, he settled it back atop the table, this time much more gently than the last.

Mulling over his words carefully beforehand, he said finally, "Burying husbands always seemed such an easy chore for you. I'd no idea . . ."

"Nay," she said, nodding, "of course not." Her stout shoulders slumped forward, as though the anger that had stiffened them only seconds before had suddenly begun to dwindle away. "You couldn't know that which I refused to tell or show you. Of course not. The decision to keep my grief to myself was my own, freely made.

"Ah, Willie, what can I say by way of explanation? I simply did what I thought best at the time. Mayhap 'twas wrong, I cannot say. All I know is that you were so very young when your father died, and so very devastated by it all. Watching you struggle with your grief . . . well, how could showing you the depth of mine have helped? I thought at the time, and still think now, that displaying my grief would have served no purpose other than to make your grief harder to bear. Don't you see, Willie? 'Twas the last thing I wanted, the last thing any mother would want for her young son. If you had a bairn of your own, mayhap you'd understand better . . ."

William's shrug was vague. "Aye, mayhap I would," he replied distractedly. His gaze had settled on the empty, shadowy depths of his tankard. In the last few minutes, he'd felt a sudden weariness descend over him, loosening his already tired muscles, and seducing his mind into thinking that mayhap 'twas time to seek his bed, and sleep. Finally. With luck, tonight's dreams would not be the same as those that had plagued him last night . . . dreams filled with visions of a slender, platinum-haired vixen whose attractive violet eyes were heavy lidded with passion, and—

". . . at least think about what I've said."

With a shake of his head, William snapped himself back to the present. His gaze lifted, and he was surprised to note his mother had stood up, as though in preparation to leave. Whatever she'd said, he hadn't heard a word, so lost had he been in thought.

Apparently, she didn't expect an answer, for with a nod of her head, Lizbet turned and, side-stepping sleeping bodies, made her way from the hall.

William watched her go. His gaze was riveted to her excessively wide, familiar back. Nay, more accurately, his concentration focused on the fat red braid trailing down her spine.

As a child, he remembered sitting for hours in her abundant lap—a lap that hadn't been quite as abundant as it was now—twirling thick strands of her hair around his bairnishly-pudgy fingers.

At those times, she would whisper in his ear, or stroke his hair or cheek. Many times she sang lullabies. While her singing voice was deep and abrasive and more than slightly off-key, to his young ears she'd had the voice of an angel.

Sometimes the lullabies were sung in Gaelic, sometimes in French, sometimes in Welsh. William hadn't known the words, was far too young for that. Instead, he'd reveled in the simple feel of his mother's closeness; his small body had absorbed her warmth as the parched roots of a tree drew in moisture during a sudden summer storm. He couldn't recall another time in his life when he'd felt so safe, so protected, so loved.

Everything had changed when his father died.

His life changed still more when Lizbet's second husband died.

And her third.

Watching how easily his mother slipped through her grief, while he could barely contain his own . . . ah, well, it had managed to shatter his trust and belief in her, had raised doubts about her loyalty and devotion to anyone.

Like an unfading scar, those doubts had followed him into adolescence and beyond. They'd ridden him hard, still did. At some indiscernible point, the doubts had ceased to be directed entirely toward his mother.

William swallowed hard. Dryly. His fingers curled around the tankard handle, lifted, only to remember abruptly that he'd drained it already. Scowling, he considered refilling it, then decided against the idea.

His mind had swerved in another direction—upstairs, to one bedchamber in particular and the woman who slept there—and now it refused to fix itself elsewhere.

Moyra.

I understand ye want me, William Armstrong. Almost as badly as I want ye.

The muscles in William's belly clenched. Lower, he felt a more integral stirring. The memory of those words, and of the passion-husky way Moyra had uttered them—the way her lips had brushed against his skin as she'd spoken and her breath had kissed his flesh like a warm, dewy mist—kindled a fire in William's bloodstream.

Aye, he'd wanted her.

So very badly.

The lightning-quick, lightning-*hot,* reaction of his body to the memory—not her absolute touch, but merely the *memory* of it!—said . . . Ah, blast it, he couldn't deny it any longer.

He wanted her again.

Wanted her still.

Wanted her equally as badly.

Nay, that last wasn't quite true. If possible, he wanted her *more.*

The legs of the wooden bench scratched harshly against stone as he pushed himself to his feet. William barely realized his mind had given his body the command to move, for it seemed to be moving of its own accord.

Past a woman sleeping on the hard, cold floor, a tiny babe nestled close to her body.

Past a young girl curled up trustingly in the crook of her ancient grandfather's age-withered arm.

Past all of them.

Seventeen

Moyra Elliot snored.

Not a lot, and not loudly, but 'twas noticeable.

William eased the bedchamber door closed, and paused when but a step within. A grin tugged at one corner of his mouth.

Soft and breathy, the slight, gentle rumbles tickled his ears and made a tingle work its way down his spine. It seemed crazy, but there was no denying he found the sound charming . . . and more than a wee bit endearing.

He took another step into the room.

Another.

He didn't stop until he was a handsbreadth away from the oversized bed.

The night was clear and cloudless; shards of moonlight slanted in through the small, single window carved into the far wall, forming streaks across the stone floor. The silvery hue was a rich parallel to the color of Moyra's hair.

The bed was the only piece of furniture in the room—the interior of Smailholm was as stark as its exterior, although, thankfully, not as stark as Wyndehaghen. The size of the bed made the already small room feel cramped, while the straw-filled mattress seemed to stretch on endlessly, swallowing up the tiny figure huddled in the middle. She looked like naught more than a bulge beneath the thick woolen blankets.

Only the very top of her head peeked out from beneath the covers. Curling his fingers into a tight fist, William resisted the urge to reach out and run his fingertips over those pale, softer-than-silk strands. 'Twould have been a simple touch, aye, but, once started, he wasn't entirely sure he would be able to *stop* touching her.

Moyra muttered something under her breath, the words too sleep-slurred to be understood. She tossed onto her back, heaved a restless sigh, muttered again, then tossed onto her side. The rest of her head came out from underneath the covers. Hers was no relaxed and peaceful sleep; her features were tight, the creamy skin between her eyebrows pinched with alarm.

Again she mumbled. Did she call out his name? William wasn't sure, but he thought she might have.

This time when she tossed onto her back, it was with enough force to make the mattress rustle beneath her. Her hands came out from beneath the covers, searched blindly, then crunched closed until the thick, coarse cloth was trapped in small, white-knuckled fists.

"Nay, William! Dinna go in there!"

Moyra's voice cracked through the chamber like an unexpected bang of thunder penetrating a warm, sunny spring morning. Even William was startled by the sheer force of it, as well as the way she abruptly sat bolt upright upon the bed.

In the unnatural silence that followed, the ragged soughing of her breaths seemed alarmingly loud.

Her eyes were open now, although their heathery depths looked glassy from sleep. Jerking her head from one side to the other, she scanned her surroundings with panicky swiftness, as though she expected the very devil himself to be crouched somewhere in the shadows clinging to dark stone corners.

Finally, her gaze came to rest on William. She blinked hard, then shook her head.

"William," she said, her voice a quivering, breathless rush. With trembling fingers, she tossed her hair back over her shoulders, then hugged her arms protectively about her waist. "Wh-what are ye doing here, mon?"

"I came to check on you before seeking my own bed. You were . . . er, having a nightmare?"

"Aye, and well I ken it." A shiver skated over Moyra's shoulders, trickling down her spine. Closing her eyes, she pulled in a long, deep, calming breath. Released it with equal deliberateness. After repeating the process twice, she opened her eyes. " 'Twas a maun awful dream, and . . . Och! well, that's all ye be needing tae know aboot it."

His eyes narrowed. Mayhap 'twas all *she* thought he needed to know about it, however, he thought otherwise. Turning, he settled himself on the edge of the bed. The mattress dipped and crunched beneath his weight.

"Another vision . . . ?" William asked. Although he tried to keep the sarcasm he felt from creeping into his voice, a bit must have crept into his tone, for she fixed him with a furious glare.

"We'll nae know unless it comes tae pass, will we?" she answered irritably. "Nae that it matters. Ye'd ne'er believe me. And e'en if, by some far-flung miracle, it *did* come tae pass, what then? Would ye attribute it tae naught more than coincidence?"

The mattress crunched again as William shifted his weight from one side of his hips to the other. "You have to admit, Moyra, in the time I've known you, you've had several visions, most of which proved wrong."

"Will ye ne'er let me forget that night, mon?"

"I'm not trying to be insulting! Honestly, I'm not. However, that night of all nights, 'twould have helped a great deal if your vision had been a wee bit more clear. Had I listened to my instincts, which said the Douglas *would* return—"

"Och! mon, I canna control that! The Sight may nae always be crystal-clear, I'll admit as much, but 'tis been clear on enough occasions tae make me take notice. I'll nae be ignoring a single one of me visions simply because ye dinna believe in them."

"I didn't ask it of you." Sighing, William dragged his fingers through his shaggy blond hair, then shook his head. "Let's leave the topic be, lass. I didn't come here to fight with you."

"Really?" Her snow-pale brows lifted as she assessed him skeptically. "Then what *did* ye come here for?"

Ah, 'twas an excellent question.

Pity William had no ready answer!

He'd told himself, told her, his reason had entailed nothing more sinister or complicated than the desire to check on her before retiring himself. Only now did he recognize that for the lie it was.

Truly, there'd been no great need for him to slip into her bedchamber. Smailholm was a sturdy tower-house, built to withstand assaults. Besides, assaults themselves were rarely quiet. Had they been under attack, had even the vague threat of one been hanging in the chilly night air, the entire keep would be aware of it. Instead of sleeping soundly, everyone in the chambers below would be hustling to ward off the intruders while battening down for a siege.

Nay, there was no attack to worry over, just as there was no reason on earth he'd had to check on Moyra.

At least not a definable reason.

Yet he'd *had* to do it.

The compulsion to see her had been like an unseen hand shoving against his back, propelling him forward, dictating his every step. 'Twas far too overpowering to resist. He should know, he'd tried his best to resist it—and failed miserably.

In the end, he had decided that peeking in on her would be a harmless enough way to satisfy such an inexplicably strong urge. Afterward, he would seek out his own bed and, with just a shred of luck, spend the night entrapped in a deep, dreamless sleep. A sleep unplagued by the slender, platinum-haired temptress who'd haunted his every waking and sleeping minute for too long to tally.

The platinum-haired temptress in question was glancing at him now as though patiently awaiting an answer to . . . ?

Then what did *ye come here for?*

Like the tip of a feather brushing against bare flesh,

an answer tickled the back of his mind. 'Twas an odd sensation, that of being within grasp of a rationalization, yet the counterfeeling of not wanting to extend his reach. He didn't dare look too closely for fear the explanation would do naught more than reveal another layer of confusion and mayhap a bevy of even more complicated questions, the answers to which he was not ready to examine too closely.

At some point Moyra had crawled out from beneath the covers and knelt beside him on the bed. William noticed this fact only when he felt her small hand settle on the shelf of his left shoulder. Through the thin layer of his tunic, her touch warmed his skin.

Glancing up, he met her inquisitive gaze with a guarded one of his own. " 'Tis late, lass," he said finally, his tone as shielded as his expression. "We both need sleep."

"Aye," Moyra agreed, yet her soft, breathless tone lacked sincerity. Her gaze had dipped, settling on his lips.

It felt like a hot, tangible caress on his skin. William's tongue darted out, dragging over suddenly parched flesh. The gesture was a mistake. He knew it the second he'd completed the act, for her gaze shadowed the movement. Her intriguing, heather-colored eyes narrowed perceptibly, and darkened.

Was Moyra even aware of the way her own lips parted so invitingly, or of how she instinctively leaned toward him?

William didn't think so.

But he was.

Excruciatingly aware of it.

Her hand on his shoulder felt suddenly heavy, as

though the simple touch weighed him down, pinned him to the bed. Odd. He knew he could have broken the contact at any time. Didn't. Couldn't.

Instead, his body responded on its own, swaying toward hers. He didn't give his head permission to angle, it seemed to do so of its own accord. When his lips sought out and brushed against hers, the sensation that erupted inside of him was one part surprise, countered by three parts raw pleasure.

Were I to allow myself to take you into my bed again, I swear by all that's holy, 'twould be as my wife.

Sooner than he could have expected, the words came back to torment him. They pealed through his mind like a score of church bells . . . even as his mouth opened hungrily over hers.

The moist puffs of her breaths, shallow and rapid, warmed his skin, made the blood surging through his veins swiftly heat to the boiling point. His own breaths turned deep and ragged, clogging his throat and blocking any words of resistance he may have voiced.

When he'd made that vow, he'd meant every word. But then, he hadn't had the feel of Moyra Elliot's sweet, sweet lips to contend with, had thought it an easy vow to keep. Truly, he should have known better, just as he should have known 'twas a vow he could never honor.

The fingers on his shoulder tightened, biting into his skin as she leaned into him, lifting her chin, deepening the kiss to a dizzying pitch.

Turning toward her, he felt his breaths shudder through his chest when she pressed the upper front of her body fully against the upper front of his.

The world spun and tilted.

It took William a moment to realize what had happened.

Suddenly, he was no longer sitting up, but lying on his back atop the bed. The cool, hard mattress pushed against his spine, while Moyra's softer, and infinitely warmer, body blanketed his front.

Ah, but the small curve of her breasts felt good pressing against his chest! Touchably firm and hot and tempting beyond all reason.

The way her hips ground against his, nudging at the long, hard proof of his desire . . .

Now it was *her* mouth on his, *her* hunger devouring his last crumbs of his resistance. Moyra's hands had shifted, her open palms now cupping the sides of William's head as if she were afraid he would turn away. With his ears covered, he could hear the ragged pounding of his heart in his ears, each beat echoing with a passion so strong it would have sent him to his knees had he been standing.

"Och, William," she murmured, her breath hot and misty against his lips. "I beg of ye, dinna leave me. Nae now. Nae this way."

Lifting his arms, he coiled them about her waist. He held her to him with breath-snatching tightness, not with a crushing pressure but rather with one born of equal parts desperation and desire.

Leaving was no longer an option. It hadn't been from the instant he'd felt her sweet lips beneath his, or her breaths puffing warmly against his skin. Even the vow he'd sworn not so long ago and had been determined to maintain fell away and became insignificant as his hands traversed restlessly over the slender length of her back.

Her bottom felt rounded and firm to the touch. So hot. So enticing. The kilt covering it was a scratchy contrast to the smoother-than-silk flesh beneath. Flesh he wanted oh, so very badly to feel gliding beneath his searching palms.

Her mouth turned its attention from his to nibble, lick, and kiss its way to the hard line of his jaw. William swallowed a groan.

His fingers closed around fistfuls of wool. Tugged. The garment dragged its way higher up her thighs. Moyra squirmed atop him, and a bolt of pleasure-pain shot through his body when he realized she was not trying to move away, but instead helping him to disrobe her.

Was she as impatient to feel him skin-to-skin as he was her? Aye, she seemed to be quite eager for it. The idea was thrilling in itself, for never had William bedded a woman so openly enthusiastic or so quick to respond to his touch.

He'd not have thought it possible to want this woman more badly than he already did. He'd never been so wrong.

Moyra's uninhibited response fueled his desire, heated his passion to an unprecedented degree. The need to feel himself buried deeply inside of her—ah, Lord, to possess her just this one last time—rode him hard. It drove all rational thought from his mind, all other needs from his body. As a mirror with a stone thrown at it, the vow he'd made shattered; each shard of it now seeming abruptly small and inconsequential.

Her mouth had found his earlobe. Her hot, moist

tongue licked around the curl, her teeth nibbled and tasted and teased.

William's breath caught in his throat and his body stiffened as a shiver of pleasure tingled its way down his spine. Her hands skimmed his shoulders, stopping occasionally to lightly test and squeeze the hard bands of muscles playing beneath.

His hands shifted to her waist—so thin and tight. Exerting gentle pressure, he lifted her up off his body. Bending until he was in a sitting position, he settled her on her feet on the floor next to the bed.

Moyra whimpered a protest, but he leaned forward, capturing the airy sound with his mouth. "Nay, lass, I'm not pushing you away," he whispered against her mouth. "I want only for you to undress for me."

He felt her stiffen, hesitate. Then, as though the reluctance had never been there at all, she took a step backward and stood under her own power. Even though she was standing, and he sitting, William noticed that the top of her head reached only a scant few inches above the top of his.

She was so small, so delicate, so . . . ah, aye, so infinitely appealing.

The silvery glint of moonlight streaming in through the lone window barely reached this far into the room, yet there was enough light for him to make out the flush of desire heating her narrow cheeks, and the hot-violet glint of passion darkening her eyes. The curve of a sexually confident smile tugged at her mouth as her hands traveled to the waist of her sleep-wrinkled kilt.

William's breath trembled in his lungs as he watched Moyra work the garment free. When she was finished, she did not immediately drop the kilt to the floor. Rather, her gaze lifted, locked with his. The confident grin on her lips deepened.

Blast it, the woman was teasing him! William realized it in the same instant he realized 'twas working quite well. The anticipation of seeing the swatch of plaid drop to the cold stone floor clawed him up on the inside; 'twas almost beyond his control to sit placidly upon the bed waiting for her to complete the chore herself. His hands itched to reach out and grab the skirt away. He resisted, but only barely.

Cocking one eyebrow high, he let his gaze travel slowly, meaningfully down the length of her body, pausing at the hands at her waist, then going back up again. Was it his imagination or was the color in her cheeks even higher now?

There was no time for an answer to form itself in his mind, for suddenly Moyra had opened her hands, letting the thick cloth go.

As though in slow motion, he watched the cloth slide down her creamy thighs, lower and lower, until it formed a wrinkled puddle at her feet atop the bare stone floor. 'Twas as he was staring at her skirt that she must have also removed her tunic, for the next thing he knew, that garment was falling atop the heap of the other.

William swallowed hard. Twice. Dryly. Like a thirsty sponge, his gaze roamed upward, absorbing the perfection of her bare form.

Moyra Elliot stood naked and proud before him. Her only covering was a thin gleam of moonlight; the faint sheen enhanced the silvery strands of hair waterfalling down her slender back, and cast her skin with a pale tint that made it look smoother than expensive porcelain.

He reached out, his need for her throbbing inside him now, too intense to ignore or deny. His fingertips brushed soft, warm flesh . . . but only for one torturously short second.

No sooner had he touched her than Moyra took a step backward, placing the sweet promise of her naked body just out of reach.

William groaned low and deep in his throat. 'Twas a feral sound that echoed throughout the abrupt stillness in the bedchamber, rivaling the ragged soughing of both their breaths, for prominence.

The mattress crunched beneath William as he leaned down and swiftly removed his boots. They landed upon the floor with twin *thuds*.

He pushed to his feet. 'Twas impossible for him not to notice how Moyra's grin broadened when she took another step, this one to the side, moving toward the foot of the bed.

"Play fair, Armstrong," she said, her voice a breathless rush in his ears. "I undressed for ye. 'Tis time ye do the same for me, dinna ye know?"

She kept moving. If she was at all self-conscious to be unclothed in front of him, her discomfort was not evident. Her spine was straight and proud, her steps long and confident. If anything, she gave the impression of being content and secure with herself as she rounded the foot of the bed, moved to the other side. Her grin, William noticed, never wavered as she perched on the very edge of the mattress.

One platinum brow rose defiantly as her gaze, dark and hungry, traveled over him in much the same way his had traveled over her only a few short moments before.

"Weel," she asked, "what are ye waiting for? 'Tis a maun brisk night, m'lord." As though to prove it, a shiver skated up her spine. He could not decide if it was genuine or not. "Dinna keep me waiting o'er long, or I'll be forced tae find me way under these nice, warm covers and go back tae sleep again. *Alone.*"

"Ah, you're a minx, woman," William grumbled, even as he reached for the waistband of his trews.

This time it was *his* fingers that quivered over hidden fastenings, *his* skin that chilled to the slap of icy winter air as he quickly peeled the trews down his legs, cast them aside, then dragged his tunic up over his head. The body-warmed garments landed in a rumpled heap atop hers; both were forgotten the instant they left his hands.

The mattress crunched and sagged as he rested his right knee, and the bulk of his weight, atop it. "Come here, Moyra," he beckoned, his voice rough and throaty. " 'Tis time to finish what you've started."

She shook her head, her grin melting away. "Nay, William. If ye be wanting me as badly as I'm thinking ye do, badly enough tae break a vow so recently made . . . then this time, *ye* come tae *me.*"

Like a dense, inviolable ground fog, the challenge swirled between them, electrifying the frosty midnight air.

To his wary eye, she did not look nearly as confident now as she had before. Instead, she looked determined, her finely etched jaw set in an uncompromising line as she met his gaze with a level one of her own.

The Armstrong pride racing through William's veins was thick and unyielding. But no less so than the staunch streak of Elliot pride racing through Moyra's.

Was it his desire for this woman—pure and strong and distracting beyond reason—that forced William to speak when it was obvious Moyra would not?

"I suggest a truce. A compromise, if you will."

"Aye?" she asked suspiciously. "And what sort of compromise would ye be suggesting? Nae one that's only made on me own part, I'm hoping."

"Nay, lass. The compromise I have in mind need be made on *both* our parts." His gaze dipped to the expanse of mattress stretching out endlessly between them. "I'll meet you halfway. Does that not sound fair?"

Moyra pursed her lips. A frown pinched her brow as she seemed to mull the suggestion over. Eventually, she glanced back at William and, smiling slightly, scooted a wee bit closer to the center of the bed.

William's heart skipped a beat, then hammered to frantic life. He placed his other knee atop the bed, inched in the same direction.

They met in the middle.

Both held their breath as slowly, slowly, Moyra's hand lifted, palm out to face William. His gaze volleyed between her eyes and her hand before he mirrored the gesture.

Simultaneously, they reached out to each other.

Their palms came together; hers small and soft and delicate, his big and callused and powerful. Fingers splayed, trembled, curled inward and entwined.

A sigh whispered from one of them, but William was never sure which. His attention had dropped to

Moyra's lips, and suddenly he could not think beyond the hauntingly sweet taste of her, or his hunger to savor that flavor again.

Tugging gently, he pulled her closer, not satisfied until he felt the front of her body once again pressed against the front of his. Her breasts pushed against him, their nipples achingly rigid.

His head dipped, and his mouth crashed down upon hers for a kiss that was long and hard and thorough.

William's free hand slipped around her waist, hauling her closer still, as though trying to melt her body right into his even as he shifted.

This time it was Moyra's back which came up against the mattress, and William's body which instantly followed.

She felt good beneath him. Torturously good. Small and soft and oh, so very right. Her skin was passion-hot, warming his wherever they touched. Where their chests pressed together, he thought he could feel the pounding of her heart. The rhythm was fast and erratic, a perfect match to the ragged beat of his own.

As his mouth devoured hers, he let the hand not clutching hers roam over the side of her body. The indentation of her waist, the silky curve of her hip, the upper portion of her thigh. Finally, shifting slightly, he captured her breast in his hand. The nipple was indeed rigid, pushing into the center of his palm as though eager for attention. His fingers closed around the firm flesh surrounding it, kneading her.

She moaned with pleasure, and he captured the sound with his mouth.

His fingers turned their full attention to the pearled,

sensitive peak. He rolled her nipple between his thumb and index finger, then tugged very, very gently.

Moyra gasped.

Mo chreach, but that felt wonderful!

Her free hand clutched William's shoulder, the fingernails digging into his skin, not quite breaking the flesh there, but coming excruciatingly close. Her spine bowed and she arched greedily into his touch. Keeping her hips still was not possible; the now-familiar pulse of desire insisted they move.

A heady burst of triumph shot surged through her bloodstream when her hips pushed upward. Hesitantly at first, then with more confidence, the satiny nest of platinum curls between her thighs nudged at the long, hard proof of his desire.

This time, it was *she* who captured *his* throaty groan.

That she had been the one to set aside her staunch Elliot pride and boldly initiate their lovemaking bothered Moyra not at all. To have William so close yet not be able to touch him was unbearable. Och! nay, she felt no guilt and . . . Dear Lord, when he touched her like this, not a shred of remorse.

His hand tickled the flat plane of her belly before slipping between their bodies. The roughened tips of his fingers abraded her tender flesh as he inched his attention lower.

Catching her lower lip between her teeth, Moyra turned her head to the side, her chin lifting, straining for a more intimate touch.

William did not keep her waiting.

The feel of his hand between her legs was comparable to being tossed headfirst into a steaming pot of liquid fire.

Moyra inhaled sharply. Her desire intensified, flaming through her bloodstream. No visions edged her mind tonight. Instead, there was naught but white-hot, wondrous sensation.

The ends of his sandy blond hair teased her shoulder when William turned his head, applied his open mouth to the sensitive side of her neck.

She squirmed beneath him, the feelings raging inside her suddenly too strong to bear. He must have sensed how close she was to the edge, for he eased her legs apart, then guided himself between her creamy thighs.

One quick, sure thrust of his hips and he was buried deeply inside her.

The breath Moyra only now realized she was holding shuddered past her lips, washing over his shoulder in a warm, misty rush of air.

He did not move inside her. Not yet.

She did not encourage him to. Not yet.

For the length of a handful of heavy heartbeats Moyra was content to savor the blissful sensation of fullness and closeness that came from having this man buried deeply within her. 'Twas unlike anything she'd experienced before and she was reluctant to let the heady sensation slip past too quickly. She wanted to enjoy it to its fullest.

His mouth on her neck moved. She felt the graze of his teeth, a wee bit cooler than his breath, and the hot tip of his tongue, stroking and laving at her skin before suckling a patch of it into his mouth.

A shudder curled down her spine as an uncontrollable spasm of pleasure seized her.

Only then did his hips lift. Slowly. He pulled back so far that at first Moyra feared he planned to leave her. He didn't. Instead, this next stroke as slow and as deep as the last, he plunged back fully inside her.

Again.

And again.

And again.

Their fingers were still entwined; her grip on his became white-knuckled tight against the moonlit mattress beside her head. Despite the chilly night air, a fine coat of perspiration beaded on her flesh. Her breathing was rapid and choppy, and as she rose to meet his every thrust, it became more rapid and choppy still.

She reached her peak quickly. Too quickly, she thought, but there was no stopping it.

When the first pulse of climax trembled through her, Moyra did not try to fight or deny it. Instead, she greeted it with a breathless enthusiasm that wrung a groan from William. With his chest pressed firmly atop hers, she could feel the sound rumble through his body as well as her own, and at the same time felt the spasms of her completion pulsing lower.

'Twas Moyra's climax that proved the undoing of any restraint William may have maintained. Like a brittle twig, his control snapped. The hot, moist core of her quivered around him, milking him to his own fulfillment.

Unlike Moyra, William tried to fight the sensation. Couldn't.

Ah, God, she simply felt too good!

His grip on her hand tightened, his thrusts quickened. Finally, left with no alternative, he surrendered what was left of his self-control and tumbled blindly over the edge of completion, a mere heartbeat behind her.

They lay there, motionless except for the inner quivers of their climaxes, still trembling softly inside their bodies, for what seemed like forever.

It took a long while, but eventually, their breathing smoothed, their heartbeats regulated, their sense of the world around them returned. Their entwined fingers relaxed, yet neither let their grip fall away.

Beneath him, Moyra sighed. 'Twas a long, deep pull and release, the undisguised sound of a woman happy and relaxed and entirely sated.

A satisfied grin tugged at one corner of William's mouth as he broke the intimacy of their embrace, then rolled onto his back.

Her body followed his. Finding the natural indentation beneath his shoulder, she cushioned her cheek there even as she curled up sleepily against his side. Lifting and bending her right leg, she draped it over his hips and snuggled more securely into him.

Her breath felt warm on his skin, the ends of her long platinum hair silky soft where it tickled his belly.

Only then did William realize that, atop the firm plane of his chest, their hands rested directly over his heart.

Their fingers were still linked.

Eighteen

"God blast it, Willie, have you no common sense at all? Methinks you really *have* lost your mind!"

The words slammed through the bedchamber like a clap of thunder. The angry tone was reinforced by the crash of the wooden door careening shut.

Gray Collingwood took one long stride into the room, then hesitated. He dared not move closer for fear his anger would get the better of him and he would do something he would sorely regret.

Crossing his arms tightly over his broad chest, he stood glaring down at the couple who lay sprawled upon the bed.

The woman's long platinum hair was lover's-fingers-tousled, her large violet eyes heavy-lidded with recently abandoned sleep, her lips full and moist as though she'd just been thoroughly kissed.

His gaze narrowing furiously, Gray speared his half brother with a glare. William's shaggy blond hair was equally mussed, his dark brown eyes also heavy-lidded and sleepy.

Gray watched his brother sit abruptly, the blanket once draped over William's shoulders falling unnoticed to his waist. That William was as naked under the covers as he was above them, Gray did not doubt.

Moyra also pushed herself up until she sat with her back pressed hard against the carved oak headboard of the bed. The fingers of both her hands closed in white-knuckled fists around the blanket she'd hauled protectively up to her chin.

Dear Lord, 'twas the second time in as many days Gray had stumbled upon the two in such a blatantly compromising position. And this time, 'twas in his mother's own house!

Did they have no idea the sort of scandal it would cause had someone besides himself discovered them? Did they not care that centuries-long blood feuds had been waged for far less significant reasons?

Gray clamped his teeth together so tightly his jaw ached. Somewhere behind his temples, a dull ache began pounding in time to his every furious heartbeat.

After dealing with that old nag, Queen Elizabeth, for more months than he cared to remember, he'd thought to have seen the last of such flagrant self-centeredness. Such was not the case, apparently, for the nasty trait seemed to have followed him home and invaded his own family!

Either William and Moyra did not fully realize the repercussions of what they were doing or, worse, they knew but did not care.

Gray's attention shifted between the two, settling finally on his brother. Through gritted teeth he said, "I'm going to say this but once, Willie. I suggest you listen closely and heed my advice." He jerked his chin in Moyra's direction. "Unless you've a taste for siring bastards, you'd do well to get this lass to a church, make her your wife. Do it, and do it quickly. Before the sun sets would be ideal. Afterward, the two of you can mate like rabbits, but you'll do so *without* jeopardizing the peace of this entire family."

"No one tells me—!" William began, only to have his voice overridden by Moyra's indignant, "Och! 'Twill be a frigid day in Hades afore I'll *e'er*—"

Their mouths snapped shut simultaneously.

The bedchamber suddenly became quiet.

Too quiet, Gray thought.

He couldn't help but notice the way both shifted uncomfortably, the mattress crunching beneath their weight as they directed their attention to opposite.walls. Each seemed to be struggling not to give in to temptation and glance at the other. The silent inner battles being waged were as telling as the crimson stain of embarrassment warming Moyra Elliot's cheeks.

"Did you barge into my bedchamber only to lecture me?" William growled.

One dark brow arched. A hint of a smile played about the corners of Gray's mouth. " 'Tis not *your* bedchamber, Willie, it belongs to our newest stepfather. And, nay, lecturing you was not my intent . . . albeit, 'twas a nice bonus." Sighing, he shifted his gaze to Moyra. "I came to tell you you have a visitor." He then looked back to William. "It could be said you'll soon have one, too."

"A visitor? *Here?*" Moyra frowned, her attention snapping to Gray. "Who is it?"

"Truly, lass, I've no idea. Mayhap you should get dressed and go downstairs to find out?"

"Aye, I will." She nodded, then frowned. "Ye said

William should also expect a visitor. Och! mon, dinna tell me 'tis . . . ?"

Gray sighed. "Aye, I'm afraid 'tis. Duff spotted Iain Douglas a few hours ago, then rode hellbent back to Smailholm to sound the alarm. While 'tis rumored my newest stepbrother has the fastest mount this side of the River Esk, methinks it doubtful the Douglas lingers far behind. The keep is preparing for the . . . er . . . *visit* as we speak."

Gray's attention shifted back to William; his brother's spine and shoulders had stiffened, his brown eyes narrowing warily. Gray turned toward the door. Directing his next words over his shoulder, at William, he said, "You'd do well to dress and come downstairs, too. With Olen away, all able bodies are needed to secure this place."

Gray left the room. The door closed behind him, much more gently this time.

Still clutching the blanket protectively beneath her chin, Moyra scooted to the side of the bed and swung her legs over the side. Her plaid and tunic lay in a hopelessly wrinkled heap atop the icy stone floor. Beneath the larger pile that was William's clothes.

Slipping off the bed, she bent at the waist and retrieved the pile, separating her garments from his, then tossing the latter across the bed to him.

She still didn't glance in his direction. She didn't dare. Feeling the heat of his eyes on her was distraction enough, as were Gray's words prowling her thoughts.

Unless you've a taste for siring bastards . . .

That she might have conceived William's bairn had

not occurred to Moyra. Oh, aye, she knew it should have, but it hadn't.

It occurred to her now, though, and the realization hit her with enough force to push the air from her lungs. Without her consent, her hand strayed to her abdomen. Her palm opened, her fingers splaying over the flat, firm expanse of flesh and muscle.

Flat and firm now, aye, but for how much longer? Was it possible . . . ?

Behind her, she heard the rustle of cloth that suggested William was dressing. Voices in the courtyard outside strayed in through the lone window. Rumbles of commotion echoed throughout the chambers on the floors below.

Somewhere in the keep, a visitor awaited her.

Not far from Smailholm's sturdy stone walls, the Douglas was coming for herself and William. Again. Och! but the man was relentless!

And yet . . .

The fingers over her abdomen flexed self-consciously.

Moyra shook her head, as though trying to dislodge her distracted thoughts and instead concentrate on the situation unfolding around her. Now was not the time for retrospect, it was the time for action, swift and sure.

Still . . .

Her chin lifted. Slowly, slowly, her head turned. Instinctively, and definitely against her better judgment, she directed her gaze to William.

He was standing at the opposite side of the bed, not dressed after all. His clothes hung limply from his left fist. The window at his back cast the sculpted angles of his face in dark, clinging shadows. Although 'twas impossible to tell exactly where he looked, somehow she knew. The feel of his eyes on her was a warm, tangible caress.

Moyra was aware of the precise instant his attention skimmed her shoulders, trailed down the length of her arm, settled finally upon the hand unconsciously cradling her middle, and settled there hard.

Tension crackled in the cold morning air between them.

Unspoken words played on slightly parted lips, but remained unsaid.

In this light, at this angle, 'twas futile to try to judge his expression. Not that she needed visual proof; anger and indecision rolled off him in waves, every bit as palpable as the feel of his eyes on her. Every bit as palpable as the fear and indecision that coiled throughout her own body.

She opened her mouth to say . . . something. She was never quite sure what, she simply knew she had to hear the sound of her own voice, had to somehow break the tension sizzling between them.

William held up his free hand, cutting her short before the first sound whispered past her lips. When he was sure she would remain silent, he used that hand to rake his fingers through his hair, hauling the bulk of the shaggy strands away from his face.

He shook his head, started to sigh, swallowed the breath midway, then shook his head again. "Nay, lass, not now. We've too much to do this morn to waste time discussing that which we cannot change. Once you've attended your visitor, and Gray and I have made sure the keep is secure, there will be plenty of time to discuss the matter. Mayhap by then, we'll even know what to say to each other. Lord knows, right now, I don't have the words."

Moyra nodded, suddenly not trusting her voice. Her hand dropped to her side, yet even as she dressed she noticed her palm still burned with the imprint of her own flesh.

Much the same way her mind continued to burn with the notions Gray Collingwood had kindled there.

Nineteen

She found him in a corner of the great hall; 'twas the only spot in the keep not teeming with activity.

Jared Elliot sat upon an unwelcomingly hard, straight-backed wooden chair. His back was to the wall. Attention carefully averted from his surroundings, he fixed his gaze upon a spot on the floor where gritty bits of mortar fused two cold stone slabs together. His spine was bowed, his shoulders slumped, his elbows rested atop the thin cushion of his thighs.

As though sensing her presence, he glanced up when his sister approached.

Moyra faltered in midstep. Her gaze raked her brother, noting his pallid complexion and the smudges of exhaustion beneath his eyes that looked like bruises. The hazel eyes themselves were red rimmed and bloodshot.

Her heart skipped a panicked beat. Her breathing wedged painfully in her throat like a handful of dirt. A sensation not unlike that of a fist's snapping reflexively closed spasmed the muscles around her heart.

"Jared . . . ?" Moyra asked, her voice thick with the fear gripping her. She completed the step she'd hesitated over, her pace quickening as she hurried to her brother's side. When he didn't answer, she reached for him. His shoulder felt too thin and prominent beneath her fingertips as she gripped him tightly. Even through the thick padding of his jack, her fingers dug into his flesh. Her Scots burr thickened with distress. "Dinna be sitting there staring at me like that. Talk tae me, Jared. Tell me what's happened."

"I think ye already be kenning it, lass," he replied, and his voice cracked. "Yer the one gifted with The Sight, after all."

" 'Tis nae a gift I cherish. And I know naught. I dinna e'en suspect anything at home was amiss." 'Twas true enough. What Moyra didn't say, but thought, was that her mind had been too occupied with worrying over William Armstrong for other thoughts—or visions—to tarry in it overlong. "Tell me it's nae our mother."

His answer, a mere sobering of his already alarmingly somber expression, was nonverbal, yet as substantial as if he'd spoken aloud.

Moyra inhaled sharply. A shiver curled down the length of her spine; the tremor spread rapidly throughout the rest of her body in ever-increasing waves. Hugging her arms tightly about her, she asked tightly, "Is she . . . ?" 'Twas her voice that cracked this time. She couldn't complete the sentence, couldn't even complete the thought.

Jared's answer was to close his eyes, wearily lower his head.

"Nay." Moyra shook her head, slowly at first, then with more force. *"Nay!"*

The people closest to her turned at the outburst,

glancing at her curiously. Moyra paid them no mind. The grip on her brother's shoulder went desperately tight. "Tell me 'tis nae true. Tell me 'tis naught but a cruel joke. Tell me . . . Och! Jared, I dinna care what ye tell me, so long as ye *dinna* tell me our mother is . . . is . . ."

"Dead," Jared said, cutting her short. His tone sounded abrupt and final and oddly flat to her ears. "Our mother is dead, Moyra. 'Tis nae a subject I'd e'er joke aboot."

He sighed, opened his eyes, looked at her.

The truth was there, easily read in the ghostly pallor of his cheeks, in the unshed tears blurring his painfully familiar hazel eyes.

Understanding surged through her like the rush of a mountain-fed stream.

Her mother was dead.

"When?" she asked, and her voice was cracking so badly now her words could barely be understood. "How?"

"The night before last. In her sleep. We dinna know how, although maun than one Elliot assumes 'twas a broken heart. One of the serving wenches found her"—he hesitated, the line of his jaw clamping around words he did not wish to voice, but knew he must—"found her body in the morn. She was fine the night before, but . . . If it sets yer mind tae rest, 'twas a maun peaceful passing."

"She dinna suffer?" Her throat closed around the words, and she had to concentrate very hard to push them forth. "Yer sure o' it?"

"Aye, lass, ver' sure."

Moyra reeled as the finality of it all settled around her like a thick, oppressive cloak.

Mo chreach, *her mother was* dead!

Unlike Jared, she did not try to conceal her tears or hold them in check; big, warm droplets pooled in her eyes, dripped over her lashes, splashed onto her cheeks before trickling down past the trembling line of her jaw.

A sob hitched in her chest. Another. She did not try to fight those, either. When the strength drained out of her legs, she collapsed weakly to her knees on the hard stone floor beside her brother.

Jared reached out with fingers that shook visibly. A single tear dripped down his cheek, even as the backs of his knuckles stroked a tentative line over the moisture glistening on her own.

When Moyra made no move to push him away, he cradled the back of her head with his hand and, turning toward her, pulled Moyra into a fierce embrace.

She hugged him tightly, crying in great, gulping sobs as the pain overtook her. Sharp and intense, the all-too-familiar grief stabbed into her from what felt like a thousand different angles. Had she been standing, she would have toppled over from the sheer force of the emotion. As it was, the only thing that kept her from sinking even further onto the floor was the solid strength of her brother's arms.

William found her shortly before noon, sitting beneath a thick-trunked, sprawling oak tree.

The tree's branches were depressingly bare of leaves, like skeletal arms reaching out to the cloud-strewn sky above. Her spine and the back of her head were propped wearily against the trunk. Her eyes were closed, but she wasn't asleep. Her breathing was choppy, and her brow pinched, as though the thoughts scrambling through her mind caused acute physical pain as well as harsh mental anguish.

From her slender shoulders hung a jack that was several sizes too big. The heavy leather and steel-padded coat engulfed her tiny body, making her look unusually small and fragile.

Gone was the woman who'd fearlessly stood toe-to-toe with the Douglas, exchanging pointed barbs. There was no stubbornness in the line of her jaw, no impudence in the set of her shell-pink lips. She looked vulnerable, he thought, and was reminded of an abandoned newborn kitten; frail and helpless, in desperate need of shelter and care.

A twig snapped under his bootheel.

If Moyra noticed she was no longer alone, she gave no outward indication.

William stopped beside her, hunkered down. Up close, he could smell the worn leather of the jack and, he thought, the salty scent of the tears streaming with silent dignity down her cheeks.

He reached out and, with the tip of his index finger, captured one of those tears, rubbed it into his skin. Warm and wet, it was quickly absorbed by the callused pad of his thumb and index finger.

"What can I do?" he asked gently.

"Bring me mum back tae me," she replied, and sniffled loudly. William found himself straining to hear; her voice was as soft as the cold breeze rustling the platinum wisps against her brow. "Tell me this is naught but a bad dream, a vision gone horribly amiss. Och! William, truth tae tell, I dinna care what ye do, so long as ye make it all go away."

"I cannot do that."

"Then there's naught I want of ye but tae go away and leave me in peace tae me grieving."

William hesitated, sighed, shook his head. "Nay, Moyra, I cannot do that, either."

She opened her eyes.

Their gazes met and held.

The pain he saw shimmering in the deep violet pools of her eyes was so intense it stole William's breath away. A dull, throbbing ache clamped around his heart; the sensation was as powerful as it was inexplicable.

Had he grown so close to this woman that he could actually feel her pain as though it were his own? Aye, 'twould seem so. The idea was frightening . . . yet not nearly so frightening as the strong, sure knowledge that, given the ability, he would take the pain away from her and shoulder it himself.

That 'twas the most altruistic notion he'd ever had, William didn't doubt or deny. He knew it as instinctively as he knew the sun would set, as instinctively as he knew each of Moyra's ragged breaths would mist the cold winter air separating them, as instinctively as he knew each of her quiet sobs was tearing a small but very real part out of him.

There was no sense of pride in the acknowledgment, only a sharp pang of regret that the ability to take away her pain was not within his grasp.

"There is one thing I can do for you, lass," he said finally. When her brows arched slightly, he continued,

"I can hold you whilst you cry. 'Tis not much, and well I know it, however—"

William was never given a chance to finish the statement. No sooner had the words slipped past his lips than Moyra thrust herself into his arms. Her own arms coiled about his neck, her fingers twisting into his hair so tightly his scalp burned with the pressure.

She pressed her cheek against his neck, and he felt the hot dampness of her tears streaming over his flesh. Stroking his open palm down her back, over her long platinum hair, he murmured, " 'Tis all right, love. Let it out. Cry until you've no tears left to cry. I promise you, Moyra, I'll not go anywhere. I'll stay right here and hold you."

And he did.

'Twas hard to believe she'd spent the better part of the last few hours crying, for when the tears started anew, they felt fresh, the pain inside every bit as biting and intense as when her brother had broken the heart-wrenching news to her.

Her sobs were quiet, but gut wrenching, as though they were torn from the very core of her. She clung to William, absorbing the feel of his strong arms around her, the security of his closeness.

Moyra didn't know how long she cried. Time had ceased to exist in any recognizable form. It seemed to take forever before the tears finally slowed, longer still for the sharp, stabbing pain inside to ease a wee bit. Her body gradually relaxed against William's.

True to his word, he did not leave her, did not once try to pull away. For that, Moyra was more grateful than she could ever have expressed.

At some point, he'd shifted positions; it was now

his back propped against the gritty tree trunk, while she was curled up snugly in his arms like a wounded pup. Their fronts were pressed together and she found herself sitting upon his muscle-hardened lap.

The comforting circle of his arms around her loosened slightly, but did not drop away. With William's every breath she could feel the easy lift and fall of his broad chest. Subconsciously, her own breathing slowed and regulated to match. His heart drummed a reassuringly steady beat beneath her open palm.

"Better?" he asked, after a few less emotional moments had slipped past. The time was marked by the stirring of branches overhead as a dove left its shelter and propelled itself into the cloudy gray sky.

"I feel . . . drained," Moyra replied, her lips moving against his neck. She pulled in a shuddering breath, released it on a sigh and shook her head. "I dinna think I'll e'er feel better."

"Aye, 'tis a feeling I know well. The same one I had after my father died. I was but a wee lad at the time, but even wee lads have long memories for pain so sharp." Moyra started to lift her head. The gentle pressure of his big, warm hand against the much smaller, cooler nape of her neck returned her cheek to the sculpted hollow beneath his shoulder. "The feeling will pass, Moyra. Eventually. If I can promise you naught else, I *can* I promise you that."

"I'm nae asking for any promises from ye," she said, fully aware that the intimation lent the conversation a subtle undertone not present a few seconds before. Did William realize it? Aye, she guessed by the way his arms stiffened around her that he did. Had he any idea that her abrupt swerve of topic was really naught more than a deeply rooted need to avoid her grief, and distract her mind from the pain cutting her up inside?

"You've a right to, you know. All things considered, Moyra, you've the right to ask for that promise . . . and more."

"Mayhap, but I'll nae. Ye dinna understand, do ye, William? Och! mon, let me explain. I dinna want yer promises. They be words and naught more. In fact, I dinna want a cursed thing from ye if 'tis nae freely given."

"Who says 'tis not—?"

"*Ye* do. Nae with words, aye, but then, ye dinna need words, dinna ye know? I saw yer face this morn when Gray mentioned yer obligation tae wed me. Ye looked"—she swiped away the remnants of tears clinging to her cheeks and took a thoughtful pause—"horrified." She nodded. "Aye, there's nae other way tae describe yer expression. 'Twas as though the idea of taking me as yer wife proved a worse fate than being caught by the Douglas with yer trews down and nae sword at the ready. Lizbet warned me 'twould be yer reaction. I dinna want tae believe her, but apparently she was right."

"Don't fool yourself, Moyra. And don't allow my mother to fool you, either. She doesn't know me nearly as well as she thinks she does." His tone was as stiff as the arms encircling her had become, as hard as the chest she rested against.

"I'm nae so sure. Judging by yer expression this morn, she knows ye maun well."

William shifted uncomfortably. "Truly, lass, now isn't the time—"

"And what better time could there be? With me mother d-d—" She sniffled loudly, then cleared her throat. Nay, she could not say it, not yet. 'Twas difficult enough to even *think* of the reality of it. "I'll be returning with Jared tae Glentroe Tower. He leaves early tomorrow morn. Och! William, dinna ye see? This is the ideal time tae discuss it. Dinna ye think it best tae settle things between us now, afore I leave?"

"We don't know for certain there's anything *to* settle. Yet. There's a good chance a few fortnights of time will show the urgency to even consider a union between us has passed."

It was Moyra's turn to stiffen. "Ye mean if I'm nae carrying yer bairn, we'll know it then and ye'll have nae need to worry o'er having tae wed me?"

"Aye! Er, nay. Blast it, Moyra, I was trying to not be so crass about it."

"Methinks crass isna so bad. At least it tells me exactly where I stand. And with ye, I maun obviously stand nowhere at all."

The pain that had engulfed Moyra when she'd first sought out this peaceful, secluded place suddenly channeled into a different, yet equally as potent, emotion.

Anger.

Hot bursts of fury pumped through her bloodstream; the emotion radiated swiftly throughout the rest of her until she was literally shaking from the intensity of it.

Moyra pushed away from William, stood. Her knees still felt weak and shaky, but stable enough to support her weight as, small fists planted firmly atop the slender curves of her hips, she glared down at the top of his sandy blond head. "Yer an egotistical wretch, William Armstrong. Tae listen tae ye, ye'd think this decision is entirely yers and I've nae say in it at all. Weel, I've a wee bit o' news for ye. 'Tis nae so. Only a self-centered fool would think I'd want tae marry a nae good reiver like yeself, e'en if I was carrying yer bairn. Mark me words, mon, I'd rather spend the rest of me days alone than spend them with a mon who doesna want me!"

The too-large jack shifted baggily around her shoulders as she abruptly spun on her heel and began to stalk away.

"Moyra—"

She held up a hand, the gesture cutting him short, but continued walking, not turning around to face him again. She didn't dare. To do so would be to show him the tears in her eyes—tears that were not for her mother this time. He'd see how badly he'd hurt her and, heaven help her, Moyra refused to give the ogre that much satisfaction. "Nay, William, I dinna want tae hear another word!"

"But—"

"Nay!" Shaking her head, Moyra quickened her pace, disappearing around one thick tree trunk, then another. She walked blindly, not caring in which direction she went. The need to get away from him was too great, the pain roiling inside of her too intense.

He wanted her gone. Abolished from his life before he was forced to participate in a marriage he obviously wanted no part of. William Armstrong could not have been more clear about his feelings if he'd carved them into her forehead and—

Mo chreach, *it hurt!*

Swallowing back a sob, and plowing sightlessly past

one winter-bare tree after another, Moyra decided that satisfying his wishes was easy enough to do.

She would leave with Jared in the morn. As soon as Smailholm's walls were a good distance behind her, she would forget that William Armstrong ever existed. The devil could take him to Hades for all she cared, she never wanted to see his arrogant face again!

Unless you've a taste for siring bastards . . .

The words echoed in her ears, making her miss a step. Her ankle twisted beneath her. She stumbled, almost falling to the cold, hard ground. Almost.

What if Gray Collingwood's prediction came to pass? What if she *was* carrying William's bairn? Would William want any more to do with his child than he wanted to do with its mother?

Moyra shoved a stray strand of hair back from her brow and shook her head. Her brow pinched thoughtfully.

The truth of the matter was, even if William's seed had taken root inside her, if 'twas even now beginning to dig in its roots and flourish . . . did he truly need to know about it?

Nay! She was leaving with Jared at dawn, taking herself away from Smailholm, away from William. Surely there was enough tumultuous distance separating Smailholm from Glentroe Tower that the news would probably never reach this far.

In which case, her secret would be safe. William need never know, *unless she told him,* and she would not do that.

Her entire life Moyra had watched her mother and father. As a child she'd basked in the love they'd shared, had vowed to never settle for anything less than the same for herself—and never, *never* with a reiver like her da!

If she had naught else, she had her dignity, and she clung to it tenaciously. She would not force a man to marry her when he did not love nor want her, even if only for the sake of giving her own bairn a name. Her staunch Elliot pride ran too deep and sure to ever allow it.

There were worse fates in life than being labeled a bastard. Being locked into a loveless marriage was one of them.

The decision, Moyra realized as she began walking once more, slower this time, was not William's. It was entirely her own. One she would make when and if the time came. Alone.

Twenty

The suspense was palpable, tearing him up on the inside.

True to her word, Moyra left for Glentroe Tower the following morning with Jared. She'd not spared so much as a word of goodbye to anyone but Lizbet and Gray.

William had not seen nor heard from her since.

Three fortnights slipped past with agonizing slowness.

The brisk chill of winter gradually surrendered to the warm, seemingly incessant rain of spring. Hillsides and valleys exchanged their winter gray for thick, lush green. Reivers, trapped for a season inside their keeps, shook off their winter listlessness and emerged with deadly intent. 'Twas a perfect time to replenish dwindling supplies with the booty lifted from the stores of more prosperous friends and enemies.

March Wardens on both sides of the Border renewed their efforts to maintain order and dole out justice. As was their habit, the reivers arrogantly ignored them. Raiding was not as bad as it had been in previous years, however, the season had just begun.

For his own part, William found no pleasure in the

changing seasons, nor any inclination to ride against his neighbors. Still chafing at the humiliation doled out to him by the Douglas when he'd launched his first raid, William had no taste for a repeat performance. The healed wound in his shoulder still ached when he overexerted himself, a firm reminder of how lucky he'd been that horrible night in Wyndehaghen.

The night he'd met Moyra Elliot.

Moyra Elliot.

Blast it! Why could he not get that woman out of his mind?!

The slender, platinum-haired vixen haunted his dreams, plagued his thoughts even when he was restlessly wide awake. Wondering if she did indeed carry his bairn accounted for only a small portion of the time his thoughts dwelled upon her. More often, he found himself remembering with bittersweet longing the way her rose-petal-soft inner thighs felt straddling his hips, or the way her warm, wet mouth opened, willing and hungry beneath his . . .

If he'd suffered from lust alone, William thought he might have been better able to put the matter into perspective. Lust was a sensation a man was integrally familiar with, one he could recognize instantly and know intuitively how to control.

But *this* . . .

Well, 'twasn't merely lust he felt when he thought about Moyra. He only wished his emotions were so simple! Nay, there was more to it. Much more.

Oh, aye, he'd be lying if he said there wasn't an undeniable hardening in his groin when he remembered the intimacy of their time together. However, there was an equally intense tightening in the muscles surrounding his heart when he remembered infinitely more simple things.

The sound of her laughter.

The glimpse of her smile.

When he saw a bed of heather, he thought of the unique color and shape of her eyes. When he glimpsed a slant of moonlight streaming in through his bedchamber window—*the same bedchamber in which they'd shared a long, hot night of passion*—he remembered the way her thick platinum hair flowed down the delicate length of her back like a drift of freshly fallen, unblemished snow. A juicy red apple reminded him of her lips, a freshly laundered sheet of her skin. He could not hear a Scots woman speak without hearing Moyra's voice echo hauntingly in his ears. Unfortunately, residing as he was in his mother's newest home on *this* side of the Border, a Scots accent was something he'd heard daily these last few fortnights.

"I propose a trade."

The sound of his stepbrother's voice startled William back to the present. He glanced up sharply, in time to see Gray slam a tankard down on the table directly in front of him. The bottom of the ceramic mug collided with the pitched wood with a bang that echoed throughout the deserted great hall. The rich amber contents frothed over the top and over Gray's hand.

William's gaze shifted warily between the tankard and Gray, then back and forth once more. One sandy blond brow arched curiously high. "Trade what for what?"

"I'll wager the contents of that tankard"—Gray waved a hand at the mug in question—"for whatever 'tis on your mind."

"What makes you think anything is on my mind?"

Gray smiled, a sloppy tilt of one corner of his mouth. His silvery eyes glistened, and when he spoke there was a distinct slur to his words. That he was well into his cups would be obvious to a blind man. "Men rarely seek out an empty hall, in the wee hours of the morning no less, when they've nothing of import on their minds, brother. They seek out their beds and sleep most soundly."

"You're here," William pointed out.

"Aye, I am." Gray sighed, and smothered a yawn with the back of his fist. "Hence, I know whereof I speak. Tell me, Willie, what are you doing up and about so late? Yet again. And does this recent bout of insomnia have aught to do with a certain violet-eyed, platinum-haired temptress who may or may not be—?"

"Have a care, Gray," William snapped, his tone suddenly low and deep and threatening. "I don't wish to discuss it."

"Ah, well, more's the pity, because I *do*. I've watched you brood about this place for the past several fortnights, and, quite frankly, I've had a belly full of it. And I'm not the only one. You're obviously not handling the situation very well on your own, so I've decided to help you."

"How . . . generous of you."

Gray nodded, as though William hadn't uttered the words in a voice dripping sarcasm. "You're my

brother, 'tis the least I can do. Now, tell me, when
was the last time you spoke to the wench?"

"I haven't."

"Since . . . ?"

"She left with her brother."

It was Gray's turn to look surprised; one thick, dark
eyebrow cocked high with skepticism. "God's blood,
Willie, that's been"——he hesitated, sloppily pursing his
lips as he tried to get his whisky-soaked mind to count,
a chore he quickly abandoned——"well, 'tis been quite
a while."

"I don't need you to tell me how long 'tis been,
Gray. Believe me, I'm aware of every minute of it."

"Aye, I'm sure you are."

Reaching out, William grabbed the tankard and, lifting it to his lips, swallowed a deep gulp. The whiskey
made his eyes water as it cut a fiery path down his
throat. He choked back a harsh cough, then took another equally long drink. When he finally settled the
tankard back atop the table, the contents were half
gone; the rest swirled in a nice, hot pool in his stomach.

William's attention, which had settled on the tankard, lifted. His gaze locked with Gray's.

"Ah, Willie," Gray said, his drunken smile widen-
ing, "I was wondering how long 'twould take. Truth
to tell, I thought 'twould happen long before now."

"What are you talking about?"

"You. And Moyra Elliot. You've fallen in love with
the wench."

"You're drunk, Gray. You don't know what you're
talking about." William's eyes narrowed. "I'm not in
love with her."

"Drunk, mayhap, but not blind. And aren't you?"

"Bloody hell, no!"

The lopsided grin locked itself firmly back into place on Gray's mouth. "Methinks thou dost protest too much."

"Excuse me?"

"Never mind. 'Tis something I read by a new poet back in England." Gray shrugged and reached for the tankard. It took two attempts before he managed to wrap his thick fingers around the handle. "Listen to yourself, Willie. Hear yourself as others do. You're far too adamant about *not* being in love with the lass to be convincing."

"I've no need to convince you of—"

"Nay, of course not. You've no need to convince *me* of anything." Gray leveled him a sharp, challenging glance. "You need to convince *yourself.*"

Aye, William thought as he stole the tankard from his brother's whiskey-slackened grasp, and wasn't that precisely the problem? He could deny his feelings for an eternity or more, but what would it accomplish? He'd be fooling only himself, and it would not make them go away . . .

William shook his head. For the sake of his rapidly dwindling sanity, he swerved his thoughts, and the conversation, in a different direction. "You've problems of your own to worry over, Gray. I've heard rumors that Elizabeth misses her latest favorite."

"Aye, I've heard the same. 'Tis also rumored she's sent men out to scour both sides of the Border for me. Their orders are to drag me back to court using as much force as is necessary. I've my doubts if it's true or not. Elizabeth wasn't *that* captivated by me."

As he spoke, Gray reached out and again stole the tankard back. The glint in his eyes as he lifted the rim to his mouth, his gaze still holding William's, said that he was well aware of the abrupt change of topic . . . and the need for it.

"Ye have tae tell him, lass."

"I *dinna.*" Moyra wrinkled her nose as, using her spoon like a shovel, she dumped a mound of porridge from one side of the bowl to the other. She hadn't eaten a bite of the thick, lumpy concoction, however, nor did she plan to. The topic of discussion had spoiled her appetite.

Her gaze lifted, meeting Kenny's, and her eyes shimmered with a stubbornness that was innately Elliot. "I've a wee bit of news for ye, lad. Where William Armstrong is concerned, I dinna *have* tae do anything."

Kenny scowled at his sister. Och! but she was a stubborn one! Reminded him of his da in that respect. "He has a right tae know, Moyra."

"And what would *ye,* a mere lad, know about a mon's rights? Ye've yet tae sprout yer first whisker!"

"That isna fair." His slender chest puffed with youthful indignation even as he spooned another bite of porridge into his mouth. He chewed thoughtfully, his scowl deepening. "I'm old enough tae know the difference between right and wrong. And nae telling him is maun certainly wrong."

"Says ye. I disagree."

"Were she alive, mother would have told ye the way of it."

Moyra's jaw hardened. "Mother is not alive. We buried her fortnights ago. She . . ."

Her words trailed away. The subject of their mother was still a tender one. Not something she spoke of often. As she'd done after her father died, Moyra preferred to keep her grief private, not showing her pain to the outside world but instead tucking it away inside of her, then pulling it out like a neglected toy and examining it more closely only when there was no one around to see.

"I'm telling ye, mother would ne'er have kept such a secret from da."

"True," Moyra replied, her voice soft and haunted. "But I'm nae our mother, and William Armstrong is"—*too much like our da for me peace of mind*—"nae at all like our da."

"He's a reiver, just like da."

"Aye, and thank ye e'er so much for reminding me!" At the wounded look in her brother's eyes, Moyra reached out and covered the back of his young hand with her fingers. "Och! Kenny, 'tis sorry I am tae snap at ye like that. I'm . . . well, I'm nae feeling meself these days."

" 'Twould seem no one in this keep is. Jared has been snarling at everyone who crosses his path for the better part of a fortnight, as well."

Jared.

Moyra sighed. If anything "good" had come from her mother's death, 'twas the tentative peace she'd forged with her older brother. They'd not made up, exactly, however, their shared grief fashioned a bridge between their anger, giving them a common ground upon which to meet.

She'd be lying if she didn't admit to still blaming Jared for their father's death. She thought she always would. Yet lately she'd come to realize just how deeply he grieved over the loss, as deeply as she did, and her fury with him had subsided to a tolerable level. Aye, it had been only at Jared's insistence that their father participated in the raid that took his life. That was an undeniable fact. Yet in the last few fortnights she'd come to see how deeply the mistake haunted Jared, how it would continue to haunt him for the rest of his life. Was that not punishment enough?

"Speaking of Jared . . ." She glanced around the hall, which was deserted except for the two of them. "Where is he? I've not seen him all morn."

"Nor will you for several more. He's ridden for Carlisle. Again."

"Really? Och! that's the second time in as many fortnights." Moyra stopped shoveling her porridge. It was her turn to frown. "And what, I wonder, is so interesting in Carlisle that he'd feel the need tae return so soon?"

"Methinks her name is Eilidh," Kenny replied. "Eilidh Ridley."

The lift and fall of his bairnishly thin shoulders was endearingly sweet and innocent, Moyra thought, although she would never tell him so. He struggled so hard to give the impression of maturity that she simply didn't have the heart to tell him how far he missed the mark. "Nay, Kenny, ye maun be mistaken. The Ridleys live on the wrong side of the Border. Jared would never have anything tae do with a Sassenach lass. Mayhap Lord Dacre called him there tae discuss a complaint. The reivers are starting tae ride again, dinna ye know? Or he may have gone tae file a complaint himself?"

"If ye say so," Kenny replied halfheartedly. Finished with his meal, he pushed the empty bowl aside. "After all, Moyra, ye know best aboot all, do ye nae?"

"And what the devil is that supposed tae mean?" But, of course, Moyra already knew. Much like her thoughts of late, the conversation had traveled full circle . . . returning once more to William Armstrong.

'Twas a topic she did not care to discuss.

She pushed her own bowl aside; the container was still as full as when she'd ladled the sticky portion of porridge from the cook's kettle. The wooden bench scraped the stone floor as she stood.

Glancing down at her brother, she said crisply, "I'll be taking Demon out for a ride now."

That stated, she quit the hall before Kenny could again start lecturing her on what she should and should not do.

Pity her thoughts refused to so easily quit worrying over the problem itself. The problem that was William Armstrong.

Like a pesky fly, thoughts of him came back to taunt her.

Och! now, that wasn't quite true, was it?

Nay, 'twasn't. If she was to be honest with herself, Moyra would have to admit that in order for thoughts of William to come *back,* they would need to have *left* to begin with. They never had.

Three fortnights ago, to the very day, she'd left Smailholm and William Armstrong behind. At the time, she'd been determined to put him out of her life, out of her thoughts, forever. While she'd accomplished the former, the latter proved a task that even she was not up for.

The man was the devil incarnate; he haunted her.

She could not lay her head upon her pillow and close her eyes at night without thinking of when she'd found him wounded in her tunnels. In the darkness behind her closed eyelids, she could feel his voice wrap around her; the tone warm and comfortable and reassuring, like a thick, familiar coat settling over her trembling shoulders on a cold winter day, chasing the chilly emptiness away.

As if thinking about him—dreaming about him, *fantasizing* about him!—at night was not bad enough, during the day she thought she saw him. Twice, in the village outside the keep, she'd thought to spot him moving amongst the other men. Once her heart had jerked painfully in her chest when she'd been walking by a thatched-roof cottage and heard the abrasive tone of a clearly Sassenach voice.

It hadn't been William, of course. She'd discovered the mistake soon enough. Yet the incident had taken her by surprise, awakened her harshly to the void of emptiness stretching out inside her. She'd spent the remainder of the day trying to regain her composure. And failing miserably.

Now, as she left the keep and stepped into the bright midday sunlight—just a few shades lighter than William Armstrong's hair—Moyra remembered all too vividly the surge of joy that had swept over

her when she'd thought William had come to Glentroe
Tower.

For her?

To have believed, even for a moment, that he would
do such a thing . . .

Oh, what a fool she was!

He hadn't come for her. Nor would he. When she
did not contact him after the required time had passed,
he would drink a toast or two to his incredible luck
at escaping a hastily arranged, loveless marriage, and
forget all about her. She was convinced of it.

The thought made the black, aching emptiness inside her feel immense. Like an impossibly wide, un-
breachable cavern. Unlike anything as substantial as
a cavern, however, this obscure, inner emptiness
brought with it a profound, physical pain so intense it
stole her breath away.

Moyra stopped in the middle of the courtyard. Her
knees suddenly felt too weak and shaky to carry her
another step. Sucking in a deep breath, she closed her
eyes. She could hear people milling around as they
went about their daily chores, but she paid them no
mind. Instead, she lifted her chin, forcing herself to
concentrate on the sunshine on her face, and all the
while hoping the warmth could somehow manage to
burn all thoughts of William Armstrong out of her
mind.

It didn't.

Instead, she was reminded of the feel of William's
hands gliding over her naked body. Warm and gentle,
callused and insistent. His touch was like—

Och! What was she doing? She was supposed to be
driving thoughts of him *out* of her mind, not lingering

upon them with a wistfulness usually reserved for ado-
lescents!

Muttering a fine Gaelic curse beneath her breath,
Moyra opened her eyes. She took one step toward the
stables, thinking that a long, hard ride on Demon was
exactly what she needed. The exertion would do her
a world of good and, with luck, tire her to the point
where tonight's sleep would be deep and blessedly
dreamless.

She progressed no farther than that single step.

Her attention had strayed randomly to the gate
leading out of the courtyard, and into the rolling hills
beyond. And there it froze. More precisely, her shock-
widened gaze attached itself to the tall, broad figure
who was leading his mount through the carved stone
archway.

The muscles in Moyra's jaw must have abruptly
stopped working, for she felt her mouth sag open.
She blinked hard. Twice. Surely the image was nothing more than a vision, or a trick of the light from
her having stepped so suddenly outdoors. Wasn't
it . . . ?

Nay, it couldn't be! As she watched, unable to tear
her attention away, the vision in question stopped just
inside the gate and exchanged words with one of
Jared's men.

Images did not talk. Nor did visions. And even if
they did, no one ever talked back to them. Yet Jared's
man was doing exactly that, which could only mean
one thing.

"Mo chreach!" The familiar words slipped unnoticed past the trembling fingers Moyra pressed to her
equally trembling lips.

As though he sensed her stare, William Armstrong glanced away from the man with whom he was speaking. His gaze did not search the courtyard, did not scan faces. It went directly to Moyra Elliot.

Twenty-one

Moyra blinked hard.

Twice.

A third time.

Had thoughts of William Armstrong somehow managed to conjure the man up? Was the virile male image of him naught more than a vision sent to taunt her?

Och! and shouldn't she be so lucky?

Nay, the man standing only a short distance away from her was no image. Images did not grow a day's worth of whiskers, nor did they look so frightfully . . . aye, well, so frightfully *good!*

The man was as real as the hard-packed dirt Moyra's feet suddenly felt bonded to. If her throbbing heartbeat didn't tell her the truth of it, the way the man talking to William smiled, nodded, then whacked him soundly on the shoulder—so hard the slap echoed in her ears—most certainly did.

William Armstrong was here.

In Glentroe Tower.

Moyra had dreamed of this moment. Fantasized about it. *Yearned for it.* In the long, dark, lonely hours between dusk and dawn she'd clutched her crumpled blankets tightly to her body, imagining the cold, life-less wad of cloth to be William's body.

Although the prospect had always seemed dim, she'd wondered how she would react if she were ever to come face-to-face with him again.

Now that the dream had ended and the sharp truth of reality began—now that William was actually *here*—och! well, the joyous reaction she'd dreamt of experiencing scattered like thick ground fog before a harsh morning sun.

'Twas all well and good to dream of abandoning all thought and reason, of throwing herself into his arms while she slept, but to think of it while she was *awake* and *sensible* . . .

The reaction that pulsed through her was a marked contrast to what Moyra had imagined it would be. 'Twas harder, hotter and so all-consuming she had no choice but to spin on her heel and turn away from it before the bitter flames consumed her.

Gravel crunched beneath her heels as she swiftly retraced her steps to the keep. Any plans for riding Demon were promptly forgotten, overridden by a sudden, desperate need to run.

She almost made it to the doorway.

Almost.

Moyra's trembling fingers were in the process of gripping the latch when she felt stronger, untrembling, *familiar* fingers close around her upper arm. Her mind flashed her a memory of that night in the tunnel, when she'd found him.

His grip now was equally as firm, the tug intracta-ble. Before she could stop it or utter a refusal, she felt herself being spun back around.

Her breath caught in her throat when she came face-to-face with William's chest. A faded gray tunic covered that broad expanse; the thin sheet of cloth could not conceal the intriguing play of muscles beneath. She couldn't see it, yet she was very much aware of the wound in his shoulder, now well healed.

'Twas a chest her fingers had explored to its fullest not so long ago. A chest her fingers longed to reacquaint themselves with and explore anew.

Closing her hands into tight fists at her sides, Moyra let her gaze travel upward. The shaggy fringe of his hair grazed the impressive breadth of his shoulders. A pulse drummed at the base of his throat, the tempo rough and erratic. The sculpted line of his jaw was harder than the thick oak door Moyra leaned weakly back against.

Her attention settled finally on his face. A frown creased her brow. William's complexion was pale; amidst the sharp planes and angles, his face looked haggard. The remnants of more than a few sleepless nights left smudges beneath his dark brown eyes, while the eyes themselves were heavy lidded, red rimmed and bloodshot. The vague scent of whiskey lingered on him.

All in all, he looked like hell.

Nay, that was a lie. Pale and haggard he may be, yet to her wistful eyes he looked like heaven.

Thankful for the firm support of the door behind her, Moyra lifted her chin. Her gaze met and locked with his.

There was a shimmer of emotion in William's dark eyes that she couldn't quite define. Exhaustion? Longing? A combination of both? Or was that nothing more than wishful thinking on her part?

"Ye've traveled all this way for naught," she said finally. Her voice rang crisp and clear on the warm morning air, its tone calm, collected, colder than the winter so recently past. 'Twas surprising, that . . . especially since her insides felt so warm and weak and quivery beyond reason. "I'm nae carrying yer bairn."

He cocked one sandy blond brow high. 'Twas the only outward sign he was startled by her bluntness. The shimmer in his eyes changed almost imperceptibly as his hand released her arm.

Moyra's own eyes narrowed assessively. Mayhap she'd been mistaken? Mayhap the emotion she saw playing in those devilishly dark eyes was neither exhaustion nor longing after all, but hopefulness melting away to disappointment? Och! aye, and she was really stodgy old Queen Bess . . . 'twas about as likely!

"Weel?" she said when he continued to stand there, silent and staring. "What are ye waiting for? I've told ye what ye came tae hear, there's nae need tae tarry. If ye leave right now and ride hard, ye can make Smailholm by dawn tomorrow." She nodded curtly to the gate behind him, but her gaze never left his. "The exit is that way. Should ye nae be remounting that huge horse of yers and leaving?"

"Aye," he replied, and Moyra tried to ignore the way his breath misted warmly over her upturned face as he spoke. Tried to, but couldn't. "Thank you, lass, but I know exactly what I *should* be doing."

"Do ye? Och, weel, why are ye nae doing it?" Hopeful, she felt her heart skip a beat. Swallowing hard, she squelched the shiver of anticipation rippling through her.

"That I don't know." He hesitated thoughtfully, then shook his head. "Now that I'm here, I find I've no desire to leave."

"Ye speak in riddles." Her frown deepened. "Truly, there's nae reason for ye tae stay."

"Isn't there?"

Again, Moyra's heart skipped a beat; hope radiated through her, warming her in ways she hadn't been warmed in several fortnights. Not since that rapturous night when this man had held her in his strong, comforting arms. This time, the feeling was much harder to squelch, and impossible to ignore. Her voice cracked slightly when she said, "Y-Ye play a sore cruel game with me, William. I'll warn ye now, I'll nae play along."

"Is this a game?" he asked and, lifting his hand, cradled her cheek in the cup of his palm.

His flesh was warm and rough against her much cooler, much softer skin. Not turning her head and nuzzling instinctively into it took more self-control than Moyra thought she possessed, but she managed it. Barely.

"Or this?" he asked as, angling his head, he lowered his mouth to hers.

The kiss, if it could truly be labeled such, was soft and fleeting and more gentle than the stirring of a dove's wings. His breath kissed her skin, making it burn and tingle, even as his lips brushed teasingly back and forth over her own.

He didn't close his eyes.

She didn't close hers.

Their gazes were still locked when the tip of his tongue skated over her full, moist lower lip. A lip that quivered in response.

Only a moment before Moyra had been glad for the door pressing hard against her back, holding her upright. Now she resented it. Were the door not there she could have stumbled backward and escaped the confusion that was William Armstrong's kiss. With the door there, she had no ready escape. She could not back up, and William's broad, virile body blocked her from moving forward.

She was trapped.

Nay, that wasn't quite right. Creatures who were truly trapped did not feel sparks of desire kindling deep down inside them . . . did they?

To not return his kiss with all the pent-up passion burning inside her strained Moyra's normally good self-control to the limit. She longed to wrap her arms around his neck, pull him closer, melt right into him. She wanted to meet the tentative strokes of his tongue, to deepen the kiss until he felt as weak and dizzy as she did.

His chest was so close; if she splayed her hands over the center of it, would she feel his heartbeat drum against her fingertips? And would its rhythm be as wild and erratic as her own?

Did he sense her vacillation, somehow feel the white-hot need clawing her up on the inside? He must have, for his hands stroked down the lengths of her arms and his fingers wrapped around her wrists, tugging her hands upward until the outer sides of her palms rested against his breastbone. Of their own accord, her trembling fingers opened, and her palms turned inward until they were pillowed atop the hard, hot expanse of his chest.

He captured her sigh with his mouth.

'Twas madness to let him kiss her this way, here, where anyone could stumble upon them and see. Yet the door she leaned against was tucked into a shaded, stony crook at the side of the keep. No one was close enough to see. Or to stop them.

A blessing or a curse? Moyra wondered vaguely, in that corner of her mind still rational enough to wonder at anything. She decided 'twas both.

As she'd imagined it would, the beat of his heart felt strong and irregular beneath her abruptly sensitive fingertips. Wonderful. It felt wonderful. In her dreams she'd never imagined details—the beating of his heart, the feel of his breaths on her face, the way the heat of his body penetrated her clothes and warmed her more thoroughly than the strong, midmorning sun.

The reality of it all was shocking—a thousand times more potent than all of her midnight fantasies woven together. Her head spun even as she opened her mouth beneath his, let the tip of her tongue play with the tip of his, teasing and coaxing him deeper.

He groaned, low and deep in his throat, as though he'd also dreamed of their next kiss and had also found the reality more shocking than he could have imagined.

He swayed forward, his chest coming into contact with hers, pushing her more firmly against the door. She couldn't decide which felt more solid: the door pressing against her back, or the hard male chest pressing against her front. In another instant, she ceased to wonder about it.

William had let go of her wrist, slid his hands around her waist. He lightly stroked the line of her spine before closing his fingers around thick fistfuls of the coarse plaid at her hips. He tugged, pulling the front of her hips hard against the front of his, and his breathing went choppy.

"Madness," she whispered against his mouth, even as her eyes fluttered closed. " 'Tis pure madness tae let ye kiss me this way."

"Aye," he agreed. His mouth was still against hers; she enjoyed feeling the way his lips moved when he formed the words. " 'Tis reckless. 'Tis indecent. And 'tis not at all what I came here for, Moyra."

The statement, no matter how breathlessly he rasped it, reminded her painfully of what he *had* come for. To find out if she carried his bairn, and for no other reason than that. Certainly not to tell her he missed her, wanted her . . . loved her.

The realization poured over Moyra like a bucket of icy mountain water. She stiffened in his arms. The hands that had been loosely splayed atop his chest now went rigid. She shoved, trying to push him away. Useless. Trying to move a man of William Armstrong's size and strength when he didn't want to be budged was akin to single-handedly relocating the towering stone keep at her back. 'Twas impossible.

Lifting her chin, she used the little space available between the back of her head and the door to dislodge his mouth from hers. Her voice, when it came, sounded breathless and strained, even to her own ears. "Let me go!"

"Nay."

"Dinna toy with me, William. I mean it. Let me go. Now. *This instant!* If ye dinna, I'll screa—"

His mouth closed over hers once more, sealing the rest of the threat on her tongue.

Unlike the last, this kiss was hard and ruthless and draining. His arms crushed her to him. She didn't struggle; suddenly, she didn't have the willpower for it.

Or the desire.

Not when he held her so very closely, as though he never intended to let her go again. Not when his mouth consumed hers with a force that obliterated her reasons to push him away. Not when she'd longed for this moment for what felt like an incredibly long, lonely lifetime . . .

Her parents had often kissed like this, deeply and with a heartfelt, barely restrained passion that was a flagrant display of the love they shared. As a child, Moyra had watched the way they touched, the way they gazed at each other when they thought no one saw, the way they put their heads together and laughed with such easy abandon.

Until she'd met William Armstrong, it had never occurred to Moyra that love could be anything but light and uncomplicated. Easy. Natural. Certainly 'twas not supposed to be a struggle. 'Twas not supposed to cause a pain so deep and intense and all-consuming it rivaled that of the losses she'd so recently suffered.

Love . . . ?

It seemed to take forever before William pulled back, easing the kiss enough for them both to catch their breath. Her small body felt good in his arms; warm and wonderful and oh, so very right. Her soft curves fit the hard planes and angles of his body to perfection.

He'd been more than a wee bit soused when, thanks to Gray's encouragement, he'd ridden from Smailholm with the intent of finding out whether or not Moyra carried his babe. Two hours out, as he'd passed through a ragged-looking village, he'd learned that the Douglas had launched a successful raid. Against Smailholm. The reiver had captured several Pringles. Gray was one. Thankfully, death had not been his stepbrother's fate. Rather, the Douglas had decided on a fate even worse . . . he'd sent Gray back to Elizabeth.

Knowing there was naught he could do about it even if he did turn back, William had ridden on.

By the time morning had broken, he'd been nursing a hangover that had made even the roots of his hair hurt. Yet he hadn't stopped, hadn't even slowed. The need to know had been overpoweringly strong, clawing at him for weeks; it had taken very little instigation on Gray's part to bring the emotion to a head and set William's course of action.

It hadn't occurred to him that the Douglas, upon not finding William at Smailholm, could have set out after him. Either the man had not, or William was simply too far ahead to be overtaken.

Whatever the reason, William's focus had been so intent on reaching Moyra Elliot that it wasn't until he'd finally breached the thick, safe stone walls of Glentroe Tower that the idea of the Douglas in hot pursuit had crossed his mind. And even then, only in passing. Rather, the entire time he rode, his thoughts

had been consumed with his platinum-haired temptress.

Then, across the sunlit courtyard, he'd caught a
glimpse of her. His heart had skipped a beat before
thundering to life in his chest; the harsh pounding had
reawakened the dull ache in his head, but the pain
there paled in significance when compared to the ache
that squeezed like a fist around his heart as he
watched her violet eyes widen, watched her delicately
molded cheeks drain of color . . . watched her spin
on her heel and hurry back toward the keep.

She was running away from him!

The thought made something inside of William
snap.

His need to go after her was no longer an urge, but
a strong, blinding *force.* She was so close, yet she
seemed an eternity away! As though he'd been hooked
by an invisible string, yanking him reluctantly forward,
he'd felt himself placing one foot in front of the other,
clearing the scant distance separating them.

There was no way to describe the emotion that shot
through William when he'd reached out, wrapped his
fingers around her slender upper arm. Words were inadequate, the emotion too overwhelming and strong.

His grip had instantly molded to the shape of her
arm, the heat of the skin beneath her tunic warming
his palm in ways he'd only dreamed about. The heat
had seeped up his arm, spread in waves throughout
the rest of his body. It melted away his concern for
his stepbrother, melted away the remnants of his hangover, melted away his anger . . . indeed, it had melted
away everything but the bittersweet knowledge that he
was touching Moyra.

Again.

Finally.

Kissing her had been a mistake, but God help him, he hadn't been able to resist. The need had been too strong to ignore or deny. He had to know if she tasted as good as he remembered, if she would respond with the same wild abandon that had kept him awake for too many long, sleepless nights to count.

She had.

The urgency in her kiss had been a tangible thing, matching his own and taking it to unheard of heights. Heights he wanted them both to soar to together.

'Twas then William realized he was lost.

Holding her in his arms again, kissing her so very deeply when he'd thought never to hold and kiss her again . . . oh, aye, he knew with the same surety he knew his own name that he never wanted to *stop* holding her, never wanted to *stop* kissing her . . . never again.

Now, he glanced down at Moyra's upturned face—her cheeks were rosy with color, her violet eyes dazed with ill-suppressed passion, mixed liberally with restrained fury—and briefly considered turning away.

Remount. Ride back to Smailholm. Quickly. While I still have the presence of mind to do it!

Yet he knew he could not. The idea caused a pain to run jaggedly down the length of him, pushing the breath from his lungs.

In the hours he'd spent riding toward Glentroe Tower, William had told himself his reason to seek Moyra out was nothing more complicated than the need to discover if she carried his babe. What other reason could there be? Now he knew, and the sheer force of the unexpected discovery was staggering.

"Are ye ill, William?" Moyra asked, her voice equal parts leeriness and concern. "Ye dinna look well. Yer cheeks be maun pale than a freshly shorn sheep, yer breathing is hard and irregular and . . . aye, ye be swaying like ye just stepped off a ship and havena found yer land legs yet."

"I'm fine." His voice sounded weak and shaky, entirely unconvincing.

"Ye *dinna* look fine tae me. Ye look dreadful. Mayhap ye should sit down for a wee bit? Have ye broken yer fast this morn?"

He shook his head and took a small step back, putting some much-needed space between them. "I don't need to sit, or to eat."

"Then let me draw ye a cool drink of water from the well."

"Nay, I don't need that, either."

"Och! mon, then what *do* ye need?"

"You."

Moyra gaped at him. She shook her head, as though to clear it; the thick platinum braid trailing down her spine swayed against her hips. "Wh-what did ye say? Repeat yeself," she demanded, "for I dinna think I heard ye correctly."

"Liar."

"I'm *nae* a—"

"You *are*. You heard me just fine, lass, and well you know it."

" 'Tis impossible. What I *thought* I heard ye say was that ye need"—she gulped, and felt her heart skip a hopeful beat—"me. But o'course, that canna be right."

"Why not?"

"Because . . . och! weel, because . . . it just *canna* be." She swallowed hard as her attention lowered, then just as swiftly rose again. This time she did not meet his gaze head on. She couldn't; to see even a hint of duplicity shimmering in his dark brown eyes would surely kill her. Rather, she peered at him questioningly through the thick, protective shield of her lashes. Then, so softly the words were barely discernible, she added, "Can it?"

"Aye, Moyra," William replied, his voice equally hushed as he reached out and dragged the tip of his index finger along the quivering line of her jaw, Hooking the crook of his finger under her chin, he lifted her gaze back to his. "It can. It *is*. 'Tis exactly what I said. What I *meant* to say."

Moyra opened her mouth to speak. Twice. Both times, no words came out. She cleared her throat and tried again. "Wh-what a mon says and what he actually means isna always the same thing," she reasoned. "Aye, ye may have *said* ye need me, but mayhap what ye really *meant* was—"

"I love you."

It was Moyra's turn to pale, her turn for her breath to go hard and irregular. Her limbs drained of strength, and she couldn't stop herself from swaying toward William.

His powerful arms wrapped around her in the instant that she would have collapsed in a humiliating heap. He held her to him so tightly she could feel the erratic beat of his heart against her breasts. The puffs of his breaths, as labored and irregular as her own, pelted the top of her head, penetrating the layer of her hair, warming her scalp.

I love you.

The words echoed through her mind, over and over like the repeating clang of a church bell. She thought at first that she was experiencing another one of her visions, but immediately dismissed the idea. Never had a vision made her feel like *this!*

Did William mean it? Or was he only saying what he thought she wanted to hear because of the . . . ?

Nay, of course not. It couldn't be his reason, for he didn't know about *that*. She hadn't told him. Instead, she'd chosen to lie, after deciding firmly that if he didn't want her for herself, she didn't want him to want her at all.

Moyra swallowed hard. Tears of a joy unlike anything she'd ever known before blurred her vision. She steadfastly blinked them away.

Pillowing her head against the hard cushion of his chest, she weakly placed her arms around his waist, her hands splaying his back. Her fingers closed around body-warmed clumps of his tunic as she leaned hard against him, drawing from his virile strength, reveling in the comfort that was William Armstrong's embrace . . . something she had dreamed of nightly but had thought she would never feel again.

He loved her?

Mo chreach, he loved her!

That the admission had been heartfelt and unforced only served to make it all the more touching. There wasn't a doubt in Moyra's mind that William's declaration was sincere, that he truly did love her.

"Moyra?" William turned his head, nuzzled her ear with his nose.

"Hmmm?" she replied dreamily.

"Have you nothing to say to me in return?"

A playful smile curved over her lips, but of course, he could not see it. "And what would I be saying tae ye, William?"

"Usually when a man proclaims his love, the woman he proclaims it to responds in kind."

"Och! is that the way of it? Ye be wanting me tae tell ye I love ye?"

"Suffice it to say, I wouldn't object if you did."

Moyra pulled back a bit. Not enough to break their embrace—she couldn't bear to let him go just yet—but enough so she could gaze up into his eyes. Those brown eyes were narrow and guarded, but she detected a hopeful glint shimmering in them.

"Yer a reiver, William Armstrong," she said finally, a frown marring her brow. "I've told ye afore how I feel aboot spending me life with a reiver."

"Nay, lass, I *tried* to be a reiver." It was William's turn to grin. "There's a difference between trying something and succeeding at it. Even you cannot argue that my sole attempt at reiving was . . . well, suffice to say, 'twas not entirely successful. I've no doubt that 'twill be remembered for naught so much as its blunders."

"Aye, 'tis true enough. Ye werena ver' good at it, were ye?"

"I was pitiful."

"Truer still." She nodded slowly, thoughtfully. "Given the time, and a good deal of practice, ye'd get better. I'm sure of it."

As though he couldn't resist, William's head dipped and he planted a light, fleeting kiss on the tip of her nose. "Thank you ever so much for your confidence. I'm sure you're right, I would get better at it. However, truth to tell, I've lost the taste for it."

"What are ye saying, mon?"

"Isn't it obvious?" His hand shifted, brushing back a stray platinum strand of hair from her brow. "I'm saying that I don't wish to spend half of my life raiding and pilfering from my neighbors, the other half running and hiding from March Wardens on both sides of the Border. 'Twas my father's way of life. It's not mine." He cupped his hand around the tapered length of her neck and sighed. "If it succeeded in doing naught else, spending the last several fortnights enjoying the relative peace of Smailholm has taught me as much."

"Then what *do* ye want tae do with yer life, mon?"

"I honestly don't know. Crofting is a possibility. Mayhap merchandising. Or smithing. All are honorable trades, Moyra. Stable and nonviolent. I thought we, er . . . that is to say, if you're agreeable, mayhap the two of us could answer that question together . . ."

He shrugged, glanced away. Uncertainty and apprehension were sculpted in every hard plane and angle of his handsome face. Seeing those expressions on a man like William Armstrong . . . Och! but Moyra would be lying if she claimed to find the sight anything less than heart-tuggingly endearing.

"Is this yer roundaboot way of asking me tae wed ye, William?" Her breath caught in her throat as she awaited his answer. It seemed to take a torturously long time in coming.

He paused as visions of his mother and her many husbands whirlwinded through his mind. In the end, they were easily shoved aside. Moyra Elliot was not his mother. Indeed, she was nothing like Lizbet Armstrong. His mother would never have risked her life for a stranger.

He thought about the way Moyra had, more than once, stood toe-to-toe with the Douglas, the most feared reiver on either side of the Border. She'd faced the big man squarely, risking her very life to protect William when he'd been too weak from his wound to do it himself.

Would Lizbet have done the same? Never. Nor would his mother have tended those same wounds with the care and gentleness Moyra Elliot had shown.

Last, he thought of the fortnights in which he and Moyra had been apart. In truth, they hadn't been separated that long . . . It only *felt* like a dozen lifetimes. Yet Lizbet Armstrong had found more than one husband in the same amount of time. Moyra Elliot, on the other hand, had not even looked to another man.

William swallowed hard, his attention swerving back to her. Their gazes met and locked, and this time he did not even try to keep the emotions coursing through him from entering either his expression or his voice. "If I was asking, what answer would you give me, Moyra?"

"Yes," she replied without a second's hesitation. Her voice rang sharp and clear, the sincerity in her tone unmistakable. "I'd be saying yes." Her gaze searched his. "That is, *if* ye be asking . . ."

A groan rumbled low and deep in the back of William's throat as, bending at the waist, he slid one arm beneath her knees and scooped her delectably slender body up into his arms. "I'm asking, lass."

Her arms coiled around his neck, and she clung to him fiercely. "And I'm answering in kind."

William's smile was broader and more heartfelt than she'd ever seen it before. It matched her own to perfection.

Moyra opened her mouth to say . . . something. She was never entirely sure of what, for William's mouth crashed down upon hers in a kiss that was hard and fierce and possessive. Anything she might have said faded, overridden by the surge of passion this man's kiss and embrace always inspired within her.

In the corner of her mind not clouded with desire, she thought about the babe growing inside of her.

She had lied to William about that. She'd had to; her pride had demanded he declare his love for her willingly and without coercion.

Eventually, she would have to tell him the truth, as well as her reasons for the deception. Mayhap he would be angry with her for keeping the secret from him, but Moyra doubted it. Surely he would understand her reasons, would share her joy.

Aye, she would tell him of the babe, soon, before Kenny had the chance to impart the news for her.

But not now.

After all, she and William had their entire lives stretching out before them. Lives that, as she'd predicted many years ago, when she'd been naught more than a bairn herself, were destined to be infinitely entwined.

'Twas another vision that had, in the end, proved accurate.

Mayhap her Sight was clearer than she'd once thought? For this had proved to be the best vision of all.

BOOK YOUR PLACE ON OUR WEBSITE AND MAKE THE READING CONNECTION!

We've created a customized website just for our very special readers, where you can get the inside scoop on everything that's going on with Zebra, Pinnacle and Kensington books.

When you come online, you'll have the exciting opportunity to:

- View covers of upcoming books
- Read sample chapters
- Learn about our future publishing schedule (listed by publication month *and author*)
- Find out when your favorite authors will be visiting a city near you
- Search for and order backlist books from our online catalog
- Check out author bios and background information
- Send e-mail to your favorite authors
- Meet the Kensington staff online
- Join us in weekly chats with authors, readers and other guests
- Get writing guidelines
- AND MUCH MORE!

Visit our website at
http://www.zebrabooks.com

ROMANCE FROM JO BEVERLY

DANGEROUS JOY   (0-8217-5129-8, $5.99)

FORBIDDEN   (0-8217-4488-7, $4.99)

THE SHATTERED ROSE   (0-8217-5310-X, $5.99)

TEMPTING FORTUNE   (0-8217-4858-0, $4.99)

ROMANCE FROM JANELLE TAYLOR

ANYTHING FOR LOVE   (0-8217-4992-7, $5.99)

DESTINY MINE   (0-8217-5185-9, $5.99)

CHASE THE WIND   (0-8217-4740-1, $5.99)

MIDNIGHT SECRETS   (0-8217-5280-4, $5.99)

MOONBEAMS AND MAGIC   (0-8217-0184-4, $5.99)

SWEET SAVAGE HEART   (0-8217-5276-6, $5.99)

ROMANCE FROM FERN MICHAELS